ABOUT THE AUTHOR

Sam Youd – who would go on, as John Christopher, to write *The Death of Grass* and *The Tripods* – was born in Lancashire in April 1922, during an unseasonable snowstorm.

His teenage love affair with science fiction was short-lived, and by his mid-twenties his ambition had turned to literary fiction. His first novel, *The Winter Swan,* came out in 1949; he brought out a total of ten non-genre titles, before turning his attention entirely to genre fiction.

As a writer of genre novels his range was extensive. Alongside John Christopher the dystopian and young adult writer, there was William Godfrey the cricket novelist, Peter Graaf the thriller writer, Hilary Ford whose stories centred on female protagonists, Stanley Winchester who chronicled the carnal tendencies of the medical profession …

But writing literary fiction meant a lot to him, and he turned his back on it reluctantly. The novels written under his own name are eclectic in their themes and outlooks: from a woman's life told in reverse, to crises of faith amongst Jews and Catholics, to anti-heroes and deserters in World War II, to séances in post-war London. The last of the series, a bitter-sweet comedy of errors set in a large decaying country house, was published in 1963. He would continue to write, in a more popular vein, for several more decades.

ALSO PUBLISHED BY THE SYLE PRESS

Sam Youd

The Winter Swan

John Christopher

The Death of Grass

The Caves of Night

The White Voyage

Cloud on Silver

The Possessors

Pendulum

Hilary Ford

Sarnia

A Bride for Bedivere

BABEL
ITSELF

...And o'erthrew them with prophesying...

SAM YOUD

THE SYLE PRESS

This novel is respectfully and gratefully dedicated to the members of the committee of Atlantic Awards in Literature

Published by The SYLE Press 2018

First published in 1951
by Cassell & Co. Ltd.

Copyright © Sam Youd 1951

No part of this book may be reproduced or utilized in any form or by any means, electronic or mechanical, without prior permission from the Publisher.

All rights reserved

ISBN: 978-1-911410-08-9

www.thesylepress.com

Introduction

> We came in to hear the most incredible succession of
> bumps, bangs and rattles proceeding from Benson's room.
> At its height it was punctuated by a scream – 'For Christ's
> sake put the light on!'

It was early 1947, and Sam Youd and his wife Joyce had moved into shared quarters at 24 Drayton Gardens, as subtenants in Benson Herbert's flat. In lieu of rent, they provided editorial services for *New Frontiers*. This magazine, launched by Herbert, was intended to report on research into the veracity of 'psychic' phenomena. It folded after two issues. The Youds, meanwhile, were not entirely comfortable in a situation where Herbert brought his own investigations into the domestic surroundings, preferring to get out whenever 'Benson and his dubious friends' were about. The morning after that particularly violent séance:

> Gwen and Benson fell over each other in telling us what
> had been happening. They had smashed two tables, one
> that they were using and one lying peacefully in the corner of the room. Cushions, papers, splinters of jagged
> wood, and copies of *Kiss of Youth* ... flew through the air,
> and the table, supposedly motivated by one Gobi, a guide
> of Gwen's, attacked Benson and Gordon viciously, but
> did not harm G. herself. Benson, wild-eyed, professed
> himself completely disabused of any idea that the subconscious of a sitter could have been doing things, and when I
> attempted to reason with him was content to say that I'd
> have been convinced if I'd been there.

It was thus no accident that the events, and the Bohemian assortment of characters who populate the Regency Gardens of *Babel Itself,* would bear some resemblance to those of Drayton Gardens. But what might have been autobiographical in a novice writer was in this case only loosely so. The shared lodging house and the séances may have been real enough but, as revealed in Youd's later memoirs, the situation at Drayton Gardens was rather one of creative chaos, with no hint of the darker side portrayed in the novel. In 1947 he had been working on his first novel, *The Winter Swan;* by the time of starting *Babel,* two years on, he had already had one novel published and a second completed.

Benson Herbert had trained as a physicist, but took a particular interest in the occult. Youd would later refer to him as a would-be tycoon, and in his career as a publisher he showed himself to be something of an opportunist, at one time publishing pulp westerns for American GIs, and later moving into soft pornography. But opportunism aside, he bore limited resemblance to Piers Marchant (the Svengali of *Babel*), and in fact Youd maintained cordial relations with him after both had moved on from Drayton Gardens (they shared acquaintances in the world of British Science Fiction).

Another regular at Drayton Gardens was Quentin Crisp, who would later write *The Naked Civil Servant.* He provided copy for *New Frontiers,* in the form of verse and drawings, although – unsurprisingly – artistic integrity took a hit, as Youd recalled at the time:

> Quentin has just been up … We have just shown him the cover of NF 2, in which his drawing has been mutilated for the sake of sensation. And he was very nice about it.

But although the world of *Babel* has its poets and painters, it would be a mistake to try to associate any too closely with Crisp.

Babel Itself, then, is not essentially autobiographical, and indeed the author uses the middle-aged, genteel first-person narrator Tenn to distance his own person from the story. He also introduces the theme of the occult as a tool for manipulation, underlined in the novel's epigraph: *And o'erthrew them with prophesying* (like the title, a citation from Arthur O'Shaughnessy's *Ode*). This theme would later provide material for other novels, notably the Young Adult *Sword Trilogy*.

A contemporary reviewer of *Babel* found little to approve of in the 'rag-bag of untidy people, untidy in habits and untidy in morals' that made up its characters. Today such disapproval would attract less sympathy. For despite its dark moments – and surely Piers shares with Pirrie, the ruthless gunshop owner in *The Death of Grass,* more than just a likeness of name – *Babel* is far from the dystopian universe that the same author, writing as John Christopher, was later to explore.

During the writing of *Babel* Youd was becoming caught up with personal explorations of religion, including Catholicism; this may go some way to explain the surfacing of the themes of redemption, and divine intervention, in the latter part of the book.

According to the story of Genesis, God punishes humanity's arrogant assumption that they can build a tower tall enough to reach heaven, by confounding their speech so that they can no longer understand each other, and scattering them around the world. As *Babel Itself* draws to a close, whilst the close-knit community of Regency Gardens is largely dissolved, confusion has yielded considerable ground to clarity. But can there be a 'comfortable explanation' for the paranormal events? Or have the 'powers of good and evil' been at play? In this novel, at least, neither alternative is fully dismissed.

July 2018

BOOK I

CHAPTER ONE

While waiting for Helen to call us down to breakfast I went out on to the balcony in front of my rooms and stood looking down the deserted vista of Regency Gardens towards old Brompton Road. It was a raw morning for July; the air had a damp sharpness that was both a recollection and a promise of chill rain. But for the moment the rain had stopped. Clouds raced senselessly overhead, bursting forward in unending chase over the rooftops opposite, at once individual and part of a crowding mass. I went back into the room and brought out one of the wicker chairs. Seated on it I was a spectator of nature's consuming ordinariness; a tedious mediocrity of grey formless shades, dampness and uncertain chills. It was a reassuring scene.

Along Old Brompton Road there was activity with the constant press of cars and vans and lumbering buses passing processionally across the brief transverse that I could see from my balcony. People, too, passing on their diverse and futile errands. On the corner, at this early hour, the saloon door of the Little Lion stood open, with a barricade of chairs on the threshold and a glimpse of someone washing the floor behind them. Regency Gardens was a channel of emptiness, leading down into the main road's gustier activity. As I watched the milkcart broke it, turning into the emptiness, bringing echoing noise into the damp silence.

I rented the first floor at Number 36. It comprised one large and one rather smaller room, divided by a retractable screen, together with a dubious claim on the tiny room eight steps down. This, being mid-way between the first and ground floors, was a kind of no-man's-land which I sometimes used when Helen was not already using it to house some passing acquaintance. Helen

Drage and her daughter Cynthia shared accommodation similar to my own on the ground floor; Helen having the front half for the convenience of being able to greet people from the window without getting out of bed. Between the first and second floors was one bathroom; the other was down in the basement. Piers Marchant had the second floor, sharing it, at this particular time, with Olivia. Another tiny room made up – as one might say – the two and a halfth floor; there Rupert Harbinger lived in the interspaces between a disproportionately large library of poetry, which occasionally stirred him to emulation but more frequently inhibited. The top floor was also shared; Lulu Cartesian had the front room and Helen's son, Howard, the rear.

Number 36 was thus comparatively empty. There was no one in the little room between Helen's domain and mine, and the basement, which we used for meals and access to the garden, was, except for the badger, untenanted.

I looked at my watch. It was almost eight o'clock. Above me I heard the clatter of Piers's window being opened, and looked up; but neither he nor Olivia was looking out. I glanced down again, watching the street through the superimposed pattern of fretted, rusty ironwork. The milkcart was ambling nearer. It stopped approximately opposite Number 30. The horse shook itself and lifted its long head, as though towards me, as though in greeting. It was quite a handsome chestnut. Forty years ago it would have fetched a good price as a carriage horse and would have trotted down these streets, a symbol of the world's richness and solidity. In those days, of course, Regency Gardens would not have been so badly in need of a coat of paint. And milk had certainly gone up in the world. Tuberculin-tested, pasteurized, dehydrated – and with the final accolade of scarcity. I gave the horse a salute. It pulled its neck down again and began to move forward.

I had left the door of my room open and I heard the clatter from the stairs now as Piers ran down to the bathroom. He shouted something up to Olivia and I heard the even vaguer sound of her reply. The furious running of water garbled their words. On a third level I caught the deep moaning bass notes of a 'cello. Necessarily Howard. The house was awake. Day was begun.

From the depths Helen's clear contralto, echoing, unforced.

'Breakfast!'

I had to pass Cynthia's room on my way down. She called me huskily:

'Is that you, Tenn?'

Her door was ajar. I pushed it open and went in. She was sitting up in her divan bed with a silk scarlet bed jacket over her shoulders. Her face, not yet made-up, was pallidly and fascinatingly ugly. She gestured towards her tortoiseshell compact which was lying on the small table by the door. I picked it up and took it across to her.

She smiled. 'Thanks, Tenn. Would you tell Helen just some thin toast and butter, and coffee – white if there's any milk?'

'Aren't you getting up?' I asked.

She smiled more confidingly.

'Feminine frailty. Any aspirin on you? It doesn't matter. Ask Helen to root me some out, will you?'

Down the deep well of the staircase the 'cello's resonance romped exuberantly. Her face changed, shrinking into petulance.

'Blast Howard ... Close the door behind you. Don't forget, darling. Toast, coffee and aspirin.'

I left her and descended the remaining stairs to the basement. The dining-room was empty but with the big table laid for breakfast. I heard Helen clattering pots in the kitchen and went through. She made an admirable figure, white-aproned, deft. Matronliness became her; she had kept extremely good lines and her cheeks, always naturally coloured, were now finely flushed from cooking. She half-turned towards me as she shifted a frying-pan.

'It won't be a minute, Tenn. You could go in and sit down.'

By the door Brock was delicately drinking coffee from his pan. I went over and stroked his fine white blaze. He looked up a moment, bracing himself back against my hand, before resuming his drinking.

I said: 'Cynthia would like toast, white coffee and aspirin.'

She looked up quickly. 'Oh. Tenn, would you look after your own omelette? It's been folded. I have some toast and coffee made. I'll just take it up to her.'

I was lifting the omelette out as she came back. I carried my plate into the dining-room, leaving the communicating door wide open. Brock, having finished his coffee, ambled after me and settled down on the carpet. He looked towards the inactive fire reproachfully. It was rather cold. I walked over and switched it on.

I said: 'I'm putting the fire on, Helen. This omelette's delicious.'

She came through the door carrying a tray with the coffee percolator and a plate holding another omelette on it. She sat down beside me.

'I'll have mine now before they come down,' she said.

I took another mouthful of my own.

'Dried egg?' I asked.

She nodded. 'And ... different things. Tenn. Can you let me have an advance?'

'Damn it, Helen,' I said, 'I'm paid up to the end of September as it is. If I give you October's rent now how are you going to manage for the next three months?'

She smiled vaguely.

'Something will turn up.'

I said: 'Cynthia might even get a job.'

She took it seriously.

'I think she would like to. Don't you know someone, Tenn, who might have the right kind of vacancy?'

'And what is the right kind of vacancy?'

She said: 'Oh, receptionist ... something like that.'

I finished my omelette. I said wearily:

'I'll write you out a cheque when I go upstairs. But you'll have to start organizing things better, Helen.'

We heard the clatter of feet descending the stairs and she picked up her plate and retreated into the kitchen again. Surprisingly it was Lulu who came in. She was wearing her green, Paris-tailored costume and her face was sallow and looked stiff with her customary ochre cosmetic. She sat down, pulling her skirt up, and I noticed silk stockings and snake-skin shoes.

'Early, Lulu,' I observed. 'And dressed.'

She said: 'I'm going out. I told you. Leslie's exhibition.'

'Opening this morning?'

She nodded. She called through to Helen.

'Darling. Just coffee, I think. Unless ... Is there any grapefruit?'

'One left,' Helen said. 'I'll cut it for you.'

Lulu got up restlessly and went over to where Brock was lying. She kneeled down and took his head between her hands.

'Lovely Brockie ... wasn't he a beautiful badger?'

I said: 'I'll have to find time to drop in. It is the Bowman Galleries, isn't it?'

Lulu bent her own head down, ruffling her silk blouse carelessly against Brock's fur.

'Darling, darling Brock ... Yes, the Bowman.' She turned the ochre mask of her face up towards me. 'I hope he gets some decent notices. He's terribly sensitive.'

'Can he paint?' I asked.

'Water colours,' she said, explaining. 'Klee – but more dynamic. More intense.'

I buttered my toast and applied the marmalade. I said: 'I hope so.'

Helen brought her grapefruit in and Lulu came back to the table. She was not still long. When Piers and Olivia came in there was plenty of room for them to pass her but she nevertheless started up noisily, and carried her grapefruit round to the other side of the table, away from the door. Piers sat down beside me, but Olivia followed Lulu round. I noticed that she looked tired; her hair was braided tightly back, making her face seem narrow and accentuating the shortness of her upper lip and the vague protrusion of her front teeth. Instead of the usual voluptuous rabbit she was a weary and nervous one.

Piers, buttering bread, looked at me in sideways speculation.

'Still got that stock of *Mirror to the Ballet*?'

I nodded. Lulu began telling Olivia about Leslie's exhibition.

Piers said: 'How many were there?'

'Just over three thousand.'

He pretended to make mental calculations.

'I might be able to get you ... twenty-five quid for them.'

'Tuppence each,' I said. 'Retailing at two shillings.'

He said: 'You won't get rid of them any other way.'

'I've still got a ninety quid printer's bill to pay,' I told him. 'Your twenty-five won't help much.'

'Ah, omelette,' he said. 'Good old Helen. If you will do this highbrow stuff, Tenn ... Westerns now. One hundred and twenty-eight pages with a nice bright cover and selling at a shilling ... I'll take as many of those as you can provide at less fifty. It's easy.'

'Look, Piers,' I said. 'If there's all that easy money in them why don't you publish yourself? Are you thinking of my old age?'

He laughed. 'Just helping you to make more money with less risk. I don't take any risks at all – it's bad for my nerves. Those ballet things, now. I might get as much as thirty for them.'

I didn't bother to reply.

Lulu said, fairly loudly: 'He has a water-colour temperament of course – pastel shades with subtle nuances of depth. And a wonderful instinct for group patterns.'

'And how young is he?' Piers asked.

She quite genuinely missed the sardonic overtone.

'Only twenty-three,' she said. 'When one thinks ... Haven't you met him, though?'

Piers shook his head, his lips pursed up in regret.

'I'll bring him round to the Regent to-night,' she said. 'You should meet him.'

I wondered again what impulse of masochism it was that made her betray herself so continuously to Piers's cynical contempt. He looked at her now levelly, curiously, an entomologist dissecting a fly, and the fly didn't even have the sense to know it should wriggle.

'Party member?' Piers inquired seriously.

She said: 'No. Not yet anyway. But his work has a real dialectical value.'

Piers looked at her again. 'Twenty-three? Yes, I'll bet it has.'

Olivia said coldly: 'Work with any kind of value is better than none.'

Piers transferred his attention to Olivia. He said, distinctly but without emphasis: 'Shut up.'

By an effort of will, that kind of half-believing stretching of the imagination to recall in winter the summer's gasping heat, I thought of the Piers of three months earlier – the hesitant, fascinated moth in its nerve-racking parabolic dance about the candle that was Olivia. If the candle had gone out another one would certainly be lit. That, of course, was his scorching and his concern. But it was Wednesday. If the split were final ... I was aware of my usual impatience towards a possible frustration. Letting my eyes rest not on either but between them, I said: 'All right for this evening, Livia?'

I saw them look at each other, hostile, wary, stubborn. After the briefest pause, Olivia said: 'Yes, of course.'

And Piers, clinching: 'Why shouldn't she be?'

That was all right, then. But it was still likely to be awkward. In their agreement and reassurance the clash between them was brought out all the more clearly. It would upset things. Lulu finished her slow, painstaking consumption of the grapefruit and glanced along the table.

'To-night's the night?' she asked. 'I'm curious. You must let me come along some time.'

Piers smiled at her politely.

'I'm afraid they haven't the very least dialectical significance,' he said.

She said confidently: 'Oh, I *know*. But just for the interest. Oh ... to-night? You won't be in the Regent, then?'

Piers wrinkled his brow, carefully, diabolically forgetting.

'To see Leslie,' she explained.

Even for Piers it was too easy. He said indifferently: 'We might. Depends how things go.'

Lulu said: 'I would like to come along some time.'

Howard came in, nodded briefly, and disappeared into the kitchen where we could hear him talking to Helen in a petulant voice. He came back a few minutes later with fresh toast, munching a piece himself. He was wearing shabby grey flannels and a torn white shirt open at the neck. His usual protest against Cynthia. He spoke to me in his precise, rather shrill voice: 'Going in this morning, Tennyson? You could drop me at the school.'

'Not before lunch,' I said.

He said wearily: 'Damn! Have I got to lug the thing in on a ninety-six bus again?'

Lulu said brightly, and as might have been expected: 'You should have taken up the oboe instead.'

Howard ignored her. Leaning back in a chair, his hand waving a piece of toast in slow revolutions in the air, he called through to Helen: 'Helen. Lend me half a crown for a taxi.'

She shouted back: 'Sorry, I'm broke. You can go in by bus, can't you?'

He shrugged. Crunching the toast between his fingers he leaned over towards Lulu. 'Not the wrong instrument, darling.

The wrong sex.' He put his hand to his mouth and began to eat the dry crumbs. 'I see little Cynthia's breakfasting in bed again.'

Helen came through, wiping her hands on her apron. She spoke to Howard: 'Was Rupert stirring when you came down?'

He said: 'I don't know. I respect his privacy. Any more coffee?'

Helen went to get it. Lulu got up.

'I must dash,' she said. 'There's a tremendous amount to do.'

As she went, Piers commented: 'And how tirelessly she does it.'

The door closed behind her.

'Off to the Bowman?' Howard asked. 'That Leslie person … quite terrible. A Bevin boy or something. Water colours of pit shafts, all dripping in blacks and greens. Henry Moore but much, much further under ground.'

'Has he a surname?' Piers asked.

'Stott or Sprott or something,' Howard said. 'Piers. Would you care to lend me ten bob? Rich man that you are.'

Piers said: 'Will you take a gift of half a crown instead?'

Howard nodded. Piers flicked the coin across the table to him.

'Financial wisdom lies in recognizing the inevitable and cutting one's losses,' he went on. '*Mirror to the Ballet* now, Tenn. Thirty quid this morning. To-morrow, who knows?'

'Who knows?' I repeated. 'But I do know the size of the printer's bill.'

Olivia put in: 'Piers specializes in Recognizing the Inevitable and Cutting one's Losses. All in Gothic capitals. To do the former you make something inevitable first and then recognize it. And if you can't lose anything quickly enough you can always throw it away. It's a gift of his.'

Howard said curiously: 'A row? How fascinating. Do let's have all the details.'

I thought for a moment that Olivia might be angry enough to abandon her usual restraint and supply them. Piers presumably thought so too; he looked at her, grinning slightly. Perhaps that sobered her into the realization that a public scene would not in any way upset him; rather, the reverse. She looked away, stirring her coffee. In the sudden lull of silence we heard the stairs creaking under Rupert's ghost-like tread, and the door opened gently to admit him. He stood just inside the threshold for a moment, precariously tall and thin and watching us with detached curiosity from behind his thick, dust-specked glasses. He had some letters in his hand, and pushed them forward on to the table.

'Letters,' he explained. 'Oh ... One of them's for me.'

I picked them up and sorted them quickly. There were only three for me, two of them ominously penny stamped. The bottom letter was addressed to Rupert and decorated with an American stamp and an airmail sticker. I glanced at the date-stamp as I handed it back to him.

'New York, Rupert,' I told him. 'A commission? A lecture tour?'

Howard laughed. Rupert took it and, with one of his rare gestures of decisiveness, ripped the envelope open and drew the letter out from it.

Howard said: 'Who want you, Rupert? The Daughters of the Revolution?'

He said: 'No. No, it's nothing like that. It's from Joe – Joe Britton. He's coming back to England.'

Howard said: 'Britton! I didn't know you knew him. A slumming holiday?'

Rupert looked at the letter again: 'He says ... for good.'

'Mad, then,' Howard observed. 'He must be.' He got up and went towards the door, which Rupert still held open. 'Where are you having lunch, Tennyson?'

'Maxard's,' I said. 'About one. But put a tie on.'

He looked at me indignantly. 'When I scrounge lunch I always appear properly dressed. I'll change before I go out. See you at one. Bye, all.'

We heard him running up the stairs. I finished my second cup of coffee and got up to follow him. As I closed the door behind me I could hear Piers's curious voice:

'What the hell does he want to come to England for?'

CHAPTER TWO

The morning passed fairly quickly. I spent some time in exhaustive wrestling with the costing estimates for a series of political pamphlets I had in mind and then Scotney telephoned with a list of queries on the Autumn issue of *Trend* that occupied us for a good twenty minutes. We were getting down to the last items when Olivia knocked and came in. I waved her to a chair, but instead she walked over to the window and stood there, looking out.

Scotney said: 'Well, that just leaves the cover. You got our rough proof?'

'Yes,' I said. 'I want a lighter blue. Can you do it?'

'Very light?'

'No. Just a shade or two. Enough to set the black off. Mediterranean sky blue – about eight o'clock on a July morning.'

Scotney laughed. 'Never been further than Ilfracombe, Mr. Glebe.'

'Ilfracombe will do,' I said. 'Anything else?'

'No. Nothing else. I'll send you some advance copies along inside a week.'

I put the receiver down and turned to Olivia. She was wearing a dove grey costume with the jacket unbuttoned to show a high-necked white blouse. She had combed her hair fluffily forward and had made her face up competently, but she still looked tired and rather nervous. I gave her a cigarette and leaned forward to light it for her. I liked her perfume. It had an edge of sharpness, of emphasis.

She said: 'Who is Britton, anyway?'

'A poet,' I said. 'A very good one, some say. Surely you've heard of him. *Castles and Kings* ... *Steel Engravings*. He hasn't published anything lately and his earlier stuff's out of fashion. But some say he's good.'

She said: 'I don't know anything about poets. Is he any good? An American?'

'No. He's English. He went over to America in 'thirty-nine. As for his stuff – I'm not fond of it myself. A bit florid. Left-wing Romantic.'

'Oh, one of those.' She paused. As usual when her face was in repose her mouth was held fractionally open, with her somewhat large but white and well-shaped front teeth resting on the bottom lip. Against the healthy curve of her cheek the gleaming teeth and red, parted lips had a demure, innocent attraction. But not, any longer, for Piers? She startled me by tackling the subject herself.

She said: 'I'm not really interested in Britton, whoever he is, Tenn. Piers is trying to get rid of me.'

I said non-committally: 'I saw that you'd been fighting.'

She said: 'No. Not fighting. It wouldn't be so bad if he would fight. He just closes up tight. He acts as though I weren't there.'

Three months. She had lasted averagely well. Longer than Jane; not as long as Hilda. I felt my usual mild distaste for the vulgarity of Piers's endless rutting – a distaste extending, naturally enough, to his various partners. The Piers and Olivia of the composite Piers-and-Olivia were different from their customary selves, and I found them embarrassing. I smiled at her, concealing my vague disgust.

'Well, it's up to you, isn't it; to both of you? It's your affair. I don't suppose you expect me to give him a talking-to.'

She sat up, bracing her body into richer curves.

'God, no! But it does concern you, in a way. If we can't manage to … patch things up, what about Wednesdays? Won't it complicate things?'

Would it? Only on the assumption, of course, that Olivia continued to take part in them after she had separated from Piers. The separation, it seemed, was inevitable. The other –

her continued participation – what did that depend on? In the event on Piers and myself; Howard was unimportant. And so, on me. I looked at her carefully.

'I don't see why it should make any difference,' I said at last. 'Anyway, we can't know until we try it. I should assume it won't make any difference.'

'Yes,' she said eagerly, 'why should it? We're independent people.'

Independent of what? Of each other? Her eagerness gave the lie to her protestation. So every Wednesday evening there would be something to look forward to, a fresh clash with Piers, a fresh hope of finding a way back into that barren past. A personal motive. But I had neither right nor inclination to exclude her because of that. Justification was everything; and justification would lie in the results. I spread my hands.

'Well, there it is. What are you going to do about things? Any plans?'

Reality crumbled her imaginings into the dust that they essentially were. She, too, I reminded myself, must know Piers well by now; more intimately, perhaps, than I did, though without the always recurring confirmation my own longer acquaintance with him had provided. Now she drooped, her brief excitement wilting in the face of her knowledge.

She said: 'I don't know yet what's happening – exactly what's happening, anyway. I want to get a job, of course.'

I said gently: 'Another job.'

She laughed. 'Yes. We have to preserve the fiction that Piers pays me for my shorthand and typewriting, haven't we? Another job, I meant.'

'That shouldn't be too hard.'

She said: 'No. People always want secretaries, don't they? What about you, Tenn? Isn't there a niche for me in Tennyson Glebe Ltd.?'

I said: 'I can't even afford to pay the Managing Director's salary. Besides, I'm a better typist than you are.'

She got up and went over to the piano, leaned against it, restlessly lifting the lid and flinging a few odd notes like withered petals of sound through the air.

'Lord, yes,' she said. 'And you'd want me to work, wouldn't you?'

She set the lid down carefully and caressed the polished wood with her small, rather stubby hands. For all their whiteness and the ten scarlet flames in which they ended they were like the hands of a sturdy boy. She was very young, of course. Young and yet quite composed in a world where my own middle-age stumbled and groped for footing. She turned to look at my Craxton, her young, well-groomed head poised in front of that tendrilled, staring face, and said irrelevantly:

'Sometimes I hate this atmosphere.'

'Come out to lunch?' I suggested.

She glanced round. 'Why not? Can the Company stand it, though?'

'Important business lunch,' I said. 'For the expense sheet. There will be Howard as well.'

She said: 'I'll slip down and tell Helen I shall be out.'

I looked at my watch. It was turned half-past twelve.

'Don't bother,' I said. 'Go up and get your things. I'll tell Helen. See you down there.'

She went out with a brief smile and I heard her running upstairs and opening the door of her room as I gathered hat, gloves, brief-case and cigarettes. I went to the window and inspected the weather. The clouds were higher, light bars of grey across a deeper background, and less likely to produce rain. I closed the window carefully and went downstairs.

Helen was sitting in her window-seat, knitting, and surprisingly was quite alone. I took the cheque out of the envelope in which I'd placed it and handed it to her. She caught my eye as I crumpled the envelope and threw it into the fireplace.

'Darling Tennyson! And so discreet. This really is the last advance I'll ask you for.'

'Helen,' I told her, 'if things continue to go as they are going you will be able to ask until you are blue in the face, and it won't make any difference.'

'Business very bad? Why don't you go in with Piers on some of his wonderful schemes?'

'Why don't you get your advances from him?' I countered.

She smiled vaguely. 'It's such a bother. It's different with you. Tenn, would it help if Cynthia worked for you secretarially, you know? Without salary, of course. It would be practice for her.'

'That's the second offer this morning,' I said. 'Very kind of you, Helen, but I can make my way into bankruptcy in solitary dignity. Oh, by the way, Olivia's coming out with me for lunch – she asked me to tell you.'

Helen said: 'Oh. But really, Tenn, about Cynthia …'

Cynthia herself interrupted. Helen, her attention distracted from the window, had not seen her come through the front gate. She pushed the door open and came in, a shopping bag on each arm. Helen jumped up to take them off her. Between them they put the bags on the small, baize-covered card table and Cynthia dropped back in exhaustion into an arm-chair. She was wearing a mustard-coloured tweed suit and somehow contrived to look attractive in it. Her gift for make-up and for wearing the most unlikely clothes with success was always astonishing. A common-enough talent in Paris, but in England, I had observed, ugly girls stayed ugly. Cynthia was the startling exception.

She said to Helen: 'Darling, I've been terribly wicked. I got some salmon. I just couldn't resist it.'

Helen said: 'My precious! You're a demon. But Livia's going out with Tenn. We can gorge on it together. Potatoes?'

Cynthia nodded. 'In the brown bag. I was simply weighed down.'

Helen came and stood behind her daughter, fingers reaching down to stroke her rather wide forehead. Cynthia looked up at her, smiling. I watched them, feeling myself an intruder. I was glad when Olivia called to me from the hall. Helen paused in her caresses.

'Will you be back?'

'For tea? Very likely. And early dinner to-night, remember?'

Helen nodded, returning to her absorption, and I went out to where Olivia was waiting for me by the open front door.

We walked round to the garage together and I got the car out. Isaac heard me starting her up and left a Bentley he was picking to bits to come over and drop his cigarette ash on the running-board.

'About time we gave her another overhaul, Mr. Glebe,' he said. 'Nasty tone.'

I began backing her out.

'Not yet,' I said. 'I feel so much at home with it.'

I parked the car behind Leicester Square and wondered again why I bothered to keep it up. It would be as cheap, and far more convenient, to rely on taxis. Just habit, I recognized, buying the parking tickets. It was colder here, with an edged wind blowing round the bases of the unlovely, thrusting tenements. From the other side of the street it wafted the smell of fish and chips, stewed in rank fat. In the street a crowd was patiently gathering round a man selling packets with pound notes in them. As we walked past I heard the penetrating croon of his sales talk.

'Who'll buy this 'un, then? This little packet, all sealed, you've seen me seal it. Who'll buy this 'un? Half a crown … '

We turned the corner into Gerrard Street.

Howard was waiting for us when we reached Maxard's. He took my arm with the queer, fierce, affectionate impulsiveness he sometimes permitted himself.

'I'm starving, Tenn. Hello, Livia. Joining the breadline?'

She looked round at the squalid intersection of Gerrard and Wardour Street, and smiled pleasantly at him.

'No. Just coming off my beat.'

We found a table upstairs. I left Howard to do the ordering; he could still find an adolescent delight in picking his way through the profusion of pseudo-Chinese dishes. Then I exercised my own conceit by taking chopsticks while the other two operated less elegantly with spoon and fork. Howard helped himself generously to lobster omelette, and pointed his spoon at Olivia.

'What's all the to-do with Piers? Where have you left him, anyway?'

Olivia said: 'I don't know where he is. What to-do? You know the usual procedure with Piers's women, don't you?'

Howard laughed delightedly. 'But you don't – that's the beauty of it. Or you didn't, rather. It's so nice to be anxiously helpful while innocence becomes sophistication – like an immortal asking an octogenarian how fit he feels. You're spoiling my fun, Livia.'

'I feel very fit,' she said. 'Very fit, indeed. How about you?'

He said, suddenly serious: 'Are you going to come along on Wednesdays still?'

Olivia looked at me fleetingly.

'Of course. Why not? It's got nothing to do with personal relations.'

Howard said uncertainly: 'Well … We can't be sure of that, can we?' He brightened up again. 'It might be interesting of course. The new factors it brings out. It might be very interesting.'

'Yes,' Olivia said. 'Very interesting.'

Her voice was a shade high but Howard did not notice it. Had he done so he would have hung onto the subject, worrying it engrossedly forward until the core of it lay raw and uncovered to his genial, interested gaze. Instead, fretfully, he turned to himself.

'Bust the bridge this morning. Just before I came away.'

'A bridge?' Olivia asked.

'*The* bridge,' I interpreted for her. 'On his 'cello.'

She said: 'Oh. You can get it replaced, can't you? A spare part?'

She was quite uninterested but careful to keep the conversation away from her own concerns. Howard forked the rest of the crispy noodles on to his plate and said moodily: 'Yes, I can get it replaced. By scrounging, or by bullying Helen for the money. You people seem to think I enjoy cadging.'

I said gently: 'You do, don't you, for simple needs like food and drink and taxis? But 'cellos should be presented and kept in repair by an artistic deity.'

Howard laughed again. 'I'll have it out of Helen if there's the slightest smell of money in the house. But she is broke at the moment.' He looked at me acutely. 'Unless she's had another advance out of good old Tenn.'

I said evasively: 'Good old Tenn is also in financial shoal water just now.'

Howard said: 'Well, if Helen's no go I shall have to get it out of Lulu. I've been contemplating selling her my virtue for some time now. But which is it to be, intellectual or physical? Should I join the Party or separate her knees? Instruct my youth, Tenn.'

I said: 'You don't seem to need any instruction.'

'No,' Olivia put in. 'He's quite an accomplished little swine at times.'

Her face was slightly flushed. I considered her sudden accession of partisanship for Lulu, who had been her butt in the past as much as Howard's and Piers's. A woman's confused and yearning loneliness had become less amusing to her. It was easy to see why. Howard's swift look showed that he saw too. He opened his mouth to speak, paused, and closed it again. A rush of sympathy? Or a wary retreat before a wounded, maddened animal? Yes, that was much more likely.

The waiter came forward on softly padding feet and I ordered coffee. I hesitated for a moment, observing Olivia's flushed nervousness and Howard's diplomatic, smiling silence.

'Kümmel?' I suggested.

Olivia, nodding, relaxed a little. Howard raised his hands in exaggerated benediction as I ordered. 'Thou art a good fellow,

Tennyson, a very worthy fellow. We were thirsty and he gave us drink. And the loan of a ten bob perhaps towards a new bridge? A gesture to art? Half a quid pro the very highest kind of quo.'

I took my wallet out and gave him a pound.

CHAPTER THREE

I knocked at Piers's door and entered. He was standing on a chair by the window, struggling with the black-out board. I helped him to lift it into place, and he climbed down, rubbing his hands. He stepped back to examine with satisfaction the two blacked-out and curtained windows.

'Now we're really inside,' he said. 'Four walls round us and a blaze of electric light.'

Blaze was a false description, of course. I had always been vague as to the number of lights he had rigged up in his room; now, counting them, I found eight, but all so concealed that their diffuseness drifted through the room like a bright cloud. Piers followed my gaze, and with a gesture of restlessness walked over to his desk and flipped a switch, bringing on a ninth light from a low-set, brooding globe I had failed to notice. I walked over and sat on the edge of his double divan. My fingers rested with sensuous delight on the plush surface of the crimson bed-cover.

I said: 'You always black-out very early, Piers. Howard at any rate won't be along for another half hour.'

He said: 'But now we're enclosed. Less than six yards to the edge of the visible universe. Everything docketed and known.' He smiled his thin, severe smile. 'Or – if you prefer it – a neat reversion to the womb. Warm and limited. The rest's a waste.'

He was sitting in one of his arm-chairs in a strained awkward posture that made his slight body look more puny even than it was; he looked like a prematurely aged child. Aged and tired. I felt both affection and pity for his lonely smallness.

I said: 'Busy day?'

'Whisky,' he said. 'There are two dozen cases kicking around somewhere and with luck I can get not only a finger but a whole hand in the pie. But it's a hell of a job bringing the right people together and keeping the wrong people apart. When I have a buyer I can't get hold of the seller; when I finally get the seller' – he shrugged – 'the buyer gets cold feet. Now it will have to wait till to-morrow. And I don't like leaving things.'

'Who was the buyer?' I asked.

He looked at me carefully as though to reassure himself that I was not likely to profit by the information.

'Carson.'

'And the cold feet?' I asked. 'Did he find out where it was coming from?'

'I don't know where it's coming from myself,' Piers said. 'I don't ask silly questions.'

Nor, I reflected, was Carson the kind of man who asked questions in the normal run of things. Some of the private rooms at the Three Bananas were evidence enough of that. So the whisky must be more than usually doubtful.

'What do you stand to make?' I asked him.

'Five bob a bottle with luck,' he said. 'With luck and some very delicate work on the telephone.' He glanced towards me swiftly. 'I'm beginning to need a partner. Someone I can rely on and who can take part of the weight.'

I added for him: 'And without any great moral scruples – or even little ones.'

He said: 'You're not the kind of person who fools himself with imaginary ethics. I know you better, Tenn. You're too intelligent for that.'

'I'm a publisher,' I said.

Piers laughed, cynically but with disarming friendliness.

'Mushroom variety! There's no reason why you shouldn't carry on with it. You do too much donkey work anyway. You need a secretary, perhaps a couple of clerks.' He sat up, his small body poised and suddenly alive. 'We could take an office in town and get a small staff. Run your publishing as a front.'

Why did he want me? Did he really want me at all? I was wondering about this – watching Piers and trying to get behind the tight blandness of his face – when Olivia pushed the door open.

In this room she had been at home and at ease. I could remember how often I myself had entered to see her sprawling with casual grace along the great scarlet oblong of the divan, or in her preferred arm-chair underneath the window. Three months? It seemed longer. I did not associate Piers's earlier women with the room to a like extent because my own acquaintance with him had only really begun to ripen in that same recent period. Now I watched Olivia come into the room, cautiously and defensively, like a stranger. Piers watched too, smiling tightly at her from her usual arm-chair. She paused for a moment, irresolute in the centre of the carpet, and then moved decisively, flinging herself down beside me on the divan. Her hair fell, more blonde against the sultry red, like fine, soft straw.

She said: 'Howard will be up in a minute.'

I looked at my watch. 'So soon?'

She said, eager to talk to me, eager to forget the straining, nervous hostility that stretched between her and Piers: 'You remember? No practice to-night. He's bust his fiddle – or something.'

Piers said: 'His 'cello.'

It was impossible to classify his words either as statement or interrogation; the tone of his voice hovered between the two, between casual innocence and subtle, didactic sneering. Too trivial a point for malice? But I was continually being amazed by the trivialities which Piers found it worth while to seize on as minute springboards for his darting, cool attacks. Olivia, catching the nuance better, probably, than I did, looked up quickly, and then mutely looked away.

Howard came in through the door she had left ajar, and

pushed it back with one thin, white hand to slam behind him. He was wearing a pair of trousers that I recognized as part of Rupert's Army kit; khaki-drill gabardine with ridiculous drainpipe legs. And above the waist a tattered red shirt under a shabby leather jacket, open down the front.

He said cheerfully: 'Everybody ready?'

Having offered the invitation he stood on one side, watching with interested friendliness while the rest of us made the necessary preparations. Olivia and I pushed the carpet back, drew the four chairs up to the small oblong table and cleared it of a litter of American illustrated magazines, ash-trays and other articles. Piers attended to the radiogram. When we finally sat down Howard and I were facing each other, and Piers and Olivia, with Piers in his usual place for access to the light and radiogram switches. I took Olivia's left hand with my right, Howard shifted his chair awkwardly, there were two separate clicks, and in the swiftly plunging blackness I felt Piers's hand on mine. His hands were peculiarly large for his small frame; in the enveloping darkness, with only his hand for witness, he was a giant.

Holst's music leaped and glimmered about us, its fantasy transmuted into shivering, insubstantial eeriness. Mercury, Venus, Mars. Then Jupiter – by day, by sunlight or lamplight, the rich, honest sureness of a major key wedded to strong, bare melody. But now, in the enclosed and wanted night, full of dark undertones, its laughter tinged with something less definable, something unreal and absurd by day but now real and quivering at every nerve-end beneath the blunted senses. Outside a car changed gears and the harshness of the sound, found and swiftly lost, was a raft to snatch at. Jupiter, an obliterating wave, rolled over it, sweeping it away beyond reach, beyond hope of recollection. We waited, mute, sacrificial.

This was the point where we expected things to begin. I thought I felt the table give minutely beneath my balancing finger-tips; I heard Olivia draw in breath and her hand, half covered by my own, twitched sharply. But the tremor died away, the table was firm. There was only Jupiter, riding the sightless air.

All this, I remembered, had begun by accident; it was difficult to remember precisely when. Soon after Olivia came to Number 36 – at the end of April? A joke first; a noisy gathering round the table in sceptical pursuit of a hint in a magazine. Something to do one evening before going round to the Regent. And from that, from the disbelieving laughter when the table tilted for the first time beneath our careless fingers, had come curiosity and repetition and an increasing refinement of techniques. Now Wednesday evening held a major part in our separate weeks. We had the comradeship of the hunters and also, perhaps, of the hunted. I wondered suddenly what we were really doing.

Howard said softly: 'Nothing much to-night.'

As though in answer the table jerked quickly, pushing against us, coming down again on the floorboards with a clatter of wooden feet. Jupiter had given way to Saturn. Over the silvery notes, Piers's voice was clear and gentle.

'Is anybody there? Knock once for yes. Is anybody there?'

Now a more subdued, a rocking motion. The table swayed backwards and forwards under our hands, faster and faster, and for a moment I felt the fantasy that it was absolutely still and that it was we, and all the black room about us, that were whirling into this furious, unconscious dance. Piers's voice repeated, steadying:

'Is anybody there? Knock once for yes.'

Gradually the rocking died away. As it did so a record finished, and there was silence as the auto-change made its substitution. Across the first notes of the new record the table lifted, lifted and crashed down again. Howard, his voice lacking the sure control of Piers's and a little harsh with excitement, took over the questioning.

'Who is it? Will you spell out your name?'

He began to recite the alphabet slowly as the rocking began again, and in the darkness I thought of Burkie, and myself stumbling over J and K in the dusty, inky sunshine of the nursery. And the voices through the open window of the men pruning the wall-trees, calling to each other and laughing; slow, contented, sunlit laughter. For a fraction of a second even the distinctive powdery smell of Burkie's well-scrubbed hands was as vivid and unmistakable in my mind as it had been then. But the instant went and smell, scene and sunlight were lost in Howard's rhythmic recitation.

The table stopped at G. From that to L, to Y, to a confused indecision between B and C. Howard said impatiently:

'Start again. I'll spell out. Start again.'

It started again; rocking forward alongside Howard's enumeration. To G to L. To an uncertain S, and subsequently a sullen, irresolute silence. Howard said: 'Is Ming there?'

On the back of my hand I felt the lightest suspicion of coldness, the shadow of a chill breath. The table lurched, and settled again into silence. Howard repeated: 'Is Ming there? Knock once for yes.'

We waited in lengthening silence. After a few moments Olivia said: 'I could do with a cigarette.'

Howard said uncertainly: 'There doesn't seem to be anything doing.'

Piers's voice sounded, for him, lazy, and reflective. He said: 'Give it time. What about you taking over, Tenn? Coax him along.'

I said: 'Is anybody there? Knock once for yes.'

It always embarrassed me to have charge of the questioning at this stage; dropping these queries into the black pool around us and the intermittently attentive unknown. I preferred to leave it to the others; to Howard's unselfconscious excitement or Piers's detached coolness. Olivia and I were the foils, the inactive partners in the awakening. Once awake, once the table was alive, and responsive under our control, there was less difference in the parts we played as all four merged into a partnership of thought and action.

I said: 'There's nothing there.'

We waited in the dark for perhaps twenty minutes more; our challenges becoming more and more perfunctory. A strange restlessness crawled about us. Since Olivia had mentioned it my own vague wish for a cigarette had stretched over my body to the very nerve-ends, becoming a desire and then a craving. Eventually it distracted my attention altogether from the object of our sitting; there was just this mouthless longing, and darkness, music and the unmoving table were irrelevant beside it. As a record ended I said to Piers:

'Put the light on, will you? I'm dying for a fag. You can see it's a wash-out.'

The darkness flaked away at the click of a switch and I closed my eyes against the swift rush of light; diffuse and shaded but still overwhelming to unprepared eyes. I looked again to see Howard and Olivia also squinting, but Piers was gazing directly in front of him, his small, deep-set eyes unwavering. I reached for my case and tossed cigarettes to Olivia and Howard. Piers watched with tolerant contempt.

'You are like children,' he said. 'Half an hour without the little white cylinder-dummy in your mouths and you can think of nothing else.'

Howard grinned, tapping the cigarette I had thrown him and reaching down with it towards Olivia's lighter.

'Labial erotics, every one,' he agreed. 'May I say I've never known the infantile urge as strong as in the last five minutes? If I hadn't been the tough, reserved fellow I am I should have begun screaming for tobacco; I sat tight just to teach myself a lesson.'

Olivia looked at me.

'Were you anything like that, Tenn?'

I said: 'Very much so.'

Olivia said: 'I think perhaps I started it. I felt it growing –

down my throat, in my fingers, my nostrils itching for the smell of tobacco smoke. And it went on to all three of us?'

Howard laughed. 'Perhaps Ming wasn't as far away as we thought, then. A new trick.'

Piers said: 'That's interesting. Working on your vices now.'

Olivia said softly: 'And you, Piers. Were you wanting anything very badly?'

He looked at her, his eyes steady and cold.

'Nothing that you can give,' he said.

Howard, his glance darting warily between them, said: 'Well, well!'

I stood up and pushed my chair back against the wall. In the soft wash of lights the table was very ordinary; rough wood with a badly stained top and the drawer underneath missing. I hadn't noticed before how out of place it was in the impersonally tasteful atmosphere of Piers's rooms. The floorboards underneath were pitted and scarred from past buffetings. Looking up I saw Howard preparing to speak again, and forestalled him.

'I want a drink as well. It might buck things up. Shall we adjourn to the Little Lion?'

Olivia nodded uninterested acquiescence. Howard said: 'Brilliant suggestion.'

Piers got up and switched off the electric hum of the radiogram; it dropped from our consciousness like a veil discovered only in the lifting. Another car went down the street outside, its engine harsh in a new, unmuffled dimension of sound. Piers said: 'Right. But the Regent; not the Lion. We might see Lulu and the boy friend.'

CHAPTER FOUR

There was no sign of life in the house as we made our way down to the street, although the front door was wide open. We called perfunctorily for Helen and, receiving no reply, closed the door behind us as we went out. A cat was sitting on top of the bird-bath in the centre of the tiny scrap of front garden; a ginger-red monster with a long, silky coat and emotionless yellow eyes. Piers stepped across to stroke it and bury his face against its casual, yielding flank. As he straightened up again it arched its back suddenly and he pressed his hands lingeringly about it; down each side and cupping under its neck.

We waited for him to join us on the pavement, and I wondered why he had bothered to suggest the Regent. It had been tacitly out of favour with us for some weeks. For no clear reason we had changed over to the Little Lion on the opposite corner. I remembered Lulu saying she would probably be in the Regent along with Leslie but it was unusual for Piers to pay any attention to the suggested arrangements of so casual an acquaintance as Lulu was. Was I wrong, it occurred to me, in looking for motive in his most trivial actions? Perhaps I was paying too much attention to Piers's actions altogether.

All day there had been sharp, cold showers of rain, interspaced by longer but no more promising periods of grey, damp winds sweeping down from the unfriendly, tattered sky. Now, too late, the sky had turned serene – deep, delicate, virginal blue with only the last spur of the retreating cloud-mass standing up on the Chelsea horizon. The wind had dropped, too, into a flustering breeze that seemed to fan phantom stars into brilliance just beyond the edge of vision; brilliance vanishing, as one looked for confirmation, into the extending blue. Outside the Regent two American soldiers stood holding pint tankards of beer, their backs pressed against the wall and their feet sprawled so far forward that they could hardly be comfortable. We heard them arguing with each other as we passed, in slow, melancholy Southern drawl.

'Hell,' one of them said, 'you ain't been where I wish I was goin'.'

The swing doors were wedged open and we walked through and along the hall into the Lounge. It was pretty full but in several places there was room for three or four people to stand together without excessive crowding, not a very frequent phenomenon in these days. One of those places was beside a table in the corner by the door to the Ladies' room, where we saw Lulu sitting with Helen, Cynthia and a young man who was probably Leslie. We pushed our way through to join them.

Cynthia was the first to notice our approach; she caught sight of Howard and I saw her face crinkle into the knowing, confident smile of one in possession who sees the dispossessed hopelessly watching and waiting. She called out: 'Hello, people. No spooks to-night?'

Her voice was a huskier version of Howard's. He bent towards her, his hands reaching to grasp her hair. She swayed away from him, rocking her chair back.

Piers said: 'All drinking beer? I'll get some. Come and help me carry, Howard.'

Lulu said: 'Tenn, you haven't met Leslie, have you? This is Tenn, Leslie. And Olivia.'

Leslie's hand was flabby and nerveless; I dropped it and saw it sink down slowly to lie, palm uppermost, on the table top. His face was wedge-shaped, with a sharp, narrowly-protruding chin and a broad high forehead above it. His eyes were long-lashed behind black horn spectacles. I saw them glance at Olivia with the spontaneity of unappeasable lust; glance and retreat to the safer contemplation of Lulu's ochre cheek. She, I observed, was looking happy, the happiness reflected in her ability to sit motionless, vaguely smiling at us all. Her restlessness for the moment was allayed.

Howard and Piers came back, pushing their way through the crowd, each with four glasses balanced between his fingers. Howard, putting his consignment down, darted to one side where a middle-aged Jewish couple, rising to leave, presented two vacant chairs. He picked them up and Cynthia and Lulu made room for them at the table between their own chairs. Howard gestured Olivia into one and took my arm to press me towards the other.

'Come on, Tenn. You carry too much weight to stay on your feet unnecessarily.'

I smiled; the fat man's unembarrassed mirth to mask the bitterness of his embarrassment. Even as I winced inwardly under the lash I realized my own stupidity; my fat was there all the time for all to see and none who knew me could picture me without it. But references, casual or friendly, still cut deep. I wanted to turn the subject elsewhere and, wanting that, had to dissemble it.

I bowed to Howard. 'More consideration than you thin-fleshed skeletons normally show. I gratefully accept.'

Piers, leaning against the wall behind Helen, said: 'So this is Leslie, Lulu? You haven't introduced me.'

And I was free again; unwatched and unconstrained.

Piers said: 'How did the exhibition go?'

Leslie looked round obliquely at him. Lulu said rather quickly: 'You never sell anything the first day. But we've had a lot of people looking round.'

Piers said: 'You can get notices into the Party press, can't you, Lulu? Get the masses swarming round what's good for them.'

Leslie pushed a hand back through his bushy, square-cut mop of hair.

He said: 'I'm not a Communist.'

His speech was careful and only lightly accented. A certain stress, an accompanying lilt. Durham, perhaps.

Piers said: 'No. Lulu is. And she must find something dialectically significant in your work, mustn't she?'

Olivia said: 'Oh, give it a rest.'

Piers looked across at her. He said softly: 'I always give you good advice, Livia. You ought to take it. But I don't like repeating myself on the same day.'

I was watching Lulu and Leslie. Lulu genuinely bewildered, lost as usual in a world whose hints and vague apprehensions outraged her blacks and whites. Leslie, quicker to understand, glanced again at Olivia, finding in her an unexpected champion and so a hope for his ever-leaping yearnings. Beside me Cynthia drank from her beer and put down the red-smeared glass with a bump that splashed beer frothily over the table. She said loudly: 'I've asked you once – what became of the spooks to-night?'

She was looking at Howard and he picked his glass up from the table, pointedly ignoring her. He would have liked the rest of us to do the same, I knew, but I saw no point in complying with his malice. I said: 'They weren't very sociable. We haven't any reason for expecting superior manners from the disembodied.'

I saw Piers glance at me, so seriously that he might well have been secretly laughing and caught the implication. Embarrassment shivered down my spine again, fading away in a few seconds but leaving its tiny scar. To add to all the rest.

Leslie said: 'What are they – table rappers? Red lights and tambourines and pennies on the drum?'

Piers, surprisingly, smiled at him. He said: 'No. The Regency Gardens Society for Psychical Research. All derived from the very highest motives of scientific disinterest. You should come along some time.'

'Can we?' Lulu said. 'When – to-night?'

'To-night, if you feel like it,' Piers said. 'A few strange faces may brighten things up. One never knows.'

Lulu said: 'Oh, good! I've always wanted to attend a séance.

What about some more beer first, though. Or should we have spirits?' She laughed happily and turned to catch Leslie's arm just above the shoulder. 'Your turn, Les. Drinks wanted.'

She watched his progress towards the bar with naïve pride in her ability to make demands on an escort and have her demands obeyed. She clearly did not suspect that every one of us knew he would be paying with her money. When he returned with the half-pint glasses on a tray she accepted his offer of the first one with royal complacency.

Leslie asked: 'What does happen, anyway? Ghosts? Long white figures?'

Howard had found another chair for himself and carried it round to wedge himself in between Leslie and Helen. I saw Cynthia lean forward on her elbows, her body slackly drooping towards the table, to look at Howard as he sat down. Then deliberately she leaned sideways against Helen, and Helen put her arm out to draw her closer and to hold her.

Piers, still blandly informative, said to Leslie: 'No long white figures yet. We've only been sitting for three months. Some very queer stuff, though. Messages through table rapping – very interesting, some of them.'

Leslie's small mouth smiled watchfully.

'In the dark or with the lights on?' he inquired.

'We sit in the dark,' Piers said, '– at present.'

'That will suit us,' Leslie said. He put his arm round Lulu's waist, paying her, pitying her. 'That will suit us all right.'

'It suits everyone,' Howard said. 'Everyone. What about you, Cynth? Do you feel like joining us round the table when we go back?'

Cynthia smiled at him and looked up at Helen.

'Shall we, darling? Do you feel like giving the spooks a fling?'

Helen said: 'I suppose we might as well, if it's going to be a sort of party.'

Piers said: 'Well then. Let's be moving.'

The two Americans were still leaning against the side of the pub as we left. I was on the outside of the group and one of them came over and accosted me.

'Can you tell me, friend, how I should get to Piccadilly Circus?'

'Gloucester Road Station,' I told him. 'First on the left.'

'Thanks,' he said. 'I aim to get me a piece of old England.'

I watched him with some interest as he turned away, trying to fit my alternative translations of his idiom into the right context. He jerked his companion's arm and they moved off down the road. It seemed probable that 'old' had an affectionate rather than an objective significance. And that England was strictly feminine gender.

As I climbed the stairs at the tail of a noisy procession I saw that one of the doors to my rooms, which had been closed when we went out, was now open. I looked in, straining my eyes to see through the darkness. There was a dark bulk lying on the floor by the window. I recognized it as Rupert, lying on his back with his head towards the last glimmer of daylight, reading a book.

'Want the light on?' I asked him.

He turned a page, the rustling unaccountably vivid in the shadowy room.

'You, Tennyson? No thanks. I'm quite all right. I've borrowed your Cowper. Close the door, will you?'

I closed it, and followed the others to the next landing. Halfway up I stood aside to let Leslie come out of the bathroom. He ran lightly up the last half dozen steps and I followed him more slowly, hearing the noise of the cistern behind me like a river of iron.

They brought chairs in from Olivia's room and one downstairs from Lulu's. Eventually the eight of us were grouped round the table. The sixteen hands resting on it seemed, as they were massed, peculiarly detached from their owners. They were sixteen five-fingered small animals, hairless, crouching, waiting. I twitched my own left hand, in reassurance.

Darkness again; and a long lake of silence breaking now and then into giggling crests. With a preliminary scratching hiss the radiogram swelled out into Debussy – 'La Mer'. Sound without shape or colour, only the remorseless logic of return and repetition; the drifting and drifting without anchor or harbour. It stilled the giggling and the cramped, uneasy movements. Here there was neither land nor sky.

Above it, Piers's voice, matter-of-fact:

'There may be nothing at all, of course. Eight may be the wrong number – too many. Or some person may be unsuitable.'

Lulu said: 'Oh. Can we talk?'

Piers said: 'You can talk if it has any relevance to the sitting. The atmosphere need not be one of fear or worship. It can be …'

'Clinical?' Olivia's voice suggested softly.

Piers laughed, a laugh edged with hardness. 'Yes, clinical.'

And on that suggestion the Debussy was clinical also – a grey, antiseptic rhythm, dulling and weakening and almost smelling of sickness.

Nothing happened. 'La Mer' ended, and was started again. Cynthia's voice, more husky and more animal in the darkness, drifted across the table:

'I'm getting rather frightfully bored.'

Lulu said with prim enthusiasm:

'Scientifically we have to give it … them … every chance. I find it absorbing. You have to relax – is that right, Piers?'

Piers said: 'If you like. It doesn't make much difference.'

There was a fretful tone about his speech. It was natural, I supposed, that he should want to impress even these with the reality of what we sought; I did myself. Seeing the strange wings the child will call: look, look, the white blackbird! – and his son, the grown man, never tires of seeking witnesses to his own amazing bird. Now they were here even Piers must want them to be satisfied, to be convinced, but why bring them in the first place? That was the gesture that was out of character.

Helen said uneasily: 'There's supper. I really think I'll have to be going down soon.'

And in the immediate wake of her words the air turning to the verge of frost, a chill blast from forgotten, night-bound glaciers and yet without strength or motion, the enveloping, immobile cold. Here, and as swiftly gone.

The table began to move, rocking at first and then savagely bumping and bounding until it seemed to be straining with malice and hate against our restraining hands. Piers, sharp, exultant, called out:

'We can hear you. Is anyone there? Rap once for yes.'

And listening, obeying, the table halted, and we heard the one loud rap.

Piers said: 'I'll spell out. Rap for the initials of your name.'

M. I. N. X.

Howard asked eagerly: 'Is it Ming? Once for yes. Is it Ming?'

The affirmation. Lulu said:

'Ming? Is that your ... guardian spirit? A Chinaman?'

Piers said gravely: 'Ming Chi Li. A Sung mandarin. He was tortured to death by the invading Ch'in Tartars in 1157. Very slowly.'

Lulu said: 'Oh, dear.'

Leslie broke in: 'Was he – a lover of the arts?'

The table rapped once. Olivia said, explaining: 'You can put your questions directly.'

'Right,' Leslie said. He paused briefly. 'Did you know the painter, Wu Tao-tzu?'

The table began to rock. Howard provided the alphabet recitation. We waited for this tapping, stumbling speech.

TANG NOT SUNG.

Cynthia said: 'Is that supposed to mean anything?'

I said: 'Yes. A little trap that didn't come off. Leslie asked a Sung mandarin if he knew one of the great painters of the T'ang dynasty – a matter of four hundred years earlier.'

Piers said quietly: 'And it's not evidential, of course. Since at least one of us knew who Wu Tao-tzu was, the trap doesn't spring.'

Lulu asked, bewildered: 'What trap?'

Howard explained: 'The suggestion is that one of us is Ming – doing a spot of faking.'

Lulu said indignantly: 'Oh but it couldn't be! You can tell it's real.'

The table began to rock again, more slowly, almost sedately.

Howard said: 'Is there a message for anyone?'

The answer was yes. We began to go round the circle, narrowing out. Was it for Piers? No. Was it for Lulu? No. Was it for Leslie? No. Was it for Olivia? The table rapped once. Howard began to take the message. We listened, hearing the words trickle through.

BITCH. BITCH. FILTHY BITCH. I'LL GET …

It ended in a confused flurry of bumping that tailed off gradually into silence.

Cynthia said: 'Ming doesn't seem exactly mad on you, Livia. Do you come here every week just to get insulted?'

Olivia said: 'Not exactly. He isn't usually so … violent.'

Her voice was a little shaky. I spoke across the table.

'Everyone had enough for this evening?'

Howard said: 'I don't think there's likely to be anything further anyway. Switch on, Piers, will you?'

From blackness dazzlingly to light. I looked at the circle of faces round the table. Howard excited, and trying to conceal his excitement. Helen preoccupied. Cynthia bored. Olivia, her face half turned away, still tense and nervous. Leslie off-hand, rolling a cigarette. Lulu, like myself, gazing round the assembled faces, but more wonderingly and more openly. And Piers, expressionless, withdrawn, looking straight in front of him at the table.

Helen said: 'I'll slip down and put the coffee on. You're all coming down for something, aren't you?'

Lulu said: 'No. I don't think so.' She looked at Leslie, and I saw him nod slightly. 'Not to-night, Helen.'

Helen prepared to leave; Cynthia moving with her automatically. Howard was watching them, the excitement in his eyes dying down into some more sombre emotion. He said suddenly, blurting the words out with the doomed incoherence of a child:

'I'll come along and lend a hand, too, Helen.'

They all went. I heard Cynthia's voice float back up the well of the stairs:

'Don't slip, Howard darling. You might break your neck.'

Lulu said: 'I think I'll go up to my room. See you all at breakfast.'

Leslie drew a deep inhalation of his cigarette before following her. I turned to go myself. At the door I paused very briefly to look back at Piers and Olivia, left alone in the room together. They sat drooped in their chairs with averted eyes, like marionettes thrown down by the puppet-master; thrown down by chance in opposing aspects where they would never be able to see each other again.

'See you below,' I said, and closed the door behind me.

I heard a voice from the third-floor balcony and looked up. I could make out Leslie's face in the shadows, leaning over the banisters.

'Yes?'

He said: 'Ask Helen if she'll make up a tray – coffee and biscuits for two. I'll be down for it about' – he lifted his wrist and I saw the luminous flash of a watch dial – '... about quarter-past ten.' He laughed softly. 'You understand. Twenty minutes. The first intermission.'

I saw him disappear, heard him open a door, and went down to my own rooms. Rupert was still lying on my floor, not attempting to read any longer but simply contemplating the ceiling, his hands clasped behind his head. He did not stir when I switched the light on. I walked across and lifted him gently with the toe of my shoe. He spoke then.

40

'Tennyson,' he said, 'night is a fascinating thing. It dispels all the confusions of day.'

I put my hands under his shoulders and he allowed himself to be lifted.

'You aren't the only one who thinks so,' I said.

CHAPTER FIVE

OLIVIA MOVED her things from Piers's rooms three days later, but only one and a half flights downstairs to the little room that was nominally part of my own preserves. Helen called me into her room as I was going out, to explain matters. She was sitting on her divan under the window when I went in in response to her call, her legs silk-stockinged and drawn up neatly beneath her – a very young matron. She put her crochet work down and smiled.

'Oh, there you are, Tenn. Did you get your registered envelope from the hall?'

I said: 'Yes. I picked it up after breakfast. You saw me. Why don't you come to the point, Helen?'

She smiled again.

'Why do you always pretend to be brutal with me, Tenn? And you never pay me nice compliments. Don't you like my nylons?'

She stretched her legs out and I inspected them.

'Very nice,' I told her. 'But let us remember our advanced age. And I did notice Olivia carrying things down into the little room, so you might as well get on to explaining all about it.'

She looked shocked.

'But, Tenn, surely I don't need to? I'm sure you don't mind people who have nowhere to go using it for a night or two. She's had to leave Piers, you know.'

'Yes,' I said patiently, 'I know. And I've no objection at all to Olivia staying there until she finds somewhere else. Just about how long do you think that will be?'

Helen looked vaguely out of the window into the watery, mist-blown sunshine.

'It's very hard to find rooms now. Two or three nights – perhaps a week.'

'Helen,' I said, 'Olivia clearly has no notion of the status of the little room. She passed me on the stairs just now with a bundle of clothes in her arms and told me quite gaily that she was moving in. Now I would like you to tell me how much rent you're charging her for it.'

Helen laughed, her laughter like gold, a child innocently amused at her own folly.

'Honestly, Tenn, nothing until she gets a job. Then – it depends what sort of job she gets. You don't use the room, do you? It was just being wasted.'

'And when you do start charging her,' I pursued, 'what reduction do you propose to make in my rent?'

'But I'm so short, Tenn,' she protested. 'If I did reduce your rent by the same amount it would only mean that I should have to borrow more from you. Anyway, you're two months in advance and she may have left by then. I don't think she'll stay long in the same house with Piers.'

'Three months,' I said. I paused, considering more carefully the intricacies of Helen's financial logic and, as usual, coming finally to defeat. She looked up at me watchfully.

'I really should have been more honest with you about it,' she said. 'I'm sorry, Tenn – it's just the landlady coming out in me. But you don't mind, do you? If you have anyone down we'll fit them in somewhere.'

'That's the great thing about you, Helen,' I said. 'You manage to fit everything in somewhere – somehow.'

She smiled, accepting a compliment. Behind me I heard the sound of the wooden partition being run back on its castors. I went across to help. Cynthia surrendered the job to me gracefully and stepped through into Helen's half of the double room. She was immaculately made-up except for her hair, which hung round her face in lank curls. She sat down on the floor beside Helen's divan.

'Groom me, will you, darling?'

Helen bent obediently over her, taking brushes and comb from her outstretched hand. It made rather a pretty, sentimental tableau. I felt, however, that there was no urgent need for me to stay and contemplate it. Retreating towards the door, I said: 'Try not to move anyone into my bed, Helen, will you? At least, not without telling me.'

Cynthia said: 'Going out? Anywhere in particular? I thought you were in for lunch to-day.'

'Yes, I am,' I said. 'I'm just going for a walk.'

'The park?' Helen asked. 'You might find Rupert – and Howard. They've taken Brock along with them.'

My hand was on the doorknob.

'In that case I'll go in the opposite direction. I'm conspicuous enough as it is, without parading along with exotic animal life. See you at one.'

I heard Helen begin: 'But nobody *minds*, Tenn …' as I closed the door.

I had some vague intention of acting on my avowal but it evaporated even before I reached the street. The southern half of Regency Gardens piled up into dark and rather monstrous houses and actually ended in an unlovely modern block of flats; beyond it lay only the further desolations of the tail-end of Chelsea. Automatically I turned north, towards Old Brompton Road. And as automatically I found myself, a few minutes later, walking down the wide sweep of Queen's Gate towards the distant green.

Memories of childhood are haphazard things. They are events in another dimension, knife-edged and inapprehensible, shifting on the axis of an instant from oblivion to coloured reality and back again. At a word, a sound, a gesture, time falls away like a cast skin and the cricket bat is alive in your hands, slipping at the command of twelve-year-old muscle and nervous strength into the unrepeatable leg glide, with grass, sky and summer heat long wintered, a cloaking universe about you. Those are the memories that surprise; they come more often as the dividing years stretch longer, and flame with greater brilliance – perhaps against a world grown greyer and less real. But there are others less wilful, more ready to the tired mind's evocation. These you can call up and, more or less obediently, they come. Queen's Gate, I remembered. Queen's Gate. 1903?

'03 or '04. It was difficult to remember whether I was eight or nine. I was nine when I went to St. Nette's but I had no idea now whether my first summer in London came that year or the one before. I remembered only fragments of the train journey – noise and movement and the unbearably exciting smell of the London station; that smell that to-day is only oil and smoke. And later, drowsiness – wonder and disappointment and drowsiness in the strange house where people's voices seemed to echo from the great mirrors in the hall, and there was meaningless, tantalizing, grown-up laughter from the open door of the drawing-room as I was taken upstairs to bed.

Those were the echoes, drifting and unreliable, on the verge of reality. It was the following morning that always came at bidding, sharp and in focus.

I walked beside Burkie, my head not much higher than her narrow, belted waist. There was the sound of leaves from the centre of the square where trees tossed in sad captivity behind iron railings, and the nearer, more comforting rustle of Burkie's skirts beside me. It was all very strange; I could see three sides of the square and guess the hidden fourth and this was an almost incredible, a wonderful reversal of nature. At Thirl the house stood, as I had sometimes fancied, like a queen amongst the curtseying ranks of trees. Here the trees were prisoners and the houses massed about to watch them either in pity or curious contempt; I could not yet tell which. We reached the corner and turned our backs on the lonely plot of green, and I felt happier watching the houses, forgetting what lay behind.

And so we turned into Queen's Gate.

In July 1946, a middle-aged, a fat man, my eyes alive to the ruin behind the still noble sweep of the avenue, I could feel the large tightness of Burkie's hand on mine as I had abruptly stopped, halted by the vista that amazed and terrified me. Along this road, on which the drive at Thirl could have been set down five or six times, side by side, the carriages clipped their way towards or away from the park, behind the tight-reined horses. These by their familiarity made the scene more dream-like. In the wake of one carriage, drawn by spotless, prancing greys, I saw two ladies in identical black habit sitting side-saddle and erect on matching chestnuts. They rattled past and off into the infinity of the unbroken, converging lines. They were the known and expected, casually riding off into the miraculous. The overtones of the dread that then held me have echoed up in later years at the sight of landscapes of de Chirico or Tanguy. The overtones. But remembering I re-experienced the full terror of that original discord.

And that which resolved it also. I had been frozen against Burkie's skirts, unable to move for fear of seeing again that which so obscurely tortured me. Her scolding comforted and reassured, but could not persuade me to face that immobile, yet leaping, architectural line. I was obedient, but could not act on my obedience. Only curiosity won me round; curiosity first about the strange noise swelling towards us, and then inquisitiveness alert and eager, spurred by Burkie's words:

'Look, Master Tennyson! A motor carriage.'

I turned and looked and there was another first time, but one so ludicrous and interesting that I accepted it at a glance, and with it accepted the long wide road down which it rattled its way, all London, all the world. I walked along beside her unconcernedly after that and when we reached Kensington Gardens I was unsurprised and unenthusiastic.

Now on a Saturday morning in a dull summer, in the exhausted aftermath of the second world war to buckle the long wheel of time between me and Burkie – Burkie mysteriously dead in my first year at St. Nette's ... of cancer? – I walked where we had walked. Queen's Gate still seemed wide and long, but the houses that lined it needed painting and those that were not hotels had all too clearly been split up into flats. And here and there only the shells were left, burned out by flame from a suddenly unscrupulous sky; those, I thought, kept best their almost forgotten dignity. The sky above them was scarred also, ribbed with thick, black strokes of cloud, driving sullenly before a wind from the south east. More roofs than these were off; and a wilder east wind than this lashed everywhere.

I walked on towards the park. A taxi cruised past me slowly. Ten yards ahead a young man in flannels clicked his tongue at a mongrel dog which veered diagonally away as it ran past him. I crossed the intersection of Cromwell Road. I looked back, consciously comparing the distance I had walked with that still in front of me, but turned again without formulating my estimate. It was becoming a habit. To feel pride in walking barely a hundred yards was the harshest of self-indictments. If I could no longer take the small, ordinary achievements of my body for granted, at least I need not dwell unnecessarily on them. I walked on, resolutely unengrossed in the deliberate movements of my legs.

Here was Kensington Road, and the traffic flowing swiftly between the Park and the stubborn, stately houses. I entered Kensington Gardens through a futile, isolated gate and followed the path towards the Memorial. As I approached it the sun came out. I thought of Piers; it had roused his pedantry once.

'More accurately,' he had insisted, 'the clouds break to let through the sun's unimpeded rays. Although, of course, relatively speaking it doesn't really matter. The sun comes out or the clouds let through – it's all the same.'

Relatively speaking. Sun and shadow, winter and summer, war and peace. Nothing clear, nothing substantial. Relatively speaking black was a property of white. There was not even the consolation, I reflected, of thinking we were at the end of an era. For the end was also the beginning.

There, at least, was the Monument. The banking steps were dazzling in the sunlight, the gold inlay more bright, the pinnacled, beckoning angels more softly green. The whole great erection of white and gold and emerald seemed to take on a brilliant and emphatic reality. It rested there, existing, outlasting its detractors. The trees behind it would lose their present luxuriance, regain and lose it again; in bud and leaf and leafy fall. This foliage of marble and gold could never fail. Even the war's wound – the fourth spire broken off – only emphasized its solidity.

I looked, and turned away from it. It was of a different time than this; solid in another dimension. Now in our confusion and flux we might yearn for it, but it could point no way for us. I'm getting old, I thought, old and sentimental. There is no meaning and no objective. We learned that a long, long time ago.

The sunlight was gone again as I crossed the road into Hyde Park, and the Serpentine lay below me, black and unfriendly and ruffled into petty anger by the shifting breeze. Higher up, on the Row, a couple cantered their horses in the direction of Hyde Park Corner. The man was dressed in what looked like a grey lounge suit, the woman in fawn jodhpurs, a yellow sweater and, it would seem, nothing else. Their animals were a tired-looking pair. I began to walk through the trees behind the bathing enclosure. As I arrowed down, at last, to the asphalt verge of the water, I passed one particularly large tree, and on the other side of it found two park chairs on which Rupert and Howard were seated while Brock grubbed enthusiastically at the tree's roots. They were looking silently out across the Serpentine. Howard shifted his gaze slightly, catching sight of me almost as soon as I myself was aware of them. He sprang up, exchanging whatever silent boredom he had been practising with Rupert for the usual high spirits that I associated with him.

'Tenn!' he said. 'Sit down. Wait, I'll get you a chair.'

There was one a few yards away, at the edge of the water. He carried it back to the tree, brushed the seat with his handkerchief, and invited me to accept it. He had pulled his own chair to one side and so I sat down between them.

'Did you expect to find us here?' Howard asked. 'Were you looking for us?'

I said: 'I wouldn't say I was looking for you. Helen told me you were here. At least, she said you were taking Brock for a walk.'

'He got tired,' Howard explained. I glanced to one side where Brock was methodically taking the bottom of the tree apart, and Howard smiled. 'He's enjoying himself, anyway.'

'He draws less attention that way,' I said.

Rupert looked round suddenly.

'That's curious. The way we automatically associate introvert and subjectivist; extrovert and objectivist. It's wrong, of course. The reverse is nearer the truth. It's the extrovert who lives in a private universe, a solipsist world in which other people are no more than curious phantoms. The introvert is always trying to come to terms with an objective environment; in wondering what people think about his actions he endows them with real and separate life.'

'And we,' Howard suggested, 'what are we? All honourable introverts?'

I said, striving for avuncular, unresented patronage: 'You should make a poem of it, Rupert. Have you been writing much lately?'

He paused before answering.

'It seems unfair, Tennyson,' he said, 'that your namesake and all the rest of the bloody horde of Romantic poets should have been able to write so many thousands of lines of verse about absolutely nothing at all, while poor idiots like me, in the great intellectual tradition of Donne and Marvell, find it difficult to squeeze out a line.'

'Not as bad as that,' I said. 'Two volumes, after all, two well-regarded volumes.'

I was amused and pleased by his show of spirit, even in self-condemnation. There had been force behind that 'bloody', an adjective, anyway, that was unusual in Rupert's language. But he relapsed now into bland melancholy.

'Well regarded?' he echoed gloomily. 'Who by?

> *In the long out-wash of dream, love's ocean fringe,*
> *We beat through time's deep-mangled surf and reach*
> *The ravaged, the inestimable shore.*

Three reviewers quoted that one as characteristic of my sinewy thought. It isn't poetry whatever it means.'

'What does it mean?' Howard said.

'I don't know,' he said. He wrinkled his long, narrow brow. 'I think the shore was certainty – to be reached through love. It sounds ridiculous, doesn't it?'

'Damned silly,' Howard agreed, a shade more violently than was necessary. Cynthia would be groomed by now, I thought. And sitting beside Helen on Helen's divan, looking out of the window with her and chattering to each other as they generally did?

'Yes,' Rupert said, 'and listen:

> *The full stream feeds on flower of rushes,*
> *Ripe grasses trammel a travelling foot,*
> *The faint, fresh flame of the young year flushes*
> *From leaf to flower and flower to fruit …'*

I found myself almost irresistibly finishing the quotation:

> *'And flower and fruit are as gold and fire,*
> *And the oat is heard above the lyre*
> *And the hoofed heel of a satyr crushes*
> *The chestnut husk at the chestnut root.'*

Rupert said mournfully: 'It doesn't mean anything, of course – not even as much as my deep-mangled surf. But it's poetry. Anyone can tell it's poetry. That's what seems unfair. Swinburne could use words like that and he cheapened them, throwing them away like confetti. If I had them, if I had their mastery, I'd drive them like diamonds. Every word a diamond, set in filigree silver. I've got the ideas, all right.'

'You could be worse,' Howard said, 'you could be in my state. Now and then I think of composing but the only efforts I make are pretty little things after Mozart. And life isn't pretty any more – it isn't even real and earnest – life is just subtle. Everyone's got to be subtle – musicians, artists, sculptors, novelists … Especially poets. You can be as subtle as the rest of them, Rupe. Subtle content's the thing – forget the setting. You can't have both; you're fortunate in having the one that's popular.'

'You can have both, though,' Rupert said. 'Shakespeare did; Donne did.'

'Subtle in their time,' Howard said, 'and you can't detach them from it. No one looks at them without adding that background. But put them down in this generation and they would be lost in the subtleties we've discovered. Name someone nearer home; name a living poet who's got both.'

Rupert said: 'I can't.' He paused. 'I can name someone who might do it.'

I said interestedly: 'Who, Rupert?'

'Britton,' he said. 'He can use words; I think he may develop depth as well. It's six years since he published anything.'

Howard's mind raced away, indifferently challenging his own stated argument.

'What about Eliot?' he asked, making a discovery.

'I can only remember one line from Eliot,' Rupert said. '*The poetry does not matter.* It's from one of the *Quartets*.'

I said: 'And Britton. You think he may have developed depth during his stay in the United States?'

Rupert said slowly: 'It doesn't sound likely, does it? We don't know. He cut himself off all the time the war was on; and if he wrote anything he didn't publish it. But there was something there before. It will be interesting to see, won't it? He will be here in a few weeks.'

Brock, abandoning his tunnelling operations, came round to the front of the chairs. He stretched up on his rear legs, his long, snouted face and small front paws weaving gently as he peered up at Howard. Howard sprang up.

'More walks?' he suggested. 'Come on, you two. There's time for Tenn to buy us a few drinks yet.'

CHAPTER SIX

THE AUTUMN ISSUE of *Trend* came out in the first week of August and by the middle of the month I knew the worst. Marks, as usual, was handling the distribution. When he rang me up, on an unnaturally bright Thursday morning, he wasn't even formally apologetic. He read off the list of block sales. Eight hundred, five hundred, two lots of two hundred, one of a hundred and some odd fifties.

'That makes two thousand,' he said.

'And the other three?' I asked.

His voice was brisk, sharp, faintly cockney. No one would guess the tall, pot-bellied, immaculately dressed Marks from hearing it.

'They're still here, of course. I shall keep on trying with them. There's a chance that Smith's may be willing to increase their order. But there will be at least twenty-five hundred left on our hands. I can tell you that now.'

I said: 'But you're offering them sale-or-return, aren't you? What's the drawback? What have they got to lose?'

'They just aren't interested,' he told me. 'All the bookstalls are crowded out with unsaleable stuff already. And these arty magazines are a drug anyway. The market's …'

'Dead,' I supplied. 'Yes, I know. But I'm not asking much. I'm only asking them to find an odd space to show the magazine to the public at no financial risk to themselves and with eight-pence profit in the till for every copy they sell. I can't believe I'm being unreasonable. They don't even need to display; they could just keep a dozen under the counter – people might ask for copies.'

'Too much trouble,' Marks said. 'They can sell enough on other lines. More popular lines.' He hesitated for a moment. 'I took a copy home with me last night. I had a go at reading it, after dinner.'

'Well?'

'I suppose it's pretty clever,' he suggested, 'but it's not what the public wants. An article on Picasso and Klee, one on Stravinsky, and one on somebody called George. George who, anyway?'

'You didn't read it carefully enough,' I said. 'George is his surname. He's a poet.'

The briskness of his voice was tinged with finality.

'Well, there you are. There's over half you might as well pulp straight away. I haven't got unlimited storage myself, you know.'

'Thanks,' I said. 'Thanks for the advice.'

Marks emitted something that was a cross between laughing and coughing.

'Right,' he said. 'That's how it is. We'll do what we can with them.'

I put the receiver down and eased myself into an arm-chair. There was a copy of the magazine lying on the table beside it. I leafed through it. I knew the contents but there was always a fresh recognition, a misleading impression of the stamp and permanence of the printed page. It wasn't a bad selection at all. Stephen had done a good job, especially measured against the two previous issues. Standing apart, as he did, from all the various drifting circlets on the whirlpool of our time and culture, his editing and emphasis were detached and cool. There was one of his own short stories in the issue, knife-edged and severe. His Editorial cut sharp and cold. In the eighteenth century his austerity would probably have been appreciated. Here and now … If *Trend* must go, and the quarterly cheque with it, that was just one more step towards the film-cutting or script-writing or radio-producing, or whatever distorting mirror waited at the end of his particular corridor. At least Stephen could be relied on to accept it with ironic appreciation.

Howard came in, closed the door, and knocked on the inside panel. He gestured towards me in explanation.

'My innate breeding asserting itself,' he said. 'Better late than never.'

'Not going in this morning?' I asked him.

'Counterpoint,' he said. 'I duck it whenever I can. I find it a tedious subject. It's either boringly simple or miles away in the dim blue yonder. What – reading your own magazines, Tenn? It's not a bad issue, though. I polished it off in the bath last night. That Chagall reproduction was cute; I much preferred the colours your printer hashed up to the original. A really nice *sloppy* purple.'

'Last night?' I said. 'Do you mean about two o'clock this morning? Was that you having a bath?'

'Was it as late as that? Sorry if I woke you. I felt restless. I plunged about a bit because the water was just about frozen when the time came to stoke up after I'd finished reading. I think my idea of the earthly paradise is boiling hot water in the middle of the night.'

He began to walk to and fro along the length of my shabby plum-coloured carpet. It had been Helen's originally – I had taken the rooms as completely furnished – but in her never-ending financial difficulties she had sold me the carpet and, at different times, two or three other articles of furniture as well. The carpet had been a good one once. Even now there were several quite large patches which were individually opulent. I watched Howard nervously treading it. He was dressed in decrepit blue corduroys he had raked up from somewhere and a check shirt I could remember throwing out six months before. It hung round him in baggy folds. On his feet he was wearing battered, open leather sandals. I watched them moving restlessly across the expanse of purple, and saw them halt at the edge, facing away from me.

'Tenn,' he said, 'I think I ought to get away from here.'

I let my gaze travel upwards, resting at last on the narrow nape of his neck. He was in urgent need of a haircut, his hair curled up into a roll at the back of his head.

'Where did you think of going?' I asked.

He said: 'Oh … I could get someone to put me up.'

His voice was petulant. He was still turned away from me so that I could not see his face, but I guessed that I had not made the right comment. I tried again.

'What's wrong, Howard? Why do you want to leave, anyway?'

He turned, explosively, angrily excited.

'Because I get fed up with drifting around in this atmosphere! I get fed up with being broke and having to cart that bloody 'cello about on buses and I get fed up with living in rags. And I want to do something more than drift between the Regent and the Little Lion.'

'Right,' I said. 'You want to camp out on somebody else, in different rags, preferably on a different bus route and between two other pubs.'

He said sullenly: 'It needn't be that.'

'No,' I said. 'You could sell your 'cello and get a job as an insurance agent and settle down contentedly in Wimbledon or Croydon.'

Howard walked over and leaned against the arm of my chair, picking the copy of *Trend* up automatically. He rolled it into a cylinder and tapped it against his knees.

'I could go and live with my father,' he said.

Although I had been at Number 36 for over eighteen months this was a new and surprising factor to me. Rather absurdly I repeated his words.

'Your father?'

Howard grinned. 'Yes, my father. You didn't think Helen was impregnated by a heavenly spirit, did you? Cynthia's got a father, too. The same one.'

'She isn't a widow, then?'

'Helen? Not even divorced. Neither of them bothered about one. I think the old man still has hopes she'll come back some day, bringing her infants with her. Even after fifteen years. Great thing for hoping, the human soul.'

I said: 'Don't you go to see him at all?'

He said: 'What a lot of questions you do ask!' He had a sly, uncertain look on his face, as though he had indecently revealed himself and was remembering now the lost axioms of morality. Then, plunging, he went on quickly:

'We used to go to see him twice a year. That was at the beginning. And then, when we went away to school – the only money Helen would take off him was the money for that – we were still supposed to go for a month in the summer holidays. We did for a few years, and then we began making excuses for cutting the time short and finally dropped the visits altogether. He never said anything about it. He still writes to Helen at Christmas, wishing us all the compliments of the season.' He glanced at me with wry bravado. 'I could sponge on him, couldn't I? You could almost call it a natural right.'

'What does he do?' I asked.

Howard said: 'You've probably heard of him. He's the barrister.'

'The barrister? You mean – Sir Clifford Drage?'

'Yes,' Howard said indifferently. 'That's the one. He must have a pile, mustn't he? He's always cropping up in the papers.'

Howard's expression was still a strange one; a compound, I thought, of shame, anxiety and, in some way, relief. There were roots here which went deep; neither Helen nor Cynthia nor, before to-day, Howard, had ever mentioned this in any of the hundreds of hours of their chatter to which I had been an audience. And normally they were the reverse of reticent about their private concerns. This revelation now … Howard was under a strain, all right. I sat up, drawing my legs in close under the arm-chair.

'Well, that's easy, then. You can go to your father. He'll

probably be overjoyed to greet the returning son. You can live in luxury and take your pick of a dozen or more good, noble and true aims to follow. All this and a purpose in life too. You're made.'

He looked at me searchingly for a moment before bursting out into shaking laughter.

'Yes, I am, aren't I?' He sobered quickly and walked over to the piano, where he lifted my bust of Goethe and weighed it carefully in his hands. 'Tenn,' he said. 'Last night. You weren't doing any twisting, were you?'

I said: 'When are you going? You can telephone him from here if you like. He'll be in the Directory.'

He smiled, bumping the bust gently back on to the polished surface of the piano. He was self-possessed again, his nervousness just a part of his friendly curiosity about everything.

'Some day I will,' he said. 'When I get tired of slumming. Last night, though. Were you faking those messages about you and Livia? "Tenn Olivia true happiness." Damned funny thing for Ming to come out with. And repeating it.'

I said tightly: 'Can you give me one reason why I should do such a bloody silly thing?'

He looked at me in astonishment; with his mobility of expression and talent for mimicry it was impossible to tell whether feigned or genuine.

'Well, she's available now, isn't she? I thought you might be offering to take over. It seemed logical enough.'

'Well, I'm not,' I said. 'And if I were I could think of more effective ways of making an offer than by tilting a table.'

He looked at me seriously for a moment, and then laughed.

'Fancy me thinking you might be shy, Tenn! What a silly idea!' His amusement changed again to an almost sullen brooding. 'It's just that I get worried sometimes as to what's behind everything. I can't imagine anything more futile than our sitting in the dark round that table if someone is twisting us all the time. And I can't help suspecting …'

I said drily: 'You've always sounded convinced enough.'

He looked up quickly. 'Yes, at the time. But remembering it afterwards it's difficult to put your finger on any one point that really is convincing. Then there are these cryptic messages. Honestly, Tenn, anyone who hadn't sat in on the séances would dismiss them as phony straight away.' He paused again, remembering them. I thought he was going to cast back on to the scent of the messages concerning Olivia and myself, but he didn't. Instead he said: 'I didn't get that one about Lulu and Monday. It's weeks ago that Lulu sat in. Ming seems more than slightly imbecilic at times.'

He had lifted the piano lid and now began prodding the treble notes discordantly with one finger. He was hunched over, his face quite close to the keyboard. I watched him for a moment. Then I said, casually: 'That was quite straightforward, actually. We did have a do on Monday and Lulu was there. Didn't anyone tell you?'

He did not straighten up but reached out to strike a middle C. He said quite softly: 'No. No one told me. You didn't tell me. Piers didn't tell me. Livia didn't tell me.'

I said: 'Livia wasn't there either. If you're interested there was only Piers, Lulu and myself. It was an impromptu arrangement.'

Howard turned, half sitting on the piano keys.

'I like to hear about impromptu arrangements,' he said, 'especially when I'm left out of them. Tell me all about it.'

I heard the door open and glanced sideways over my right shoulder. Piers came in and stood just inside the door, watching us. I called to him.

'Piers. Howard wants to know all about the séance we had on Monday. You tell him.'

'Tell him what?' Piers said. His voice was brittle and rather cold. 'It was a bit of a flop, wasn't it? It never really got going.'

I looked at Howard. Now that Piers had come in he looked at once more angry and more diffident. I thought the diffidence would win, but it didn't. He spoke to Piers with a barely controlled viciousness.

'You could tell me two things. Why you think it's a good idea to start having extra séances leaving me and Livia out, and why you were so careful not to say anything about it afterwards.'

Piers came over and took my other arm-chair, sitting back in it and throwing his small legs out before him. He said calmly: 'Two questions – two answers. One. We had a séance on Monday because Lulu has been pestering to sit in with us again for the last three weeks. I don't want her in on Wednesday nights because I think the present four is the best combination. She asked again at dinner on Monday so we went up and had an hour straight away. You and Olivia were both out. Two. I can't answer for Lulu herself or Tenn. I didn't say anything about it because I rather expected this kind of childish demonstration.'

Howard's anger collapsed and with it his attack. He said weakly: 'There wouldn't have been any of what you call childish demonstrations if you had simply told me about it.' He went back to his nervous preoccupation with Goethe but this time simply stroked and tapped the plaster with his finger-nails and did not lift it. 'You're always complicating things, Piers. If it was just a spur-of-the-minute do, why keep quiet about it?'

Piers watched him, his lips thin, their edges lifting slightly.

'Yes,' he said, 'last Monday was spur-of-the-moment. Next Monday will be fixed in advance.' He glanced at me. 'Can you make eight-thirty, Tenn?'

I nodded. Howard stepped away from the piano and stood in front of Piers looking down at him. He was like a small boy in front of a garden god of his own creation, part bullying, more fearing. He said: 'Do you want Livia and me along, too?'

Piers crooked his legs up slowly. His gaze was fixed beyond Howard, on my Dürer print.

'No,' he said precisely. 'I don't. I'm experimenting.' He looked at me, a grave conspirator. 'We're experimenting.' His glance flicked to Howard, suddenly changing. 'You don't mind at all, do you? You know how it is. Lulu would muck things up if we let her into the Wednesdays, and I just want to try her Marxist reactions out on a few small séances. Probably no more than two or three times.'

His control was admirable; from unconcealed, frozen insolence to warm and confiding sympathy. He was smiling at Howard now in open friendliness. I had been watching and listening intently but I had missed the switch again. Howard's own features and voice were mobile but with a mobility that could be followed, a constantly shifting play of expression that might deceive but would not surprise. With Piers, however, an entirely new attitude was brought into play with lightning quickness, the transformation quite complete, without any trailing gesture or intonation.

Howard said, half-convinced: 'Yes, of course.'

Piers said: 'That's that. Clear off now, will you, like a good fellow. There's a little business matter I want to talk over with Tenn.' He sat forward as Howard moved hesitantly, his face cruelly bland. 'Oh, I believe Helen wants you for something.'

As the door closed behind Howard, I said: 'What do you really want Lulu for, Piers?'

He stood up and reached into a side-pocket. He said: 'Don't you start complicating things, Tenn.' He fished an envelope out and handed it to me. 'There you are. Don't say I'm not better than my word.'

It was a cheque for seventy-five pounds. I looked at him. *Mirror to the Ballet?*

He nodded. 'I've taken my ten per cent out. With what you sold before that will almost cover your losses. Charge the deficit to experience.'

He pulled up one trouser leg and began scratching the side of his calf. The shin-bone was sharp beneath the flesh, the calf itself little more than a protecting muscle.

I said: 'You know my business better than I do.'

Piers nodded, without any show of arrogance.

'I hear rumours that Marks can't get rid of *Trend* either. How many want shifting?'

'Three thousand.'

'I'll take them,' Piers said. 'Less fifty less five. Suit you?'

Forty-seven and a half per cent of retail price – that was only two and a half per cent under Marks's terms. Near enough a halfpenny a copy.

'With my blessing,' I said.

'On one condition.' I looked at him warily. 'That it's the last issue. This is genuine advice, Tenn. The market for that kind of stuff's cracking up so fast that if God Almighty turned salesman he wouldn't be able to shift them a month from now. Well?'

I said: 'The decision had been reached already. There won't be any more *Trends*.'

Piers was smiling out of his deep-set eyes. 'No more *Mirror to the Ballet*, either?' He got up again and came across to put one hand on my shoulder. 'About time for lunch. Coming down?'

As we went together down the stairs he said: 'Remember that suggestion of mine about Westerns?'

I said: 'It's no good. With the cost of off-quota printing I couldn't do anything under a run of two hundred thousand for a shilling. I've been into it.'

Piers said over his shoulder: 'Don't be too sure I couldn't sell two hundred thousand. But I know one thing. I can put you in touch with printers who will do it for two-thirds of what British printers charge. Perhaps less.'

'Abroad?' I asked. 'I could find them myself. The only trouble is a certain Board of Trade regulation. You can't get the stuff back into the country.'

We had reached the ground floor. Piers turned towards Helen's room. Just before we went in, he said: 'Can't you? You're still under-estimating me, Tenn.'

Helen's room seemed very full. There was Helen herself and Cynthia, Howard and Rupert. And a stranger. As we came in, Howard said: 'Here they are!' He was excited again by some event. He caught my hand and pulled me over towards the window. 'He's arrived, Tenn. Another bird in the little nest.'

'Who's arrived?' I asked.

I could see the stranger more clearly now. He was stockily built with square, rimless glasses and a roughly trimmed beard. He was wearing a lime-white suit of Charing Cross Road cut. He had his hands in his pockets.

'Britton,' Howard said. 'This is Joe Britton, Tenn. He got in to-day from New York.'

BOOK II

CHAPTER SEVEN

WE SHOOK HANDS perfunctorily and I moved away, finding a vacant chair in the corner by the telephone. Piers had been saying something to Cynthia but he turned, at Howard's insistence, to be introduced to Britton. I saw him looking at him with his rather blank, analytical stare, a stare that isolated and commented separately on every item of Britton's appearance. Britton flushed slightly. He said, in an embracing, general tone, his voice impersonal under a noticeable transatlantic drawl: 'The first thing I need to do is to get some decent clothes again.' He paused before going on to display his familiarity with the national scene. 'I've already got myself some ration coupons.'

I said: 'Well, as long as you don't mind waiting … The last suit I got took three months to make and things aren't getting any better.'

Britton shook his head slowly. 'No, I can't wait long. I'll have to get one off the line. I'm not staying in London – not more than a week or so.'

We were attentive, with the friendly, curious attention that was the characteristic group charm of the people who lived in or around Regency Gardens and, I felt, of the Number 36 set in particular. Only Piers stood a little outside it, in detached, non-committal appraisal of the newcomer. The rest made up for him; not effusively nor avidly but in a gently alert attitude of suspended yet favourable judgment. I had observed before the exhilarating effect this reception could have on others casually dropping into the circle. I could remember how not so long before it had loosened Olivia's tongue to garrulity, while Piers hovered beside her, his whole body nervous with the passion of his desire. Many things had happened since then, and with them Olivia had become less communicative. Now, sharing again in the atmosphere, I watched to see what Britton would make of it.

He went on, beginning to speak more rapidly: 'I was born in Presley. It's a small town in Lancashire. My father and mother both worked in the mill there. I haven't been back since my last year at the University. I feel ...' He looked around quickly, as though in intuitive suspicion of the circle of bland, friendly faces. He went on almost defiantly. 'I want to go back there. To sort things out.'

I happened to have diverted my attention from Britton's face to Piers, and so I saw, swiftly as the mask was brought down again, the sudden, revealing expression. It looked like hate; the clutching, strangling hatred of a mother for the child stepping away from her, stepping outside her orbit of possessive lust. I had to discount this interpretation; it was irrational and vastly improbable that Piers could have any such emotions for a complete stranger. But even though intellectually discarded the impression did not fade.

Howard said brightly: 'Presley? I've heard that name somewhere. One of the football clubs that let me down on my Pools coupon, perhaps?'

Britton said seriously: 'No. I don't think so. It's only a little town, you see. There's only the one mill. The population was no more than about eleven thousand when I was there.'

Howard began: 'Well, anyway ...'

I saw Helen coming towards me and guessed what she was after. She had the placid certainty of expression that generally heralded one of her more outrageous demands and it seemed to me that there was only one she could possibly introduce at this moment. She stood in front of me shielding me from the rest of the room, and spoke softly.

'Tenn, he seems quite nice, doesn't he?'

'Confidentially, Helen,' I told her, 'I don't place much faith in snap impressions. I haven't anything against him, though.'

'Oh good!' That naïve, unpremeditated enthusiasm! 'You heard what he said – about only staying a week in town?'

I took the offensive, forestalling her but without any real confidence in the outcome.

'Mine's a double room, Helen,' I reminded her. 'Why not try Piers – he has a separate single room. There's no one in it at the moment.'

She said simply: 'I know he wouldn't do it, Tenn. Anyway, he's on the trail again.'

I was interested. 'Who?'

'A girl called Blodwen. I don't think you know her; she comes in the Regent sometimes. But you'll put him up, won't you, Tenn? It's only for a few days and you can keep the partition closed if you prefer.'

I said: 'He's only just dropped in. You don't even know whether he wants to be put up. He may have somewhere – a hotel, at any rate.'

'He doesn't know anyone,' she said. 'And he can't have much money. He arrived on foot so he must have come from Waterloo by bus. I saw him coming down the street. I was looking out of the window.'

I said: 'Let's keep a sense of proportion, Helen. He only dropped in to see Rupert. He doesn't know the rest of us. Can't you see …' I shook my head, defeated. 'All right. If he wants somewhere to stay. But ask him – find out first.'

Piers joined us, putting one hand on Helen's shoulder and leaning against her. The others were still playing the good audience to Britton on the other side of the room. Piers jerked his head back.

'Quite an interesting fellow,' he said. 'All alone in the big town, too. We ought to do something about putting him up. He could have my spare room, except that …'

Piers paused slightly, successfully relying on Helen to intervene and make it unnecessary for him to complete his excuse.

I looked at him. He could easily have overheard our conversation, but whether he had or not the floated suggestion was surprising. Piers was the last person to concern himself with building any artificial reputation for generosity. A much more plausible explanation was that he had conceived one of his sudden interests with Britton as its source and basis.

Helen said eagerly: 'Do you think so? As a matter of fact Tenn has offered to let him have the smaller half of his room. There is a spare divan there.'

Howard also had drifted over. I saw that Britton was now talking to Rupert, with Cynthia sitting between them in a silence aloof but not forbidding. Howard said: 'You've arranged to put him up in Tenn's room? Oh good!'

'Excellent,' I said. 'Altogether excellent. Do you think we could tell him now what we've fixed up for him?'

Helen smiled cheerfully and moved across towards Britton again, Howard trailing behind her. I heard her begin to say: 'Now it's terribly rude of me to interrupt, Rupert, but I've got a suggestion …'

I said: 'What's all this about cheap printers, Piers?'

The chair I was sitting on was a high-backed Sheraton that had somehow passed into Helen's possession. Piers eyed it morosely as he pulled another over beside it – a cheap, cane-bottomed contraption. I guessed that the disharmony irritated him. He sat down, and said: 'It's simple enough. Eire.'

I shook my head. 'You need an import licence just as much for Eire as for America. I've tried. They're only available for pre-war importers.'

Piers looked at me, his face sharpened by the thin smile of superior knowledge.

'You need a licence for bulk imports but there's a loophole big enough for anything you are likely to want. Bring the stuff in by parcel post. There's no check, no regulation … nothing.'

I said: 'But the postage costs …'

'Eleven pounds for one and sixpence,' Piers said. 'That's a lot of copies of 128-page crown octavo. It's not very much higher than bulk shipping would be and with printing costs down a third at least … How does it strike you?'

I said speculatively: 'What are the Eire printers like, anyway? Can I get reasonably good work done by them – and without supervision?'

Piers put one hand on my arm. It was a rare gesture because in general he made a point of avoiding physical contact with other people. He said carefully:

'This is for profit, Tenn. You are in publishing to make a profit, aren't you? And I know very well that for the last six months you've gone steadily deeper into the red. Well, I'm putting something easy in front of you. Of course you can't get good stuff done in Eire; all the big boys are tied up, chiefly on pre-war contracts. But you don't want good printing for shilling shockers. I can put you on to a couple of little fellows who will do the job. And if you can get some nice flashy covers I'll promise you advance orders of fifty thousand on half a dozen titles. At least fifty thousand on the dummies alone.'

I looked at him directly. 'Why?'

He shrugged. 'I could do it myself, if that's what you mean, but for one thing I haven't got the right contacts for authors and illustrations and for another – more important – it would tie me down too much. Don't forget my status. I'm a middleman's middleman. Besides' – he smiled more fully – 'I think we might work usefully together later on.'

This was a way out, a door opening to a surprising release from the financial complications that had increasingly bogged me down during recent months. If Piers were right then everything was easy, almost too easy. I said: 'Are you sure parcels aren't checked? It seems an incredible oversight. Surely the Board of Trade …'

Piers's expression was one of surprise.

'But there always are oversights! It's part of the set-up. Their right hands never know what their left hands have issued in regulations.' He paused. 'That's why I despise them so much.'

I said: 'Well ... thanks, anyway.'

I felt relieved, but my relief was not an altogether easy one. I searched for flaws. In the mechanics of the scheme? Of course, I couldn't know that yet but when Piers got to the stage of making positive suggestions they were generally sound enough. In the conception itself? A cheapening? I saw Piers looking at me, his smile more secret. He said: 'Not worried about ethics again, Tenn?'

'Ethics?' I said. 'What are ethics?'

'They're not anything,' Piers said softly. 'Not any damn thing.'

There was a knock on the door. Mrs. Bessborough, the daily help, had come to tell Helen that lunch was ready. We streamed down to the basement, where I was surprised to notice that Lulu's Leslie had somehow managed to join us. He sat opposite me, between Britton and Howard. He nodded to me in a friendly way.

'Where's Lulu?' I asked.

He said: 'It's either a party meeting in King's Street or something at the Dorchester to promote a Czechoslovakian literary genius. I haven't seen her diary recently enough to be positive.' He smiled. 'I'm here in my own right for a change. I'm going to do a fresco for Helen – right round this wall.'

Helen, coming in with plates, heard the last sentence and glanced at me apologetically.

'It's got to be re-plastered, Tenn, and Leslie's very keen on doing a wall painting at the same time. It should look rather nice.'

I said to Leslie: '*Can* you plaster? Or are you going to follow the workmen round with a box of paints and a brush?'

He took a tureen of soup from Helen to put on the table.

'The first job I ever had was as a plasterer's assistant,' he said gravely. 'The plastering will probably be better than the painting.'

Britton had been listening, too. He turned to Leslie awkwardly.

'Have you fixed a theme for it yet?'

'Yes,' Leslie said. 'A recurring, linked *motif* of nyloned legs and sad, remorseful eyes. Or a panorama – a city of huge gleaming machines and one pot-bellied, naked little man right in the middle of them. Or my willow pattern variations, crowned by a pair of waltzing V-1's instead of doves.' He had helped himself to soup from the tureen and now began to drink it. 'The great thing, as you suggest, is to know it all in advance.'

Britton looked at him with an abashed, mournful expression common to a certain kind of American face and to St. Bernard dogs. I remembered what Rupert had said about him. Development? In New York what could he have developed into except a New Yorker? I said helpfully: 'Leslie works on impulse. He's a post-propter-post-impressionist. Don't you do much the same thing in your poetry?'

Britton said: 'It's a long time since I wrote any poetry. When I did' – he looked at me, nodding confirmation of my implied criticism – 'I suppose that would describe it well enough.'

Rupert leaned across. 'What do you think of Auden's latest? I suppose you will have seen quite a lot of him, won't you?'

Britton said: 'No. I've never met him.' His voice had a flat, seemingly weak intonation. 'I haven't read much lately, either.'

Rupert said: 'But what did you *do* in New York?'

Flatter and weaker. Britton said: 'I don't know. It's hard to say. The time seems to have gone by very quickly.'

'Yes,' Rupert agreed. 'That was the first letter I'd had from you in four years.'

Britton just smiled apologetically. We continued with lunch. When it was finished and Helen had brought the coffee in, Britton handed round a packet of Chesterfields. All except Piers took one, and as sometimes happened he excused himself from the cigarette-fumed atmosphere and went upstairs, leaving his coffee barely tasted. He paused at the door to glance back at

Britton, friendly and voluble and quite uncharacteristic.

'Hope you enjoy yourself here,' he said, 'however long you stay.'

When we had finished coffee I suggested to Britton that he come up to my room to fix his things. He followed me quite willingly. As he climbed the stairs behind me, I heard him say: 'I appreciate you putting yourself out for me this way. It is a help. There are one or two things I have to do in London. I'll try to be as little bother as possible.'

I led him into the small room and he put his bag down beside the small divan. He only had one medium-sized travelling bag with him. He saw me look at it, and explained: 'I've got a trunk as well but I left it at Waterloo. I didn't know where I would be staying, of course. And anyway, it's hardly worth while bringing it along for the short time I shall be here.'

'Presley?' I said. 'I think I've been through it. Near Liverpool?'

He nodded. 'You might have done. The main Manchester road runs through it. We lived on that road until I was twelve – over a butcher's shop. I used to spend hours in the window corner, watching the traffic. There used to be a lot of steam-trucks up and down between Liverpool and Manchester. They used to fascinate me. I don't think there are any now, are there?'

I said gravely: 'I haven't seen any.'

He began to unpack his bag; I cleared a couple of drawers in my wardrobe for him to use. He didn't have much – a couple of pairs of pyjamas, half a dozen shirts, assorted underwear, a pair of shoes, and the usual odds and ends. There were a few books on top. He put them down on the divan while he put his clothes away and I was able to read some of the titles. *The Holy Bible*, the Confucian *Analects*, the *Bhagavad-gita* and the *Upanishads*, and Sale's translation of the *Koran*. Oh my America, I thought, my new-found-land! How far, how faint now, the hissing rattle of the steam-trucks puffing between Liverpool and Manchester, passing how many butchers' shops and how many youthful eyes watching at the first floor window. One more importunate, weary of the rough breath of living, the vital stink of humanity. But why had he come back? What was there for him here?

I suggested: 'I suppose you have some plans?'

He looked up, smiling his simple, mournful, transatlantic smile.

'Nothing, I guess, beyond getting to Presley.'

'To see your family?'

Britton shook his head. 'They're both dead. I haven't any close relations.'

I said with some sharpness: 'Then why? I shouldn't think you would find much scope there.'

'Scope for living,' he said. 'More than where I've come from.' He paused. 'I aim to get a job in the mill, if I can.'

He was putting his clothes in the drawers with careful slow untidiness, taking minutes to refold a shirt into a more creased and crumpled condition than it had originally been. There was something tremendously exasperating about his small actions as though they expressed a docile but terribly stubborn wilfulness against the normal. I went across to the piano and began to play the Brahms Eb Intermezzo. For me it brought back Thirl, and especially 1918, especially September. Rodney's last three days of leave coincided with the beginning of my own. This intermezzo had been a favourite of his; the stiffness had seemed to go out of his too brilliantly gleaming Sam Browne, and he himself had looked younger and less callow as he played. And in the background our parents, and the later, unlooked-for, three-month-old Timothy. A family circle, and three days of mist and winds and driving showers of rain, burning a deeper gold than longer, sun-warmed times have done. Rodney setting out for the first time towards an adventure unknown for him; for me too well known and hated. I had fourteen days of my own, and the telegram reached us on the fourteenth.

For me, Thirl, and nearly thirty years lost in a minor key. For Britton?

He said: 'That's rather nice. What is it?'

I managed the development as well as I could, but that was not very well.

'Brahms,' I said. 'Wasn't there scope for living in New York?'

He began eagerly: 'No ...' and then stopped. He turned away in a confusion clearly genuine although I could not, at first, imagine whence it derived. Had it not been for the memory of Rodney – and Tim, too – fresh in my mind, I should not have guessed. But Britton was obviously ashamed of something. There had been scope for living in New York, scope, anyway, for escaping death. But again, why come back?

'I'm curious,' I said. 'Do you want to work in a mill?'

There was a small book-case in the angle of wall beside the divan bed I had surrendered to him. I saw him lift Marcus Aurelius, Barbellion, Pepys and Swift, glance at them uninterestedly and move them down to the lower shelf to make room for his own small library. Without looking up, he said: 'It's hard to explain ... Go on playing, won't you? I like that.'

'Do you?' I said. 'My brother did. He could play very well. He was killed in the first war. My other brother was killed in the second.'

I began to play Brahms again, watching only my fingers, plump against the narrow, shining keys.

CHAPTER EIGHT

I WENT OUT AFTER LUNCH and spent the afternoon in an exhausting and unsuccessful attempt to get a cheque from one of my few outstanding debtors to meet the more claimant of my many outstanding creditors. I came back feeling very gloomy, and too late for tea. Helen and Cynthia had both gone out. In the basement there was only the pile of tea things waiting for Mrs. Bessborough's morning ministrations, and Brock curled up on a cushion on the rocking chair. The teapot was on the table and when I patted it it seemed misleadingly hot. I got myself a cup and poured out. But I couldn't find the milk and the tea, in any case, was stewed and less than tepid. I added one more cup to the pile and went upstairs. Brock, who had been watching me with an expression I could almost judge as cynical, dropped his head again and closed his eyes.

As I climbed the stairs I saw that the door of the little room where Olivia now lived was wide open. My gaze entered the room at floor level, and rose as I did. Olivia was sitting on the edge of the narrow camp bed Helen had fixed up for her. She was dressed in her blue costume and was still wearing a hat. She looked tired. Around her the room was in a dispiriting state of confusion; presumably as she had left it on going out in the morning. I noticed odd stockings draped over my book-case and a pair of mules, a dressing-gown and a discarded slip so scattered as to produce a maximum effect of untidiness. The room was very small, of course. As I paused, coming abreast of the open door, she said wearily: 'Hello, Tenn.'

'The life of a working girl …' I suggested.

She smiled limply.

'Come on up,' I said. 'I, too, have come in feeling despondent, and found no one in to provide a modest refreshment. At least my room's not quite so depressingly small, and there will be something in a bottle. The lodger's probably out, and I don't suppose he would mind, anyway.'

I followed her up and we went through into my front room. There was no sign of Britton. I went across to the sideboard and irrelevantly tried to remember whether I had bought this particular article of furniture from Helen or not. I even felt a fleeting rage, swiftly towering and as swiftly gone again, in my consideration of the sums of money she had got out of me during my residence at Number 36. It was certainly unfair to blame Helen for them; Piers had been here longer and he, I fancied, had no such complaints.

I found the bottles. Apart from the precious whisky there was a bottle of rum, rather more than half a bottle of sherry, and three or four fingers of gin. I poured the gin into two glasses and found some rather doubtful looking orange to dilute it. Olivia was lying full length on my divan. I carried the glasses over and handed her one.

She said: 'Thanks. It's a god-send. What was that about a lodger?'

'Britton has arrived,' I told her. She wrinkled her forehead. 'From America,' I continued. 'From New York.'

She said: 'Oh. The poet? Is he staying here – in your room, I mean? What's he like?'

'It was Helen's idea,' I said, 'though Piers and Howard also helped to arrange things. He's a new toy. As for the kind – I wouldn't presume to classify on such short notice. If I were tempted …' The gin was pleasantly astringent behind the softness of the orange. 'But I won't be.'

Olivia turned over on to her face, pressing her body sensuously against the surface of the divan. Her hair fell down, hiding that side of her face which was towards me.

'Won't you?' she said. 'Not even by me?'

I said gently: 'Livia. Fight your own age – and weight. Britton is pleasant enough. In some ways he seems a little … soft, but he's been over there a long time. It doesn't seem to be a very good climate for Europeans. They go soft inside. Most Americans are the same of course, but they've generally managed to develop a firm enough exterior to hide it.'

Olivia said indifferently: 'Has he gone very American? I don't like Americans.' She stretched her arms out, spanning the width of the divan. She said curiously: 'Why do you have a double bed, Tenn?'

I drank again. The gin seemed like a warm, confiding friend in a cold world.

'Perhaps because I'm what you might call more or less a double man,' I said.

She sat up, tossing her hair back, and looked at me critically. 'You're not terribly fat.'

I walked across to the french windows and opened them. The air came in chill and damp with the very flavour of this desolate summer but the windows opposite mirrored striped fires from the briefly splendid sun. A bus lumbered across, blundering crimsonly on along Old Brompton Road, as I turned back to Olivia.

I said: 'Are you finding it very hard?'

'Bloody enough.' I waited. 'I don't like working, Tenn. I've had no practice in it.'

She gestured mutely for a cigarette and I gave her one. I reached down to light it for her, into the aura of her perfume. She inhaled heavily.

'Thanks. Do you know, I spent all spring and summer of 1939 trying to persuade my father to let me take a job? Since then – six years of large-scale fooling about in the W.R.N.S. I've never had the habit and I've lost the inclination.'

I said idly: 'He wouldn't let you take a job but he let you join the W.R.N.S.? And you must have been very young.'

'Patriotism,' she said. 'High-minded, noble patriotism. Besides, we're an old naval family; his grandfather ran a battleship or a tug-boat or something. There's the kernel of my wasted life. Six years' debauchery. Though I can't help thinking we were debauched rather less than most civilian women.'

'Where are your folks now?' I asked.

'Scotland,' she said. 'They retired there. He had a Scots ancestor too; maybe the same one. I'm welcome for holidays, of course. In fact ever since they discovered I voted Labour at the last election I've been awfully handy as a whipping-post.'

I said: 'How long are you going to stay here, Livia?'

She looked up, drawing on the cigarette. She had undone the jacket of her costume and I could see that the white blouse underneath it was grubby round the collar and even had a splash of ink on it. There was a pathos about all this that distressed me; the mawkish side of my nature responds to incalculable evocations. She said, after a pause: 'I'm using your room, aren't I? I found out from Howard. Do you want me to clear out?'

'No,' I said, 'that's not it. I don't use the room, anyway. The only thing I would be likely to mind would be Helen getting double rent for it, and she owes me so much already that I can't be bothered to worry about that.'

'What, then? Last night – those messages? They embarrassed you, didn't they?'

'Yes. But not enough to bother me. No more than your pretence at flirtation just now.'

She laughed, with weariness and some anger in her laughter.

'It wasn't very good, was it? I thought it might have been you last night. I thought I might have been expected to take a hint. I don't seem to have the equipment, though.'

I have always been surprised by the lack of faith attractive women have in their own powers of attraction, but as with stronger faith they would be unbearable I naturally subscribe to the bluff of male impassiveness. That, at least, is the reason I give myself. But what Olivia had said aroused my curiosity. I said: 'About those messages – apparently Howard had the same idea. Look, Livia, this interests me. What do you think's going on at the séances? Do you think one of us is indulging in an elaborate fake?'

She said: 'I don't know. Sometimes I think so. I don't know what's happening.' She looked at her feet, still encased in low-heeled office shoes. 'I started because Piers did.'

I suggested: 'And you go on because Piers goes on?'

There was a flash of exasperation in her voice. She said:

'Tenn, you don't understand things. You can't – you're not a woman. I'm … I'm sorry for him.'

I said: 'You have to look at things the right way up, Livia. I hear Piers may have a new tenant shortly for his spare room. By the name of Blodwen.'

She said: 'I know. You still don't understand, Tenn.'

She stood up and brushed her skirt listlessly with one hand. With the other she stubbed her cigarette into an ashtray. She said: 'Thanks for the drink, Tenn. I think I'll go down and get into some different clothes. Do you think there's any chance of the water being hot for a bath?'

I ran my recollection over the scene in the basement; the stove had been laid, presumably by Mrs. Bessborough, but certainly not lit. I shook my head.

'No chance at all.'

Olivia sighed gustily. 'Oh, well. It'll have to be a cat-lick.'

'Wait,' I said. 'I think that's the lodger. You might as well meet him first.'

Britton came through the other door into the small room. He was still wearing his off-white drape but he had a rather large parcel with him which I guessed to be his new suit. He put it down on the divan and came forward into the front room. I noticed he had a shambling kind of walk. He stopped abruptly when he saw us.

He said awkwardly: 'Oh, you're not alone … I didn't realize you were in.'

'This is Olivia,' I said, 'Olivia Pennett. She lives half a flight down from us. Livia, this is Mr. Britton. Mr. Joseph Britton.'

81

I watched them shake hands. Britton said to me: 'I hope you'll tell me if you want me to stay back there in the rear half … I believe you can close the partition, can't you?' He smiled. 'Otherwise I guess you'll find me prowling round all the time.' He looked earnestly from me to Olivia and back. 'It's so long since I've been in a decent-sized room. High ceilings, too. You feel freer.'

He glanced upwards with childish satisfaction. I said: 'The rooms are smaller in New York than in Presley, then?'

Britton laughed easily.

'Presley! No, I was thinking of when I was in London before.'

'Before the war,' I said.

He flushed. 'Yes. Before the war.'

'Prowl about as much as you like,' I said. 'Whichever of us turns in first can pull the panels across. And I may have to do it during the day sometimes; occasionally I have people here on business. Apart from that, you're welcome.'

He said: 'That's very good of you. I'll know when to stay out. What kind of business do you do?'

'I run a small publishing business. You are standing in the central headquarters of Tennyson Glebe Publications, Ltd. That is, apart from the accommodation address in Shaftesbury Avenue.'

Olivia said: 'And what do you propose to do over here, Mr. Britton? Write poetry?'

Her voice had a flat, uninterested contempt. Strangely enough, it irritated me, as though her scornful lack of interest put my own vague opinions about Britton into significant form, and in so doing usurped them. They were all too readily, too easily summarizing and docketing the man. I felt my own thoughts being pushed along by the decision of others. I waited for his answer with sardonic anticipation. It should jog her.

Britton said: 'Well, I might. But poetry never has been a living for me, and I don't expect it to be now. I'm going back to Presley – it's the town I was born in, in Lancashire. I thought I might get a job there. I'm told they're short of mill hands.'

She was jogged. Since being introduced to Britton she had been lounging against one arm of an arm-chair. She sat up, looking at him, her face ugly with astonishment.

'For Christ's sake! Are you pulling my leg?'

Britton gave a quick, embarrassed laugh. It was the first time in Regency Gardens, I reminded myself, probably the first time in England that anyone had spoken sharply to him. I wondered in what kind of dream-like society of urbane gentility he had been imagining himself to have arrived. I looked at Olivia with more affection.

Britton said: 'That's about the only thing there is to do in Presley.'

Olivia said: 'But why? What's wrong with London? You're a poet; you've had books published. I haven't read any of them but people seem to know about them. If you've got to work you could get a fat job anywhere – BBC … British Council … Ministry of Information … advertising …'

Britton said: 'I'm afraid it's just one of those things that seem silly when you try to explain them. I just … want to get back to Presley. It's something I need for my own satisfaction.'

He stumbled, hesitating over the last word. Satisfaction? Or salvation? Olivia looked at him for a moment further before speaking again. Then she said: 'During the time you've been in the States … what sort of thing have you been doing?'

Britton had recovered his composure; his awkward, irritating smugness. He produced his packet of Chesterfields again and passed cigarettes to us. Olivia took hers, looking at it curiously before tapping it against the back of her hand and accepting my lighter. I lit Britton's cigarette and my own.

Britton said: 'I went over there to teach originally. A place called Marlby, where fashionable New Yorkers can treat their male issue to a good copy of English public school life and still have them within handy reach of home. Every stone age-treated and mossed, and a Close exactly modelled on Winchester. Even flogging, to prove it was the real thing.' He took his cigarette away and coughed. I saw that he was smiling, savouring an old joke that he now pressed on people only perfunctorily. 'I was imported as the final authentic touch. Bringing with me my own background – Presley Grammar School and the South London College.'

The implied satirical comment was out of tune with his soft, Americanized drawl. Its effect was to shock and yet blunt the edge of his attack at the same time. I have always found it difficult to treat the utterances of Americans with any seriousness. They seem, when they are not being brilliantly flippant, to be both naïvely and preposterously over-solemn. Britton, having taken on much of their manner of speech, was necessarily as trite and as unconvincing.

He went on: 'I was there … about five years. Since then … A bit of everything. I worked as a – ' he hesitated, and then pronounced the word in English – 'as a clerk in a drug store for quite a while. And I picked things up – different jobs. It wasn't hard to get work.'

As though remembering why it had been easy he flushed slightly again.

Olivia said: 'You came back with a Yankee accent all right.'

Britton nodded and half-smiled.

'Yes, that's right. But it's only come on since I left Marlby. While I was there my English accent was part of my job.' He looked at us quickly, anticipating criticism. 'I picked quite a creditable one up at the University and knocking about Bloomsbury. Afterwards it was different, of course. There wasn't any point in keeping myself different from the people I worked with and lived with. You've got to surrender things to live with people.' He paused and softly repeated: 'You've got to surrender things to live with people.'

I guessed what Olivia was thinking. She had the automatic English snobbery towards Americans, a snobbery I largely shared myself. Greece to their Rome. She was reflecting that she would most certainly have kept that culture-parrying shield against the surrounding barbarian. Would I have done so? I could not imagine surrendering as Britton had, but neither could I face the thought of a lonely eminence of the speaker of English in metropolitan New York. Had that refusal been Britton's also? He would have had good reason for not attracting attention. To live with people – but for what purpose? For escape, for hiding ... for life itself?

Britton said: 'It's funny how important things like accents are. All the time I was at Marlby the Americans were foreigners to me with queer habits and incomprehensible customs. It wasn't until I made the deliberate effort – it was an effort to start with, too – and began to talk of "drug stores" and "side-walks" and "elevators" that everything else started to fit in as well. It all began to make sense; even sponsored radio and the Sunday supplements in the newspapers.'

Olivia said: 'If you got so attached to the place I'm surprised that you wanted to come back.'

He looked at her, mildly surprised.

'Did I say "attached"? I suppose New Yorkers are very much like all the other kinds of city people, when you get down to it. I liked them all right, but that had nothing to do with my going or staying. Every man's journey is his own, for his own private reason, driven by his own needs.'

She said, tolerantly amused: 'And yours drive you to some place called Presley.' She turned to me. 'What about yours, Tenn? Where do your needs drive you?'

'Just now to the sideboard,' I answered. I went over and opened it. I called to them over my shoulder. 'What are you going to have? There's no gin left. Sherry or rum?'

Olivia said: 'Sherry. I can't stand rum.'

I looked back more directly at Britton. He waved a stubby hand nervously in front of his face.

'Nothing for me, thanks.'

I shrugged, and straightened up to take two bottles over to

the table. I said to Olivia: 'Mind if it has a taint of gin?'

She shook her head. Handing me the glass to fill, her attention was directed sideways, towards Britton. She said: 'You've come back an American all right. Nothing between a roaring, fighting drunk and evangelical teetotalism – the American way of life.'

Britton said quite seriously: 'I'm not an evangelist. I just don't like drinking.' He watched with a thoughtful air as I poured myself a tot of rum. 'I think alcohol … hinders.'

I drank my rum, relishing my disapproving audience. A voluptuous nose-thumbing. Looking over her own glass, Olivia asked: 'Hinders what?'

'Thought,' Britton said. He hesitated before going on bravely: 'And the development of the spirit.'

There we were. I realized that in some way I had been looking forward to Britton's arrival and that all the small resentments he had so far roused in me had been the disappointments of expectation. It was not easy to understand why I had expected anything; true, I found this second post-war world even more depressing and unpromising than the first had been, but I was no longer a young man to hope for reversing miracles, and I could never have hoped for a Messiah out of the western wilderness. Rupert, perhaps, had fired my imagination with his suggestion of the poet returning with wisdom and mastery. I wondered what Rupert himself would feel in the realization that the poet had become a corn-fed wallower in the trough of Heard and Huxley, an ascetic smoking Chesterfields, an Auden simplified and debased. He might start writing again but although my regard for his early work was slight, for the sake of its memory and reputation I could only hope he would not. I looked at him almost with affection now that I knew the worst. A week of this would not be so bad; it might even have its points of interest. And then – the retreat to Presley, a few weeks or months grappling with the realities of human, Presleyan behaviour, and the triumphant journey back, back to Bloomsbury, back – in all probability – to New York or California with the established Creed – 'Mankind is very lovable: at a distance.' Yes, I reflected, he probably would start writing again. Writing, after all, was the great, infallible way of overcoming the paradox. One could achieve intimacy while ringing one's physical self with laborious mountains.

Olivia got up. She put the empty glass down on the table and stretched herself, yawning. 'I've got to change and have some sort of wash, Tenn. I'm filthy. What time is it?'

I looked at my watch. 'Turned six.'

She said: 'Oh, God. And your booze has given me an appetite. I think I'll go on the scrounge in the kitchen.' She smiled, leaving. 'See you both at dinner.'

I debated whether to take the dirty glasses up to the bathroom and wash them; there were half a dozen others that had accumulated on the sideboard. But I felt tired, and disinclined for anything but rest. I dropped back into an arm-chair.

'She's … she's lovely, isn't she?' said Britton.

I looked at him in inquiry. He nodded towards the door which Olivia had just closed behind her.

'There's a quality that stands out in her – not only attractiveness. Something stronger – directness, honesty.'

I examined his enthusiasm. The pilgrimage to Presley might be in danger. But perhaps he would not need Presley; there were some things he could learn as well in South Kensington. Only the establishment of the Creed was certain. I was no longer really interested. I relaxed more deeply into my arm-chair.

'Yes,' I said, 'a fine girl, our Livia.'

CHAPTER NINE

L ULU WAS NOT AT DINNER; it was the evening for a Party caucus to be held in her room and with two or three other comrades she had set the right tone by having a fish-and-chip high tea at a restaurant, thus starting real business at a proletarianly early hour. So Helen explained. I finished my own dinner early and went up to my room, leaving Britton behind me in the basement. He was talking and Piers was listening. I closed my door with some feeling of relief at privacy regained. I had not had time to settle down in the hope of savouring it when I heard the sound of feet clattering downstairs from the top of the house. I counted half a dozen pairs. Clearly the meeting was over. Unless she had come down with them, Lulu would presumably be alone in her room. Whichever alternative were true, it occurred to me that this was a useful time to return a book she had insisted on lending me. I went over to my bookcase and picked out *An Enquiry into the Decay of the Land-Owning Capitalist*, in its bright red jacket. I took the precaution of removing the bookmark from between pages twenty-two and twenty-three, tucked the volume under my arm, and went upstairs.

I followed the usual Regency Gardens custom of Knock and Enter. For the protection of intimate occasions all the rooms in the house except Howard's had locks; on the rare occasions that he felt he needed protecting he dragged his washstand across as a barrier – an embarrassingly noisy procedure audible down to the front door. Now I turned the doorknob and Lulu's door opened easily enough. She was in but she was not alone. Leslie was half-sitting, half-lying along her divan and she was resting transversely across his lap looking up at him. His hand was caressing her in a purposeful way.

I said: 'The key is in the door. I came to bring your book back, Lulu. I'll drop it on the gramophone.'

Lulu sat up quickly, brushing Leslie's hand carelessly aside.

'Come in, Tenn! I wanted to talk to you.'

While I hesitated, Leslie leaned further back and, taking a comb from his breast pocket, began to comb his hair. His expression was difficult to gauge; it could have been resentment, relief, or just boredom. He said: 'Yes, come in.'

I asked him curiously: 'Have you joined the Party after all then? That was the Party that went out in force just now, wasn't it?'

He said wearily: 'With a vengeance. No, I haven't joined. It was only a routine, non-secret do to-night. Three or four strikes arranged, a couple of minor assassinations, and a nasty letter to *The Times* signed "Lover of Fair Play" – quite routine.' His eyes gleamed into a smile behind his glasses. 'I just loved it.'

Lulu laughed a little too loudly to show her broad-mindedness and sense of humour. She patted the divan and I came over and sat beside them.

'What did you think of the Herkenheimer?' she asked me.

'The … ? Oh, yes.' I tried to remember what happened between page one and page twenty-two. 'Very – very closely reasoned.'

'His chapter dealing with the disruptive effect of capitalism on personal relationships – especially on close family relationships – I thought that very fine, didn't you? He exposes the myth of the family with wonderful subtlety.'

Thirl. Like a rose, a stone rose thrusting auriferous petals into the long morning of memory, a rose of quiet, nostalgic beauty. And all that patterned, friendly life. But the past had no arguments against Herkenheimer.

'Yes,' I repeated, 'the myth of the family.'

'The way,' Lulu went on, 'he uses their own arguments as springboards against them!'

I realized what it was that had been bothering me and my mild annoyance against Lulu was swept away, leaving only amusement and affection. The phrases were so absurdly uncharacteristic. I even guessed their source, remembering the evening I had met some of her little C.P. circle and particularly Jonathan Ritch-Davies, failed B.A. (Oxon), from whom she was now quoting. I could almost detect his mincing tones in hers.

'A very fine chapter,' I confirmed. 'Those long quotations from Pangloss are very well justified. They bring out the heart of the matter.'

She hesitated barely a fraction of a second before nodding enthusiastic agreement. Leslie put his comb away and winked at me. I wondered what Ritch-Davies would say if she carried it back. I regretted my weakness; he would probably be cruel to her. And yet, acquainted with cruelty as she was, it might be that by now she needed it. It wasn't my concern.

Leslie said suddenly: 'How's the Yank settling down?'

Lulu looked from one to the other of us in inquiry.

'Britton,' I explained. 'You knew he was coming? He arrived this morning.'

She said: 'Oh, I've missed him! What's he like?'

Leslie said: 'About five feet nine. Eleven stone. Square rimless glasses. Shaggy beard and a hair-line straight across his forehead. And a neat spiv suit.'

'Not any longer,' I said. 'He's got a new one. Rough tweed.'

Lulu said: 'If I'd known ... I'd have kept the boys here to meet him.'

'Why?' I asked her.

She looked at me in some astonishment.

'Well, naturally they would like to see him. He might do something for the *Worker* again; I'm told he did a lot of good work in the 'thirties.'

'Before your time?' I suggested.

Lulu nodded. Her expression was sad; both remorseful and regretful. She had gone late into politics and the iron embrace of the Party – in 1939, only a few months before the war had broken out. Marxism for her had been the following of a hard and tortuous path. She had missed the glad dawn of the 'thirties in that futile, thoughtless round of dancing and parties and pleasure-making from which conversion had since saved her. Missing that dawn she had missed much; false it may have been but it had glowed; and she could pictorialize and try to recapture the glow in the bound copies of the *Left Review* and the *New Statesman*; in the proletarian novels, with spines faded by climates unforeseen, and the wide margins and twelve point typefaces of that heyday of print and paper; in the simpler spontaneities of Auden and Spender and – I realized – of Britton. She was the pilgrim that came after, remembering the days she had never known, the days when the earth shook beneath the tread of the prophets. She said now, with melancholy devotion:

'He was in Spain, you know. With the International Brigade.'

I said: 'No, I didn't know. Are you sure?'

It surprised me. I thought of the Joseph Britton I had left in the basement talking in his slow, amiable drawl to a watchful Piers and tried to reconcile the opposites. It made some things different. Lulu said, citing an article of holy writ:

'He went out in the autumn of 1937 and stayed till the end.'

I said: 'Well, the end was not yet. I doubt if you will get much good out of him now. He has come back from America with the most reactionary religious conscience I've met for some time.'

Lulu said: 'Oh.' She was shocked. How much worse when the prophet, still living, turns apostate, reversing the dialectical Mass, worshipping the false, discarded gods. But it had happened before; an ex-Marxist was no new thing. Did her visible disappointment mean that she, like Rupert, had been fashioning a figure of her own devising out of the bare facts of Britton's exile and silence? For the hard orthodoxy of the true Party élite, of course, neither exile nor silence could have any meaning; there was meaning only in relentless and unswerving service and obedience. But Lulu was not of that metal, however much its gleam attracted her. She was a romantic, and prone to the apocalyptic vision. There might have been something preparing itself in the west land, something that would come when the time was ripe and lead the revolution of faith and vision in which she really believed. It was possible that some dream of that sort, vague and yet more real for its vagueness, had lifted its hovering wings in the rosy clouds of her imaginings.

And to all questions the answer had been the real Joseph Britton, no evangelist of art or politics or civilized life but the man himself, going his own private, irresponsible way.

Leslie said: 'Well, it's not surprising. The sort of mind that can kid itself it's getting nourishment from communist slop is always likely to turn to the religious trough instead. The pig-food's the same; it's only the container that's different.'

Lulu made a gesture, a feeble one, of tolerant amusement.

I said: 'You are at an advantage, Leslie, in spending your youth at the fag-end of an intellectual fashion of faith. It was much the same in the early 'twenties. In this century faiths have come and gone with some speed; we have had a whirligig of mental climates. Now, as in 1920, you may whisper that the universe is a meaningless bore. Had you been young in 1937 you would have been shouting with the rest that the millennium was at hand. And as for conversions, it isn't surprising that some people have found that shout an empty one after the first shock of disillusion. But they have learned the habit of shouting and your whisper seems a silly little blasphemy. They take up an older cry, and shout even louder.'

Leslie shrugged his narrow shoulders. His eyes were amused behind their small glass prisons. He leaned forward.

'Fashion has something to do with it,' he agreed, 'but not all. There are natural whisperers and natural shouters, aren't there? Which are you, Tennyson?'

I looked at him, and wondered why it chilled me to do so.

I said: 'I speak my lines in a pleasing baritone. Hadn't you noticed?'

'Yes,' Leslie said, 'but to yourself you whisper – I can't imagine you shouting.'

Lulu looked at us, bewildered but admiring.

She said: 'I can make you some tea. The kettle's filled and I scrounged some milk and things this morning.'

'Don't bother,' I said, but she had already jumped up from the divan and gone across to the other side of the room. She bent over the small gas-ring, striking matches. Leslie said:

'Yes, make some tea. I have a thirst.'

Sitting side by side we watched her making preparations. The silence which had fallen between us had something of deliberation in it; in a way a refusal of communication. Yet it had no awkwardness. There was as much ease in this interval as in a silence between friends, although there was no sense of friendship. We watched Lulu together. She got the gas lit and placed the kettle on it, spilling some water on the carpet. Then she swivelled round and looked up at us, kneeling.

She said: 'I like doing this.'

Her face was flushed a little from her exertions, a faint recollection of youthful colour beneath the tired yellow of her skin. I could see a long way back to the lonely, rather backward child playing by herself with the doll's tea-set, either during days when the rain whispered or gurgled or raged in sudden, pattering storm against the nursery windows, or on days when sound itself was drowned in summer's silent ocean. She would have kneeled there on the carpet in just the position her body, remembering better, chose now. And already she was ugly, and her small domestic dreams self-stultifying.

Leslie said: 'Why don't you get a flat of your own then, where you could do your own cooking just as you liked?'

The smile disappeared from her face. She said frankly:

'I should be lonely.'

I glanced at Leslie: from something in his expression, a guilty casualness, I guessed he knew the story. It was a long time now since Lulu had offended her father by the manner of her refusal of an arranged marriage but Eugene Cartesian, whose personal fortune was well and amply secured in half a dozen countries, had the tribal relentlessness of his kind. Lulu's allowance was generous but it would end were she to enter any conjugal life, legally sanctioned or not, without his blessing and approval. In earlier days she had presented one or two aspirants to him and he, with triumphant, lingering regret, had refused them, as adventurers. He had probably been justified in his description since his daughter had neither beauty, charm nor intelligence to commend her; nothing, in fact, but the promise of his fortune. But withholding that he must have known that he withheld even the chance of happiness. She might have tamed her adventurer; she could, at least, have cooked for him.

Instead there was only the bed-sitting-room at the top of the house, the various Leslies with their perfunctory, amused embraces, and now a kettle coming to the boil as she leaned with her back to the fender.

I said: 'Piers would like you to come along for another séance next Monday. Will you be able to manage it?'

She nodded eagerly. Leslie said:

'You are going in for this racket seriously, are you?'

She said: 'It's interesting. What time, Tenn?'

'Oh, after dinner. About nine. We can't ask Helen to throw her time-table out two evenings a week.'

Leslie said: 'I'm curious. I can understand Lulu going in for this sort of playtime. Howard's easy enough, too, and Piers ... and, of course, Olivia. But what is there in it for you, Tennyson? That's what surprises me.'

I said: 'It's probably good for you to be surprised a little. If you really must have an answer – might it not be the thing that makes you ask the question – simple curiosity?'

He said: 'Yes, I suppose it might be. But there's always a reason for curiosity, isn't there? It's not a pure feeling – in adults, anyway. I'm interested in people's motives because I want to paint them, and I want to paint them because it gives me a sense of power to do so. And for the reason behind the longing for power you simply have to go back to the universal cradle and the universal Œdipus.'

The kettle began to boil and Lulu turned round hastily to deal with it.

I said: 'And does the universal Œdipus solve everything as simply as that? You must remember my age, Leslie. I haven't had your advantage of imbibing Freud with my rusks and milk. Does it explain a table defying the laws of gravity?'

Leslie smiled. 'No. I should imagine Maskelyne and Devant explain that well enough.'

Lulu went hunting for cups in the recesses of one of her cabinets. She brought down three cups and saucers, surprisingly matched, and dusted them with one finger. She filled them with strong tea and poured a little milk into each from a half-pint bottle.

'There!' she said.

It wasn't very good tea but we drank it obediently. Lulu came over with her own cup and sat on the floor between us, lying back against the side of the divan. She was very scrupulous about dyeing her hair, but looking down on her head one could see the mousy brown springing beneath the blonde. She said, without looking up:

'What's Britton come back for, anyway?'

I said: 'In one sense his intentions are clear enough; in another, more obscure. He's staying about a week in town. Then he's going up to Lancashire, to a town called Presley where he was born. He says he plans to work in the cotton mill there.'

She turned her head round quickly, gazing up at me. The physical distortion drew the side of her face tight over the narrow, protruding bones.

'What's religious about that?' she asked. 'Are you sure he's religious? What makes you think so?'

I said: 'Don't build hopes, Lulu. He's going his own way, not yours. He's religious, all right, in the way most dangerous to any hopes you might have of getting him back in the fold. He's a religious intellectual.'

She said confidently: 'You're wrong there. It's the ones who give way to emotional rationalizations that we lose forever. Anyone who has once understood the dialectic can never lose it permanently while he retains an active mind.'

Leslie laughed. He bent down to take her head between his hands. Holding it with a kind of tender roughness, he said:

'Holy innocence!'

Lulu said obstinately: 'Once he gets back amongst the workers, he'll see things properly. He may be confused now. It must be hard to think clearly in America. But he'll get things right again, you'll see.'

Leslie still held her head. He dropped one hand to fondle the curve of her neck, and I saw her press back against him in sensuous pleasure. Leslie, ignoring me, whispered:

'You must never go to America, my little Lulu.'

I drained my cup and stood up. Stretching back, Lulu asked: 'Going?'

I left them, rattling the key in the door before I closed it. Howard's door was open on to the landing. He was sitting across a chair by the open window, looking out into the darkened twilight sky and the darker landscape of roof-tops etched beneath it. He was wearing only an old pair of cut-down flannels and a sleeveless vest, although the evening was damp and rather cold. The 'cello was out of its case and propped beside him, as though he had got it out for practice before this vacant, watching boredom supervened. But what made me think he was bored? Why not, instead, a mystical experience? It was certainly a private one, reducing observation and judgment to mere conjecture. Yet I knew it for boredom, and knowing it briefly was ravaged myself by that pressing, pitiless wing. The cold, wet summer, the war's aftermath, the empty evening and the quiet house ... All these seasons, all these hours, this aftermath and silence; all adding up to a long, grey futility of life. In my mind I made as though to protest. It was all right for me – bearable, and possibly deserved. There had been colour, even though I had outlived it. But for him, was it fair? His youth ... Although he must have heard me leave Lulu's room he had not turned from his preoccupied lethargy. I walked on down the stairs. Protest? To what? To Tennyson Glebe, perhaps. And hear his weary answer: not my responsibility, not my blame.

Britton and Piers were sitting opposite each other in my armchairs. They were talking. Britton broke off a sentence as I entered the room, and smiled his welcome before continuing with it.

'I was saying ... I used to think science had all the answers; all the answers that we need to know. It's a habit of thought. We accept it to-day as automatically as men looked to the Church two hundred years ago. For fifty years we have been conditioning children into it at an ever-accelerating rate. And since for the overwhelming majority of men some such pattern of thought is both automatic and essential ... But all the questions are incomplete and all the answers falsified.'

Piers sat back, hunched up small in the arm-chair, sympathetic, judicial.

'Well, of course,' he said. 'Naturally. I agree entirely. All the questions are incomplete. All the answers are misleading.'

The french windows were open and I had left a chair on the balcony. I went out and stood for a moment, hearing the murmur of conversation like a flickering fire behind me. Then I sat down and began to watch the advancing emptiness of night.

CHAPTER TEN

DURING THE NEXT COUPLE OF DAYS I didn't see anything of Britton. I was rather surprised to find that for one of his ascetic tendencies he was a late riser; both on Friday and Saturday there had been no sign of him by the time I myself had finished breakfast, and I had gone out leaving the partition still drawn between us in my room. I was under a certain amount of pressure of work. For one thing Marks, in response to my instructions to send the unsold copies of *Trend* along to the address Piers had given me, had declared firmly that he would have no transport spare for a fortnight or more. And, irrationally, I suppose, I had some vague hope that the magazine might sell well enough to justify me going back on my casual declaration to Piers and putting out another issue. Anyway, I still had a sense of urgency about it. Marks grudgingly let me have a boy for the haulage and I removed the magazines myself in a couple of taxis. It took most of Friday with the various delays and discussions and some difficulty on the part of the taxi-drivers in finding the right address. There was no sign of Britton when I finally got back to Regency Gardens.

On the Saturday morning I went along to the Board of Trade and made enough tentative, discreet inquiries to establish that Piers's tip about printing had been a good one. Although this, financially, was the most encouraging thing that had happened to me for over a year I came away with an unaccountable feeling of depression. I tried to analyse it, but got nowhere. Even though my vanity might be less responsive to the idea of associating Tennyson Glebe, Ltd., with lurid cowboy stories than with staid literary reviews, my recent bank statements had shown me clearly enough that there was only one end to vanity, and that a fast approaching one. On the other hand, if the Westerns did as well as Piers had promised they would, perhaps in six months … All the same, I felt depressed. In an unorganized attempt to dispel the gloom I had a gluttonous lunch at Elvoli's, and spent the afternoon in the hideous comfort of a cinema and the evening floating around various saloon bars on the Piccadilly edge of St. James's. I met one or two old acquaintances and there was the usual surprised pleasure in these unexpected reassurances of one's separate and individual existence. But sooner or later they mentioned Tim, and I drifted away from them to the next pub. I didn't get back until after eleven and I was drunk enough to find it too much trouble to undress. Later, sobered by sleep and the chill of the night, I took my clothes off and climbed between the sheets. I slept heavily and my subconscious alarm clock failed to wake me as usual at seven. I was only awakened by a gentle tugging at my shoulder. I turned over hazily, and saw Britton above me.

He said: 'Here we are. Take a sip of this.'

He proffered a cup of black coffee. I looked at him, trying to bring things into focus. Britton smiled understandingly.

'I heard you stumbling about a bit when you came in last night. You knocked over a table. So I had a peep in at you this morning. I thought you might appreciate a refresher so I brought something up.'

'What time is it?' I asked him.

Britton looked at the watch on my wrist.

'Quarter after ten.' He paused uncertainly. 'I'm just going down to breakfast now. Can I bring you anything else up?'

I shook my head, and became aware that it was aching.

'No. I'll probably be down myself shortly. Tell Helen not to do anything for me, though. Except some toast.'

When he had gone I drank the coffee. Then I went up to the bathroom, filled the bath with cold water (the only kind available, of course, at this hour of the day) and wallowed in it for a few seconds. I finally went down to the basement feeling reasonably fresh.

The big table had been moved nearer to the window to leave more room on the other side of the room for Leslie's attack on the walls. He was doing one side at a time, and so far had been occupied with tearing the old plaster down. It looked like a bombed site. I counted faces round the table. There were Britton, Olivia, Howard and Cynthia. Helen came in from the kitchen with more coffee.

Howard said, with a note of disappointment:

'He looks quite new-laid.'

I said: 'So you had been expecting me to totter in, bleary and of uncertain locomotion – the senile drunk in his senile hang-over?'

Britton looked up, flushing a little.

'I hope you don't think ...' he began.

Howard said: 'We all heard him coming in last night. Like the entry of the gladiators.'

I remembered more distinctly myself. There had been a light in the window of Helen's room but I had not felt like going in. Probably they had all been down there; they would not have been in bed so early on a Saturday night. I remembered slamming the front door behind me and, not bothering to put the light on in the hall, I had tripped on the stairs. I could also remember that at the time I had found something terribly funny in the possibility of my rolling all the way down, to crash on the hall carpet. In a rare moment of release I had been able to relish the idea of my own fatness sprawling its way down to a final, gasping equilibrium. The others would come out, attracted by the noise, and all manner of things would be swamped in the ensuing waterfall of mirth. But I had recovered my balance and got upstairs to my room, and now in the morning all manner of things were just as they always had been. Their amusement was friendly enough but I was the lonely target, the target that it was impossible to miss. I smiled, presenting the shield:

'The gladiators would like some more black coffee, Helen.'

I had taken the empty chair beside Britton. I accepted the coffee from Helen and drank thirstily. My disengaged right hand rested on my knee; I felt something damp nuzzle against it and looked down to see Brock preparing to rest his furry body against my leg. He was not usually so demonstrative at this time of the day. I buttered a small square of toast and gave it to him. Britton caught my eye.

'What exactly is the idea of having a badger about the house?' he asked.

His question was friendly, but there was a note of disapproval in it. Helen came between us, and stroked Brock while he turned a wary eye towards her and finished off the buttered toast.

'Dear old Brock,' she said irrelevantly. 'We've had him from a piglet.'

'But it isn't natural, is it?' Britton asked. 'They're nocturnal creatures, for one thing. And their proper environment is wooded countryside.'

Piers had come in while he was speaking, and was standing just inside the door.

'Cats are nocturnal, too,' he said, 'and also domestic. But I agree with you. I agree entirely. South Kensington is no place for a badger.'

The words were in the tradition of Piers's rather strained, malicious humour but he had never liked Brock and I couldn't help feeling that there was a good deal of sincerity in them. Certainly Britton accepted the comment as a serious and friendly one. He looked at Piers with something like gratitude. I wondered how close a relationship was developing between them. Piers had stood aloof in the hour of Britton's arrival but when I had seen them since they had generally been together and in discussion. It was easy enough to understand Britton's reaction; Piers, when he laid himself out to be charming, could be very winning, and the friendly, detached interest of the rest of us had remained just that. But Piers himself? I gave it up.

Olivia said: 'That's just nonsense. He's not unhappy. Does he look unhappy?'

They all turned to consider Brock, who was now lying across my right foot licking the butter off a second piece of toast. His tongue flicked out in evident appreciation. Britton said stubbornly: 'That's no argument. A caged skylark sings but it's not the same song. There's a fitness in things.'

Howard said: 'In this case the fitness would have entailed being torn to pieces by terriers. We got Brock in a pub in Hampshire. There'd been a badger dig. The two grown badgers had been killed and all the cubs but this one. An artful old yokel brought it into the saloon bar of a main-road pub, and got ten bob out of us for it.'

Brock looked up inquiringly, but seeking more toast rather than any information on his parenthood and origins.

Britton said weakly: 'Special circumstances don't alter things, do they?'

After breakfast there was the usual Sunday confusion as to what should be done before the pubs opened at twelve. I was feeling the need of fresh air myself and decided to go for a walk. Unexpectedly Olivia offered to accompany me. We stepped out together into a calm, grey, spiritless morning and turned our footsteps, as usual, towards the Park.

Olivia was wearing a blue, flowered dress with a white coatee that buttoned at the waist and opened out above that to the shoulders. She was looking her best, but there were still traces of tiredness and nervous strain about her eyes. She said, as we turned into Gloucester Road: 'Things don't get any better back there, do they?'

'Britton gets on your nerves?' I suggested.

She said vaguely: 'It's the atmosphere. He hasn't improved it, of course, but you can't blame him for something that existed before he arrived. I find them all pretty unbearable at times. Don't you? Helen and Cynthia hanging round each other's necks and Howard peeping round corners at them. Lulu with her clod-hopping communists and that little worm, Leslie. He tried to get into my room last night because I half-smiled at him in the Regent. And Rupert – drifting round the house like a materialized ghost.'

I said: 'And Piers? And I?'

She said: 'Piers goes without saying. Not you, Tenn. I like you. You repelled my lewd advances the other day, but we're still friends.' She put her hand in the crook of my arm. 'Oh, Christ! Look who's coming towards us. Do I look smart, Tenn?'

I reassured her. 'Immaculate. I don't know her, though. Who is it?'

We slowed our pace, and she smiled brightly.

'Hello, Blodwen. Taking the air?'

Blodwen was two or three inches taller than Olivia and rather more ample. Her hair was screwed into tight, glossily black curls under a wide-brimmed, ribboned hat, and she was dressed in black silk, splotched with scarlet carnations and tied with a green sash. Very high-heeled shoes threw her calves into long, unnatural curves. Her legs, beneath the transparent silk mesh, were noticeably hairy. Piers's taste, I reflected, was coarsening.

Her voice was husky, with a contralto lilt.

'Darling! I'm just going round to your place. You know I'm moving in next week?'

Olivia shook her head.

'I didn't. It's a delightful surprise.'

Blodwen looked down, smiling, from her extra height.

'Didn't Piers tell you?'

Olivia said: 'I haven't seen much of Piers lately. Oh, this is Tenn. His rooms will be on the floor below you.'

We nodded to each other. Blodwen drew one of her open-mesh gloves more tightly over her hand.

She went on, looking directly at Olivia:

'I think Piers is charming, don't you? He just needs a rein and someone at the other end who knows how to control it. I think that's so important.'

Olivia said: 'Have you told him that?'

Blodwen said: 'No. But you can if you want to, darling. I think he's aware enough of the truth of it already.'

As we left her behind and the clash of their rival perfumes faded into Olivia's own familiar scent, I remarked:

'So that's Blodwen. I thought you were rather subdued, Livia.'

She mused, partly to me and partly to herself:

'I wonder how he'll do it ... what lever he'll use?'

'Do what?'

She looked at me, those large front teeth resting, as though pensively, on her lip. 'Break her down. She doesn't look easy, does she? But he'll find some way.'

She had dropped her hand from my arm while we were talking to Blodwen. I took it now in my own, holding her small fingers gently.

I said: 'Don't imagine things, Livia. It isn't like that. It's no more than a weakness in Piers's sexual make-up that makes him incapable of retaining an interest in any woman for long. In that respect he's still a schoolboy. If you want reassuring, I'll reassure you that Blodwen will last no longer than you did – perhaps less. But it's no good you persuading yourself either that you can change him or that there's something sinister about the things he does.'

She laughed, on a shrill, nervous note.

'Change *him*!'

I said: 'Women get that sort of idea about the men they know.'

Her fingers gripped my own fiercely. She said:

'There is something sinister about it, Tenn. I'm not just making things up out of my own frustrations. The sexual side is nothing more to him than a blind for his real purpose.'

'And that?'

'Power over other people,' she said. 'It's the only thing he's interested in. He sniffs round them patiently until he has found their weaknesses; then, when he's sure, he puts the pressure on. He does it very carefully. You wake suddenly to find he has you tied, and his fingers are on every knot. He doesn't only do it with his women. No one's safe from him.'

It was difficult to know what to say to her; her nervousness had increased to a pitch that was not far below hysteria. I could not disregard it but neither could I, in the flat, dry quietness of the morning, take serious account of it. The suggestion itself, of course, was ludicrous, but it showed how deeply she had managed to entangle herself in her own pathetically twisted affections. In her narrow universe Piers really was, for the moment at least, a clutching monster. The disentangling would have to be patient, not scorning her wild accusations but accepting them and pointing the flaws out one by one.

I said: 'And what did he use to tie you, Livia?'

She turned to look at me, her eyes having that apparently startled expression which could often be traced in them when she was only considering some serious point. She was considering now. Then, in a barely perceptible gesture, she shook her head.

'It doesn't matter. You are drawing all the wrong conclusions as it is.' She paused. 'Tenn. You never talk about yourself. What are you doing in Regency Gardens, anyway?'

I said: 'Publishing. It's no secret.'

'But why?' she insisted. 'You must have had a career of some sort before this. You're of ... mature age. What were you doing before the war?'

'Various things. I was a director of Lucian's ... and some other firms.'

She said: 'Lucian's!' She laughed. 'And from that to running a potty little publishing firm from a couple of furnished rooms. Why, Tenn? That's what I want to know.'

The intersection of Kensington Road was only about a hundred yards ahead of us. She stopped abruptly and bent her head down, searching for what might be a run in her stocking. I paused beside her, watching the side of her face as it turned away from me. At least the brief flurry of agitation over Piers had dropped from her again. I considered the questions she had put to me; they were natural enough and it was only the general atmosphere of casualness at Number 36, I realized, that had hitherto protected me from them. But an answer? I liked Olivia well enough but she was little more than a girl, and not a source to which I could look for help. And did I need help? The thought was a confused one, stemming from the troubled illogic of the emotions. We walked, each in our own illusion, and our problems, inescapably, were private ones. Our griefs also were private.

I said: 'Too many reasons to count. Perhaps I just got idle. Perhaps …'

Perhaps all the reasons for directorships and directors' salaries had suddenly become empty and meaningless. Empty for one man; meaningless in the framework of one illusion. Past conditional, past active, past incommunicable. There were regrets and despairs for Olivia also, but they were not mine, nor mine hers. We walked for a few minutes in silence, our hands clasped lightly, the air grey and breathless about us to the cold, shadowy heights of the sky. A fat old man and a young girl walking together on a drab Sunday morning. But that barb for once was painless beneath a greater pain. People passed us; a small knot of fashionably dressed women, two of them carrying ivory-backed prayer books.

Olivia broke the silence. She said: 'Do you believe in God?'

Even Olivia's voice seriously posing the question could not give it any valid meaning. In our youth we had played with words in this way, inventing abstractions and fitting them into propositions. But what a long time ago.

'I don't believe in things,' I explained. 'I only experience them. They happen to me, in a series of events that one day, presumably, will come to an end. That's all it amounts to. I haven't experienced God, whatever it may be.'

We were at the crossroads and the traffic barred our way. Olivia said: 'I think we might as well go back.'

I took her arm and steered her across the road.
'No,' I said. 'We'll go right on.'

CHAPTER ELEVEN

During the four days he had been at Number 36 Britton had settled in so easily that I had come to think of his arrival as one of the accidents of Providence common around Regency Gardens. I became accustomed to going to sleep and awaking with a view of the wooden panels of the partition beyond the foot of my divan, instead of the distant window and the framed back view of Drayton Gardens. On the Monday evening I had brought my after-dinner coffee upstairs with me and was relaxing with it when Rupert put his head round the door. I waved him in.

He said: 'I dropped in to see Joe.'

It was only by an effort that I identified Joe as Britton and remembered that it was as Rupert's visitor that he had originally entered the house. They could have seen very little of each other since. There had been Piers's preoccupation with Britton and, according to Lulu, Rupert himself had been out most of the time in pursuit of some lad of whom he had become enamoured. He stood now in front of my Craxton, almost looking down at it, with one hand dropping from an improbably long and attenuated arm to rest on the seat of the chair beside him. His spectacles were murkier than I remembered seeing them; his shirt-collar was open and greased with dirt.

'He'll probably be up in a moment,' I said. 'You might as well wait for him. Did you have dinner out?'

He shook his head with a caution that seemed natural enough to an onlooker; any excess of vigour might well dislodge it altogether. He said:

'I'm having a fast. I started yesterday. I did one last month, you know, and got some very interesting results. Mystical.' He peered more closely at the ink drawing. The fine fuzz of dirt in front of his eyes very likely softened the somewhat uncompromising outlines. 'This is pretty awful, isn't it, Tennyson?'

'I took it for a bad debt,' I said. 'It's useful for frightening children.'

He looked at me absently for a moment, as though pondering deep subtleties in my idle remark, and then began to shuffle about the room. He found the file of *Trend* correspondence, and started to read through it. I watched him, sipping my coffee.

'Want a drink?'

'No.' He looked round briefly. 'I only drink water during a fast. The visions aren't veridical otherwise.' He probed deeper in the file. 'I didn't know Stephen had gone back to living with that Yolanda woman again.'

I put my coffee cup down.

'Well, you do now, don't you?'

He nodded, with a withdrawn, pleased expression. Stephen's love-life was inviolate with him; every item of gossip he absorbed was neatly boxed and dropped into the strong-room of his memory. If he ever counted them over it was in the privacy of his trance-like silences. With Lulu, of course, it would have been a different matter, but I should not have allowed Lulu such access to my letter files.

Rupert put the file down at last. His rather small head looked down at me from the frail mast of his body.

'So there aren't going to be any more issues of *Trend*?'

I settled back comfortably.

'You know all the relevant details,' I told him. 'There aren't going to be any more issues. If Stephen's got anything of yours he will be sending it back. You don't feel like doing a hot-blooded Western novelette for me, I suppose? Thirty – thirty-five thousand words.'

'Westerns? You mean, Cowboy and Indian stories? What are you paying?'

I said: 'Thirty shillings a thousand.'

Rupert nodded: 'I'll have a go.'

I said cautiously: 'Let me have a look at the first couple of thousand words before you commit yourself too deeply.'

He nodded owlish agreement. He had moved his face into the narrow swathe of light thrown up through the opening in the shade round the table-lamp; it marked his features in deep, almost cadaverous lines of melancholy. I wondered again about his new trick. There was a thought somewhere in my mind that would not come up; vague and inapprehensible, but even in its vagueness dismissed as fantastic.

I said: 'This fasting, Rupert. Where did you get the idea from?'

He looked surprised and rather blank.

'I don't think I know. Just an idea.'

We heard Britton come into the rear half of the room, through the other door. I gestured to Rupert an indication that he should go through to speak to him, but he made no move. Instead Britton himself came through the half-opened partition to join us. He was rapidly losing the formal American manners which would have looked for some kind of invitation before entering. He said, off-handedly:

''Lo, Rupert. Tenn, you haven't seen anything of a hairbrush of mine lying around, have you? I thought I might have left it in here.'

I said: 'Monday. One of Mrs. Bessborough's days. Have a look in the top right-hand drawer of the bureau; she generally puts odd articles in there.' I added, as he went over to look: 'Rupert dropped in to see you. He's had no chance to have a chat with you since you arrived.'

Britton said, over his shoulder: 'No, that's right. We both seem to have been too busy skipping about.' He found his brush and displayed it with a small, triumphant movement. 'Now would be a good time, except that Piers has asked me to join some kind of séance up in his room.'

It brought me up sharp, with a small shock of astonishment. Surprise had two edges; that Britton should have agreed to come to the séance, and that Piers should have asked him without consulting or even mentioning it to me. The first was the more bewildering, but the second stung like a tiny barb, carrying a shaft behind it of quite inestimable size. I looked at Britton. He had moved in front of one of my mirrors and was brushing his thick, sandy hair back. He took out a small comb and ran it through his beard.

I said: 'You needn't dash away. Piers or Lulu will come down when it's time. As a matter of fact I shall be going up with you.'

He looked round with mild surprise.

'Is that so? I didn't know you had interests in that direction.'

'I'm rather surprised to find you have,' I replied.

He said: 'But it's very interesting! Some of these things Piers has been telling me. Levitation, apports, coherent messages from the unknown. It's a beautiful refutation of materialism; a window on the real universe, the spiritual universe.'

'Piers didn't tell you that last bit?' I suggested.

'Well, no … But it's straightforward, isn't it?'

Refutation of materialism, I thought wearily. Here, in 1946, Joseph Britton, poet of the rosy, revolutionary 'thirties, proselytizer now of the perennial philosophy, stumbles on a refutation of materialism. Rest at last, Gurney, Myers, Lodge … all perturbed spirits. And let the members of the Rationalist Press Association shake in their less than solid shoes. Truth is beginning to out.

Rupert said: 'What's the latest news from these do's of yours?'

'This is a parallel series,' I said. 'With Lulu and – ' I nodded towards Britton. 'We still have the regular Wednesday evenings with Howard and Olivia. News from them? Just the usual light gossip from the depths of the infra-dimensional space-time continuum.'

Britton said, interestedly: 'Do you mean there are some other séances – and that Olivia attends them?'

I said: 'Didn't Piers mention that?'

Britton shook his head.

I glanced beyond him to where Rupert was resting his long body against the wall. He looked more melancholy than ever, although I should have known him better than to form generalizations based on his outward appearance. At any rate, I felt that Britton owed him some conversation, as a token return for his introduction to Regency Gardens and thus, at the very least, for the discovery of a stick with which to beat materialism's aged back.

I said: 'You've still not tackled your job of persuading the nightingale to start singing again, Rupert. You might as well start while you have the chance.'

Britton looked startled for a moment. Rupert said:

'I don't really see how you could have stopped writing poetry.'

Britton smiled, gently reminiscent.

'I was always a writer ... in mood, as you might say.'

'But that fluency!' Rupert objected. 'Sometimes when it reads easy it comes hard, but it came easily enough with you. That sonnet – *Orchids and tulips by their dreams devising* – I saw you throw it off in half an hour. And you sent it off without a word's correction or revision.'

Britton nodded. 'In mood. In mood it came easily, and fast. But the mood itself was hard to find, harder to pin down. I always have a strong inclination not to write. In the old days I did my best to overcome the inclination, but for years now I haven't bothered.'

'Haven't bothered!' Rupert echoed. 'But what else is there worth bothering about?'

'Surely,' Britton said, 'a whole number of things!' He glanced at Rupert slyly. 'Meditation, for instance?'

'Not by me,' Rupert said promptly. 'Verse is the end; the meditation's only an interesting means.'

'That's where we part company then,' said Britton.

He looked complacent enough about it. Rupert was less at ease. He said:

'I just don't see how it's possible to stop. And with the reputation you had.'

Britton stood up. He walked over and put one hand up to Rupert's shoulder.

'You others must have outstripped me years ago. What have *you* been doing anyway? How many volumes? I haven't kept up with things as I should, you know.'

'Only two altogether,' Rupert said. 'I never had your fluency. And then, the war didn't help.'

I watched Britton. He dropped his hand from Rupert and turned to look out through the window.

'Rupert had a long war,' I said. 'Six and a half years in the army. More than five years of it overseas. The Middle East, Palestine, India, Burma.'

Rupert said seriously: 'I didn't enjoy it very much at the time. I was a clerk with a small mobile R.E. unit. Such a lot of useless work to be done. But it was all experience of course. It will be useful later on.'

Britton turned round. He was smiling painfully.

'Good old Rupert. Nothing's lost on you, is it? All grist to the sacred mill. But what comes out of all that grist? What makes the mill-wheel turn? And who's the miller?'

'Comes out?' Rupert asked. 'Poetry, of course. And I'm the miller. Who else?'

I said gently: 'And that's where you part company again.'

This time complacency was altogether absent. Britton concentrated his gaze on me, his mild, fleshy, transatlantic face puckered into a concentration that looked like anger. He said, feeling for words in an unfamiliar way:

'We part company, all right … but there's only one way out that leads anywhere. The rest … the rest are false tracks, always winding back to the individual. On those roads you don't get any place.'

'On any road,' Rupert said, 'you can only go the way you want to go. We carry our roads with us. After all, what guides us? Only logic and experience.'

'No!' said Britton. 'That I deny.' His shapeless anger tossed his thoughts up and down, beyond his own grasp. 'There's more to it ... more to it than that.' Pausing, he tried to juggle with them. He finished weakly, 'There's ... intuition.'

Rupert inclined his small head to one side in its eminence.

'Yes?' he said politely.

Britton stared at him for a moment. I could see him fighting for calmness, and I saw him win. He looked ordinary again when he smiled, but certainly more impressive than he had during his earlier flurry of emotions. He was really quite harmless, and in his way, pleasant enough. I caught my own thoughts and pondered them. Did I despise him as much as that?

He said: 'We'll let it go, eh?'

I said: 'That's probably not the only battle you are in for tonight. Lulu has it in mind to reconvert you to the dialectic.'

Rupert said with detachment: 'Joe was strongly C.P. when I knew him. He went so far as to claim to find some merit in Mayakovsky.'

I nodded. 'Lulu was telling me. And one of the heroes of the International Brigade. She's very hopeful of winning him back.'

It was Rupert's turn to display interest.

'Did you really go to Spain?' he asked. 'I thought you went straight to America from that school in Cornwall.'

Britton retained his stolidity, but I could detect embarrassment not far below the surface.

'I was about eighteen months drifting about there,' he said. 'I didn't do anything much.'

Rupert observed him thoughtfully.

'Most unusual. Generally speaking, those who did go out never lost an opportunity of talking about it. And you were eighteen months there and this is the first I've heard.'

Britton said: 'I didn't make any secret about it. I wrote quite a few articles that were published in little reviews here.' He smiled glibly, uneasily. 'But I remember – you never did read political stuff, did you?'

'Did you do much fighting?' Rupert pursued. 'I didn't myself, of course – I was just an office clerk. In this other war, that is. I've often thought it might be interesting – for the experience.' He glanced down at his long, disjointed body. 'But I'm not really cut out for it. My muscular co-ordination isn't good enough. And I imagine it's necessary to have enough interest for it to carry you away. I doubt if I could manage that, either. Being carried away by the excitement, I mean.'

Britton said reluctantly: 'There was some fighting.' He looked away towards the room's high ceiling, and felt restlessly in his pockets. 'It's a long time ago.'

He produced Chesterfields for us. I wondered what lay at the root of his evasiveness. Time. Time – and memory. Only superficially did they run side by side. In the things that did not matter ten years ago in time was ten years in memory; a photographic print gradually yellowing, its edges imperceptibly curling, with the slow destruction of chronological time. That was the general, the over-all impression. But the particular was more important, and memory had no time-scale there. Which lay furthest from our watching present – the afternoon of daisy chains and riding on the back of a retriever dog, or last month's cloudy sunset? All rested together, jumbled beyond orderly arranging. In that vast store-house only guilt and obsession could find a way, striking unerringly to the typical scene, the unforgettable moment. And Britton? What was it he wished dead, that still dragged its wretched length across the deceptive gulf of time? I saw him draw on his cigarette, and exhale smoke with a sigh.

Lulu came in noisily. She was apparently in one of the troughs of her cyclical waves between dressiness and reacting contempt for such bourgeois fancies. She was wearing light tan corduroy trousers, flecked with darker grease stains, and her breasts drooped nakedly behind a coarse white sweater. And she had allowed her hair to fall into its natural lank strands, false, unenthusiastic gold.

She said: 'Joe! Ready to come up and tackle the spooks? Piers told me to fetch you.' She flicked her head sideways. 'And you, of course, Tenn.'

My earlier resentment was not completely gone. There was no reason why I shouldn't, if I wished, invite someone myself. Rupert was watching Lulu, his lips compressed in a dubious expression that was probably no more than boredom.

I said: 'What about you, Rupert? Won't you add another facet to your experience by pursuing the paranormal? There's plenty of room round the table.'

He shook his head slowly, a personal gesture, barely, reluctantly, conveying information to the trivial outside world. It was very final, but I pursued him.

'I thought you never refused experience?'

'Two kinds I refuse,' he said. 'The kind that seems useless and the kind for which I have no aptitude. Have a nice time, though. Mind if I stay here?'

He wandered over to my bookshelves and began hunting through the poetry. Lulu watched him for a second or two, shaking her head in wonder. She turned.

'I'm going up, anyway. You two coming?'

She raced up the stairs and Britton and I followed more sedately. He was just in front of me, climbing with steady graceless caution. A question rose unexpectedly in my mind, and I put it to him:

'Who told you Rupert went in for meditation, by the way? It doesn't date back to the time of your acquaintance with him, does it?'

Britton paused on the landing.

'No,' he said. 'I believe it's a new departure. I heard of it from Piers.'

CHAPTER TWELVE

Piers, I observed, greeted us both with the same smile, an incongruous glance of friendship from those deep, withdrawn eyes of his. He said to Britton:

'Lend Lulu a hand with the table, Joe, will you? I've got a small business matter to tackle with Tenn first.'

I noticed how willingly Britton obeyed him. Piers drew me over to his desk, and sat on the corner of it, swinging his small legs. There seemed to be more table lamps than ever on the desk. I saw that he had already fixed the black-out boards in place across the windows.

Piers said: 'I hear you've been checking up on that Eire business at the Board of Trade. Very wise of you.'

I said: 'Your spies are everywhere.'

He laughed. 'No. Only in strategic places. I'm glad you took the trouble to make sure, though. I don't want a partner who takes anything on trust.'

I echoed: 'Partner?'

He examined me intently. I had a moment's awareness of the depth of flattery in his serious regard; an awareness flaring into uncertainty and suspicion. But what foundation was there for such fantastic theories? The intentness and the flattery it conveyed were simply the normal features of his attitude towards the people about him. There was nothing there either sinister or mysterious.

Piers said: 'Well, you remember we talked of it vaguely once. I think it could be useful to both of us. But we won't press matters.' He glanced past me to where Lulu and Britton were rolling the carpet back in preparation for the séance. 'I knew you wouldn't mind Joe coming along this evening, too. Three isn't really enough, anyway.'

I remembered the nakedness of Howard's protest, its starkness yielding him up to contempt and patronage. I refused the provocation.

'It doesn't matter,' I told him. 'I don't expect much from these Monday extras, anyway.'

Piers stretched his hands behind him on his desk top, and leaned back, bracing against them. He said casually:

'We might have roped in Rupert as well, but I don't think he's entirely sympathetic towards psychical research. To anything, for that matter, but the noble hexameters and their associated metres. Still, you can ask him some time, if you feel like it.'

He looked at me and again, briefly, I was out of my depth, drifting in a sea of imaginative and unprofitable speculation. I was roused from it by Britton. He came across and put one hand on my shoulder. The familiarity was rather unpleasant, I twitched myself free.

Britton said cheerfully: 'Everything ready. Everything fine and ready. Finished your business? I'm keen to start.'

I went over to the table with him while Piers fixed the radiogram. Lulu, Britton and I took our chairs, Lulu sitting between us so that she faced Piers's empty chair. Britton gazed round at the room with interest. He said:

'Those wooden boards over the windows ... You had them made to keep the room light-proof, I suppose?'

Piers came across and took the vacant chair. He followed the direction of Britton's gaze.

'Black-out is the term commonly used,' he murmured. 'But I didn't have it made. It's a relic. They were in use over here during the recent ... war.'

The barest emphasis. Lulu didn't notice anything but she was not attuned to any subtleties, and Piers's were drawn very fine. Britton noticed it. He looked down at the table, his face mirroring the small shock of his embarrassed surprise. I felt pleased, irrationally pleased at his discomfiture. I said, hiding it:

'Has Howard rigged up that variable red light he was working on yet?'

Piers clicked a switch and darkness moved round us with its silent, intangible tread. His voice seemed to have a harsh and tremulous quality in the lightless obscurity.

'No. At any rate it doesn't work. Give me your hand, Joe.'

There was another click, marking the entry into the vacuum of silence of the radiogram's heavy purr. I felt Piers's hand searching for mine; our fingers met and hovered, resting side by side. I could feel the smooth edge of the gold signet ring he wore on his little finger. In this small intimacy of flesh on flesh I was aware of the presence of power, and in that awareness had a sudden urge to withdraw. But what excuse or justification could there be? Now the music, at first a vibration humming with the rest, became notes and melody, building its own pattern in the vacancy about us. Piers must have put the records on before he sat down. I recognized 'Le Coq d'Or', its monotonous gold surged over us like the meaningless waves of a forgotten, sunset ocean.

Lulu said: 'Would there be anything without the music? Do we have to have it? And a certain kind?'

Piers said remotely: 'We may be able to do without it eventually. For the moment, it helps.'

Britton said: 'Yes, I can see that it would help. It would be a matter of spiritual vibrations.'

He embarrassed me by the very lack of embarrassment in his voice. In the dark, accents were clearer, intonations more easily noticeable. Britton's voice had a soft sluggishness.

I said: 'Piers picks the records. "The Planets" used to be our stand-by, but we need a little variety now and then. Anything sufficiently diffuse will do.'

As though air had somehow gathered itself into a tiny sliver of venom I felt a sharp needle point of cold flick against the back of my hand and away. I waited. Lulu drew her breath in

119

with a gusty thrill of surprise and shock. Piers said softly:

'Yes?'

'Just … a touch of cold air,' she said uncertainly. 'It's beginning, isn't it?'

It was beginning. In a lull as the auto-change replaced a record the table shivered, seemed to gather itself into a hunching movement, and there was the tiny shriek of wood grating against wood. The music shrilled up again, making its empty, bombastic challenge to the waiting, watchful air. Then the table lifted suddenly, with tremendous vigour, under our idle hands. Automatically we pressed down, trying to hold and control whatever was straining upwards. There was a moment's hesitation before it yielded. The table crashed down against the floor boards and, with the final mastery of the struggling swimmer who feels the element secure and natural around him, we felt the strain and struggle lapse into the rocking, swinging rhythm with which we were familiar.

Lulu said excitedly: 'Is there anyone there? Once for yes.'

It was Ming. Lulu spelled the name out. It came correctly the first time, without mistake or fumbling. This, perhaps, was going to be a good night. The golden rooster crowed on, to inattentive ears.

Piers said, his voice so restrained beyond its usual precision that I recognized a kind of exultation in it:

'So Ming will come on Mondays, too. Ming! Will you be with us for both lots of séances in future?'

In future? I thought of this as the table slammed down its affirmation. Then the Monday séances weren't simply a temporary concession to Lulu's curiosity: or weren't any longer, whatever they had been originally. I heard Britton's voice, soft and diffident:

'How does Ming find his way here, to this place and time? That puzzles me.'

The question had been put before. Ming gave the same reply.
EXPLAIN LIGHT TO A BLIND MAN.

To three blind men and a blind woman. But what was the nature of the light that flooded round us, unseen, unwarming? A light of revelation, stretching deep into shadowy corners, illuminating to heal? Presumably Britton would think so. But for the rest of us? There was no such simple way out. We had left all that a long way behind; for us there could be only groping. But at least we groped on the sure ground of logic and experience. Ahead, obscurity; but behind, the known contours, the traversed ground.

'Messages for anyone?' Lulu asked hopefully.

It was for Britton. He counted out the letters himself at the behest of the tilting table, going too fast at first and then too slow in his efforts to find the steady rhythm of alphabetizing that we had learned. But the message came through without errors.

MUST NOT GO PRESLEY STAY HERE.

Britton said: 'Why?'

The table took up its tapping again: the speed and efficiency of its communication was surprising when viewed against the recollection of earlier sittings. It raced on, and Britton too began to find a balance and sureness in his recitation.

HERE THE BATTLE HERE VICTORY.

It was something I had been half expecting and yet I was surprised and strangely disturbed. This was no more than an extension of the original circle we had built up; there were not only Piers and I as links but Ming himself. And in that circle battles and victories were unlikely extrapolations, evoking suspicions of the despised puerility of spiritualist ethics and theology. For us facts were facts. We could smile at Bradlaugh and the great Victorian materialists, but it was their ignorance we found amusing, not their attitude. They, too, given our vantage point, would have seen with us the absurdity – the lack of utility – of their own convictions. We knew the tyranny of words, the meaning of meaning, the ultimate formlessness of a universe in which each separate electron was an individual and unique event, unpredictable because unmeasurable. The sharp sword of Analysis had pricked the zeppelin monstrosities – Ethics, Metaphysics, Philosophy, as well as Theology, their dying cousin. Battles and victories were the sum only of individual conflicts. Had the message been: 'Here the conflict: here the resolution' then it would have made sense. But it could not have had the same appeal to Britton. I checked, wondering. Was that it, then? Britton to be lured by the emotive catchphrase. Britton, the subject for – experiment? That was a possibility.

Britton said: 'I think I see … It isn't easy – to be sure.'

There was a hint of awe in his voice. I reminded myself that this was his first experience of the flattering personal attention of the Unknown. I felt a need to intervene; not to save Britton from whatever might be in store for him – I had neither sympathy nor interest in that – but to reaffirm the principle of my own free and unmastered will.

I said: 'So Ming tells us we must do things now? That's something new.'

The table reared, in a kind of fury of response. Britton recited, absorbedly.

WILL NOT GO PRESLEY WILL NOT.

Lulu said: 'There, Tenn, that's telling you.'

Piers said, quite softly: 'No, it's not. It's a correction. Not must, but will. One instructs; the other predicts.'

The music leaped to a crescendo again, catching my attention. I missed the first few words of what Britton said:

'… can break prediction. The other was more impressive. I'm going to Presley anyway. I'm going on Wednesday.'

Lulu said impatiently: 'Can't we have something more … more concrete?'

The table resumed its racketing almost before she had finished speaking. She began to pace her speech alongside its bumping rhythm. The rest of us listened, apprehending and memorizing and forming the message. We were all silent for a few moments when it had ended.

LULU RIP NINETEEN FOUR SEVEN.

Lulu's own laughter broke it finally. There was always a childish quality in her voice, a treble thinness that was as characteristic of her and generally as unremarked as the vague suggestion of continental origin in the stress she gave to certain words. But now, in this laughter, mingling with and lifting above the relentless sound of music, enclosed with it in this narrow, pressing gloom, it was the childishness that I noticed most, and felt its irony.

She said: 'Well, that's concrete enough! This year, next year …'

I said: 'It's only his peculiar sense of humour, Lulu.' I hesitated, another child within another unyouthful and alien body, but at this moment I was too deeply committed to my pity for her to be able to refuse the sacrifice. Huge, defenceless, I said quickly: 'He's like that. Last Wednesday he predicted true love running smoothly between Livia and myself.'

Piers said casually: 'Yes, we're getting a lot of predictions lately.'

Lulu said: 'We'll see if Joe manages to break his. It's only for next week. I've got a year to wait for mine.'

Piers said: 'Well, six months, anyway. What about it, Joe? Are you going to save her life by leaving us this week?'

In daylight, in vision, the bland callousness of his tone would have been modified by the fractionally lifted eyebrow, the thin lips stretching tightly into a smile. But in the dark there was no such relief; his words conveyed their meaning starkly and without humour. I heard Britton shift his feet awkwardly beneath the table.

'That would be another reason for my being determined,' he said, 'except that it makes the whole thing ludicrous. I've not been weighing up a decision – I made it some time ago. Now your table tells me first I must reverse it and then that I am bound to reverse it whether I will or not. And for good measure it tells Lulu she's going to die next year.' He said the last sentence with an anxious, quickening speed; Lulu laughed again.

'Quite apart from anything else, the two predictions are of different kinds. The question of whether I go to Presley or not on Wednesday is one in which I am, at the very least, an agent. It needs my action. But to death we're all passive. It happens to us. So it wouldn't show anything at all if Ming did happen to be right about me. And, of course, he's not. I've got all sorts of reasons for sticking to my plans. Anyway, Tennyson will want to get rid of me.' He laughed himself. 'We're being too serious about all this.'

Piers said: 'That occurred to me. I wondered when it would strike the rest of you. For amusement only, remember. I've seen some reports that atom bombs are going to fry all of us before next year. They're quite as reliable as Ming is.'

His voice was cold and impersonal; so much so that his words were the reverse of reassuring. Lulu said timidly:

'Can we have the light on? For a moment ...'

Piers plucked the switch; blinking, I saw his eyes fixed wide, in an owl-like stare. Across the table Britton caught his fingers in his beard, pulling at it, twisting the rueful smile on his mouth.

'That was interesting, anyway. Is it always like this?'

Piers switched the radiogram off also; the air was light and echoing again. I could hear the strong, leaping notes of a 'cello – Howard practising in his room. The noise of flushing water from the bathroom cut across it. Around this closed room the world was springing back to life; the sound of a taxi on the street below was almost too much – an unnecessary emphasis.

Piers said: 'It varies.' Watching him in the light I was surprised to see and remember how expressionless his features were when he talked. And yet I had blamed the darkness for hiding his body and so making his words more cold and arid. 'From the technical point of view to-night has been surprisingly good. We don't generally get things through so easily and so ... precisely. Do we, Tenn?'

As he hesitated, finding the word he wanted, there had been

the shadow of a smile. When he talked, I realized, the very economy of his gestures and expressions made them lastingly memorable. Without light, economy became impoverished blankness, leaving only the sharp edge of his voice. But solving that problem I met another, as delicate and intangible. Why this appeal to me? A simple turn of conversation, a friendly request to be confirmed? Or a thin knife probing for the wound I had so recently exposed? I cleared my head of the fantastic assembly of subtleties and counter-subtleties. The relief from tension, small as it was, brought relaxation and some contentment.

I said: 'No, it's been a good session.' I glanced at Britton. 'It's a pity, in a way, that a successful quartet like this must be broken up at once.'

Britton said: 'Do you mean that it makes a difference which people are at the séance?'

I nodded. 'It seems to. We've tried some permutations.'

Britton asked: 'And is four the special number?'

Piers said restlessly: 'None of these answers are final. We've only been experimenting for a few months. But four does seem a good number. Three's too few; five's a crowd.'

There was a moment's pause. Then Britton leaned back against his chair. He yawned, widely, amiably. He stood up, stretching his stocky, rather fleshy body.

'Well, it's been very interesting.' He inclined his head slightly forward, making what might have been a mock or the beginning of a real bow, towards Piers's chair. 'I'm obliged to you all for the chance of sitting in on it.' Piers looked at his watch.

'Don't you want some more? It's not late yet.'

Britton shook his head positively.

'It's late enough for me. I'm getting up early to-morrow.'

Piers gazed at him speculatively. I wondered if here and now he would make an effort to persuade Britton; in some way I guessed that he did not want him to leave. But Britton pushed the chair under the table with noisy assurance, and I saw Piers drop his eyes to contemplation of his own large, well-manicured hands. Lulu looked up at Britton. For a moment, from where I sat, her throat was as unlined and clear as a girl's.

She said: 'It might be a good idea if we all witnessed a document ... putting down Ming's little prophecy.' She looked round at the rest of us and giggled self-consciously. 'The one about me, of course.'

Piers said thoughtfully: 'Yes, we could do that.'

Britton leaned down towards her, caressingly protective. He said softly: 'We won't do anything so silly. We'll just forget about it. That's the best thing to do with bad jokes.' He laid one hand on her shoulder. 'It might be a good idea if you made us a good-night drink. There's a gas-ring in your room, isn't there? You could make us some cocoa. I'll come on up with you and lend a hand.'

She got up at his urging. He led her to the door, as though she were a child and he a parent. Piers called:

'Tenn and I will be up for a drink when we've cleared away.'

We rolled back the carpet and set the battered, unsteady table back in its place by the wall, with its disguising green silk cover over it. I was turning away when I felt one of Piers's hands come to rest on my own. I looked down to meet his eyes.

He said: 'It is a good quartet, Tenn. I've got an idea Ming was right about Britton. I don't think he'll be leaving ... just yet, anyway. If he's at all hesitant, you won't discourage him, will you? You can put up with the inconvenience in your room a little longer?'

I said: 'If it's as important as that to you, why don't you have him up here? You've got two rooms, after all.'

He pushed over the box of cigarettes that he kept for other people, and I took one.

'Blodwen's moving in to-morrow,' he said. 'I believe you know – you met her yesterday, didn't you? I'd cancel that if it were necessary to keep Britton here. D'you believe me?'

I looked at him and nodded. He went on, half smiling:

'Perhaps I can persuade her she doesn't need a room of her own. But not just yet. I'd be glad if you would go on putting up with Britton for a while.'

I lit the cigarette and inhaled on it.

'You are going to a lot of trouble preparing for remote contingencies. Are you so sure Ming knows better than Britton what he is going to do?'

'I think he'll stay,' he said.

'And the other prediction?' I asked him.

He shrugged lightly. 'As Britton said, there's a difference between them. Departure is active; towards death one must be passive.'

I heard his giggling laugh behind me as we prepared to leave the room. I paused, waiting.

'I was just thinking,' he said. 'There is one active form of death, isn't there?'

I still waited. He looked at me, the laugh withdrawn to the faintest smile.

'I mean suicide,' he said.

CHAPTER THIRTEEN

BLODWEN MOVED IN on Tuesday evening. I heard the racket on the stairs and her voice shrilling down from the floor above but I didn't actually see her again until the following morning. She came late to breakfast with Piers diffidently behind her. She was wearing a tight, red-silk dressing gown, with generous glimpses of fake gold lamé behind it. She had piled her hair up and tied a scarlet turban round it. Her face was hurriedly but lavishly made-up; the entire effect was dazzlingly slap-dash.

She paused dramatically on the threshold of the room.

'God Almighty!' she demanded. 'What's this?'

She was looking at the wall that faced her. Most of it was still bare to the lath, but about a quarter had been re-plastered and bore the fruit of Leslie's personal genius. Against a pale rose background half of a grey and yellow tree stretched out its contorting branches above an out-of-scale crab with a woman's, a rather insipid Madonna's, face. The crab-woman was in atrabilious green. Leslie had been working on it that morning; he had sat with his back to it during breakfast, frequently turning round to examine it briefly, and in the intervals eating toast and drinking coffee. I saw him look at her. There was the usual unabashed lust but with it went dislike and, I thought, uneasiness. He said coldly:

'A fresco. As in the Sistine Chapel.'

She stared at him for a second before bursting into throaty laughter.

'Did you paint it?'

She walked round the table and examined it, leaning back against Leslie and myself, one fleshy buttock resting against each of our shoulders as we sat together. Her scent was strong and unequivocal. Leslie got up quickly from his chair to turn and stand beside her. If he had expected to throw her off balance his expectation failed. She pushed his chair sideways as he left it, and sat down. She tapped his leg with her hand to get him to move out of her line of vision.

Leslie said: 'Well? Any criticism?'

His tone was indulgently superior, but I still detected a lack of ease.

Blodwen looked at him, broadly smiling.

'You've only just started it, haven't you?' she said tolerantly.

He was disarmed. He said, ironically courteous:

'It doesn't need to be finished for judgment. I don't ask more than three square feet. You can find the essence of my work in less than that.'

She looked at him quickly and then looked back to the fresco. She was still smiling and after a moment she began to laugh gently to herself, a bubbling, internal sound.

'There's one thing it needs,' she said. Calmly she put out her left hand towards the still wet plaster and smeared a line down from the crab through the background of rose. Leslie caught her wrist to stop her and they struggled silently until she had bent him back, helpless, against the chair.

'A tail!' she said triumphantly. 'That's what it needed.'

She walked away from him towards the chair that Piers held for her on the other side of the table. Leslie stooped to retrieve his spectacles; they had fallen off in the skirmish. He bent down silently and began trying to repair the damage she had done. Lulu came in while he was so engaged. She stood behind him, watching.

'I like that, Les,' she said. 'I like the … the vigour in it.'

I finished my own breakfast quickly and went up to my room. I ran into Rupert on my landing. He had a packet of manuscript under his arm and handed it to me. I took it automatically.

'What's this?'

'The cowboy story. I stayed up last night finishing it.' He leaned against the banisters a couple of steps above me. 'It's thirty-four thousand nine hundred and fifty words – is that all right?'

I said gravely: 'Pity you didn't quite manage the round figure. Call in after breakfast and I'll let you know.'

I examined *Smoking Guns* when he had gone. He had typed the manuscript on his old and infirm American portable; it abounded in every variety of spacing and alignment and the typing was atrocious. But the story itself astonished me. I had only suggested the idea to Rupert originally as a joke, and out of curiosity as to the kind of tangled tortuosity he would make of an attempt at simple narrative. But I didn't need to read more than a dozen pages to realize that, amazingly, he had brought it off. This was mediocrity super plus. 'Hiya, hombre!' Chapter Three began, 'yuh aimin' tuh find yuhself a dose o' lead poison?' What shocked horror from his small, eclectic public should they ever learn the truth. Adventure stories for boys and girls were the only reputable form of relaxation for advanced poets and novelists. The frankly ordinary quality of the cheap Western story would be too great a strain on their imaginative view of the creative instinct's delicate frailty.

I walked over to my balcony. This present morning was almost enough in itself to excuse the wretched summer. It had been raining during the night and the sky was sponged to a soft but sparkling blue; the air was springy against one's flesh as it is on a day when one wades out from the sea into a heatwave afternoon. The trees further down the road were a subtly greener green, as though their leaves tried to recapture the sheen of spring's first innocence and nearly succeeded. Almost opposite a window was pulled up and a red-haired girl in a soft, white polo-necked sweater looked down for a moment into Regency Gardens before disappearing again into the darker recesses of her room. Had everything – air and sky and shimmering trees – been a stage set for that one moment and that one unconscious actor, it would not, I felt, have been over elaborate.

An illusion. What else? I made my peace with empiricism. And yet in this I knew I was not convinced. Beauty, Love, Truth, and the God which they comprised; the futility of all these large essences was apparent enough. But the small things, the individual, personal shocks of feeling and apprehension, stirred by a landscape, a quality of air, by the mawkishness of bad verse or a cinema story – these remained. God, perhaps, was a meaningless proposition but a lump in the throat was its own meaning and justification.

I thought of Rupert's cowboy stories and this time the spring ran deeper, so easily and certainly that it was hard to understand how it could have failed to do so a few minutes earlier. Tim's hammock under the Keswick trees on the orchard's very edge, beside the Little Meadow, looking down to the river and the great fold of land beyond. All those sun-heavy Friday afternoons. I paused, examining, challenging memory. Only during his holidays, for one thing. And even those Tim had not devoted to hammocked leisure. Perhaps half a dozen times I had gone down from the house to bring him up for tea and once, or at the most twice, I had found him surrounded by the stacks of garish American magazines which had touched off the irrelevant recollection. I was amused by the enormity of my self-deception. A joining of felicities. Friday afternoons had represented so much – London forgotten for three days and Thirl as surely recovered – and the days when Tim was there, too, had meant even more. The wicked 'thirties … Others could hymn their wickedness well enough. Even knowing the end – the Hurricane diving in flames to the Channel, to a multiplicity of deaths – I could find no anger for those peaceful, drifting days.

The partition was noisily rolled back and I turned to see Britton stepping through from his part of the room into mine. He was wearing his faded blue dressing-gown loosely tied, and both hair and beard were still uncombed.

'Just going to breakfast?' I asked.

He said: 'In a moment. Have you got a cigarette? I'm right out.'

I gave him one and followed up by helping him to a light. As he inhaled I watched him curiously.

'I can't smoke before breakfast myself,' I said. I took another cigarette out, tapped it and lit it. 'You'll be saying good-bye to us to-day then?'

He nodded quickly, absently. 'Yes.' He came over beside me and looked out into the soft, electric air of this late August morning. He raised his hands and moved them gently as though to catch some drifting benison. 'You never get anything quite like this in the States. I don't know ... I remember a morning just like this – a long time back.' He hesitated. 'A very long time back.'

I asked him: 'In Presley?'

He smiled. 'Yes, in Presley! I remember standing in the butcher's shop before he opened, watching him cut up. There was the smell of blood and the gaslight beating against the whitewashed walls and the black shutters and the scarlet flesh. I watched him for a while and then I slipped out into a morning just like this.' He looked up. 'Strange, isn't it? Some things stay with you.'

I nodded. 'Yes, some things do.'

He said: 'That was the first morning I went to the Grammar School.' His eyes flickered. 'The whole of the first term I didn't have a school cap. We owed too much money to be able to afford that kind of luxury. It was the year of the General Strike.'

I remembered another aftermath to that notable event. The raised, cheerful voices in Clubs, confident for the first time in twelve years. 1926. Tim went to school in that year, too. I drove him down to St. Nette's and was amazed at the unselfconscious way he ran off to join a group of strange boys. My own first day had not been the least like that. I had thought I saw a new generation, clearer-eyed and happier. I remembered finding old Pismire in the Common Room, still correcting Greek exercises, and feeling sorry for him, cut off by familiar trees from the new wood springing about him.

There had been a pause. Britton said suddenly:

'Did you think it was crazy ... that idea of mine for going back to Presley – to try and pick up my bearings, as it were?'

I observed his choice of tenses. I was getting ready to reply when the door behind us opened, effectively interrupting. Blodwen came in. She stood by the door, but not diffidently. Her eyes were examining the room with cool estimation. She saw us staring at her and said casually:

'Tennyson, isn't it? Hope you don't mind my butting in. I'm just getting my bearings.'

I nodded understandingly.

'Working your way up the house? This is a double room; through the partition lies this gentleman's temporary residence. I don't think you've met him. Joe Britton: Blodwen.'

'Blodwen Geraint,' she confirmed. She nodded at Britton. 'I've heard your name somewhere. R.A.F.? Navy?'

Britton shook his head; he was colouring faintly behind his beard. Blodwen looked at him sharply.

'Conchie?'

He hesitated. 'No.'

She laughed, her sudden, subterranean laughter, the scarifying coarseness of the female. 'They had a batch of conchies stationed right alongside the A.T.S. depot at Pennicross. A couple of them tried to click with ... some wenches from my hut one night in the village pub. They got them back into the camp some way and the girls really had fun with them.' Her laughter renewed itself as reminiscence added fuel. 'They were right up the well-known creek. When they finally got away they had Union Jacks on their arses in red and blue ink.'

I wondered what quirk of modesty forbade her to reveal the obvious – that she had certainly been one of the ringleaders. I gazed at her with frank admiration and with timidity that, I hoped, was well concealed. This was Piers's strangest yet. She came over and rested her hips on the edge of my desk.

'They tell me Livia hangs out in the cubby-hole down the stairs,' she said. 'I didn't see any sign of her when I looked in.'

Britton said: 'She has to go to work. In an office. She'll have left by now.'

The dressing-gown gaped enormously from the waist down. Her Byzantine night-gown was torn across her left thigh; white flesh bulged outwards through the slit in the gold. She held one slipper by the toes of a poised, stretched foot.

'Women must work,' she said. 'Some women, anyway.'

'She only started recently,' I said.

She took my meaning. 'Don't worry about me.' She held her hand up, with the first and index fingers crossed. 'That's the way it is with Piers and me. And I'm on top.' She laughed again. 'If you'll forgive the expression.'

I wondered. In another woman such confidence would be absurd; I had known Piers, after all, in several previous affairs. But the hopes of Jane and Hilda and Olivia could hardly be compared with the mountainous vitality of this assurance. There was no scope here for secret derision.

Howard knocked before coming in. His face was pulled down into morose lines. He looked sourly at Blodwen.

'You here? Still looking for stallions?'

She smiled at him indifferently. 'I know where not to look. Schoolboy.'

Howard didn't take any further notice of her. He came over to me.

'Tenn, I'm short again. Let me have some cash, will you?'

I had been a long time in Number 36; long enough to get used to having my privacy invaded at whim by whoever happened to be passing the door of my room. I would have been deceiving myself if I had not realized that I had reasons for submitting to that state of affairs. At times, however, irritation was touched off. I saw Blodwen's opulence lounging on my desk,

Britton standing at the window in an attitude compounded of uncertainty and boredom, Howard's thin, anxious, demanding face before my own. I said viciously:

'For Christ's sake! Don't you ever stop to think how much you've had off me already? Is there no one else you can go to for a change?'

It was quite usual to insult Howard as a preliminary to giving him money. It never bothered him; he expected it, and I saw his face twist into his usual wry, appreciative smile as I began speaking. But the overtones of real anger and annoyance reached him. I saw the half-formed smile tighten into sullenness before I finished.

He muttered: 'To hell with you, then.' He paused, looking at me. 'You fat old sod,' he added deliberately.

I was caught; caught by the situation as much as by my almost hysterical embarrassment. I looked at Howard, with no desire except to avoid looking at the other two witnesses to my impeachment. I tried to rationalize, intellectually, coldly. No secret had come out of hiding, after all. Both Britton and Blodwen had the evidence of their own eyes. But rationalization failed, against a new wave of flustered shame. I sat above the fleshy mountain of my body and felt myself naked to the gaze of others, and to their pity. It was the thought of the pity that racked my mind to humiliation, even to terror. I tried to think: 'This moment will pass,' and knew it never would.

Howard was still in front of me. Some part, perhaps the essential part, of the situation remained to be saved. I smiled. In me, I reflected sardonically, an Irving lost. I said, surprising myself by the lightness and ease of my tone:

'Fat, perhaps, but no plutocrat. All right, then. How much?'

Howard watched me warily. My response was wrong; the tension between us had been too charged and too bitter to find naturally so generous a resolution. An analyst of behaviour would have known the truth but Howard was not acute enough for that. His scowl relaxed slowly. He began to smile again.

'I don't know what I'm saying half the time, Tenn. You should boot me out.' He continued to ignore the other two present in the room. 'I've been having a row with Helen again. I tried to get a couple of quid out of her. It was no go. But Sister Cynth was packed off with the cash for a perm ten minutes later. I found her slipping the money to her in the kitchen.' He pushed his fingers through his thin, grey-blond hair. 'I'm going to do one of them in some day. Probably Helen.'

The wild, irrelevant race of my mind had been slowing down while he talked, but recollection could still jab it again into its furious, threshing activity. I concentrated on the impersonal, unimportant question of Howard's need for money. I took my wallet out and opened it.

'Two enough?'

He took the notes. 'For now.' He smiled towards Britton, holding the notes in the air, rubbing them between finger and thumb. 'Tenn's a good-hearted old bastard, Joe.'

It was all right again. I managed to look at Britton's face as well as Blodwen's and surprised no malicious knowledge there; only indecision on the one and disinterestedness on the other. Blodwen's face brightened up when Rupert made a diffident appearance. She said heavily:

'Walk right on in. Tenn doesn't mind; he likes company.'

Rupert said to me: 'I just thought you might have had a look at that manuscript, but it doesn't matter. I'll look in later.'

I said: 'The needs of publishing come even before hospitality to my growing circle of friends. I've looked enough at it. It's just fine. I'll write you a cheque if Blodwen doesn't object to getting off my desk for a couple of minutes. A round fifty – will that suit you?'

He half-opened his mouth with astonishment and then, I could tell, began to work things out in his head. He was never strong on simple arithmetic and it took him some little while. He nodded; doubtfully, and at last eagerly.

Blodwen hitched herself far enough over on my desk to enable me to sit down and find a cheque book. She leaned curiously over my shoulder as I wrote out the cheque.

'Fifty!' she echoed. 'How long did it take him to earn that?'

I paused, on the point of scrawling my signature. It was a point that had not occurred to me before. I looked up at Rupert.

'Considerably less than forty-eight hours ... I don't like to think it of you, Rupert, but – you haven't been fooling me, have you? You haven't copied this from one of my rival publications?'

He looked hurt. 'Why should you think that, Tenn?'

I said: 'You're not exactly known as a *prolific* writer. Two small volumes of verse in ten years seems a little out of key with thirty-five thousand words inside two days. Damn it, it would be hard enough work to copy it in that time.'

His face cleared into guilty cheerfulness.

'It does seem a bit queer, doesn't it? But I liked doing it. I stayed up till four this morning, finishing it.' He held one hand up. 'My fingers are a bit battered about.'

Howard said: 'Right enough. He kept me awake till all hours. And the night before.'

Rupert completed his explanation: 'There's really nothing in it. I mean ... you don't have to hunt for words ... and there's no thought to hammer out. It's just a story. I should think it's easier than copying.'

I signed the cheque and handed it to him with due reverence. I said:

'I'll take another half dozen, as fast as you like. This is just what I want.'

Rupert put the cheque away and examined his fingers again.

'Perhaps in a couple of months I might do another,' he offered.

I said patiently: 'Not in a couple of months, Rupert. I want them now.'

He smiled as patiently himself.

'But I don't *have* to do anything for two or three months. I can manage on this.'

It was an entire and sufficient explanation. Howard, missing the point, said interestedly: 'But if you enjoy writing them ...'

Rupert smiled vaguely. He made a small gesture of incipient departure. His gaze drifted across, over Howard's head, to where Britton stood.

He said: 'I'd like you to drop in sometime, Joe – I've got something to show you. I'll be in my room all day. That is, if you are leaving us this evening.'

The interrogative lift in the last sentence was the barest of inflexions. Blodwen said, before Britton could reply:

'Someone going somewhere?'

I was watching Britton acutely. I saw his confusion and knew that at this moment all choice and force, determination and persuasion, came in him to decision's lasting focus. I said slowly, answering Blodwen, watching the weight of my words in the delicate balance of his will:

'He had some idea of going to live in a small town in Lancashire. Where he was born. We all try to get back to the cradle, don't we? It's a very old dream. It can almost be done, too. You gain a lot, and sacrifice ... everything.'

Blodwen's laugh rippled like meaningless thunder against a sky dark with meaning. She said something but I wasn't listening. As though there were only two of us in the room, Britton said:

'If I ... deferred it for a while – would I be in your way?'

And so it was settled.

I said: 'No. Stay as long as you like.'

Britton said: 'Thanks. I don't know how long. But if I'm getting in your way you can throw me out.' He looked at his watch. 'I haven't had breakfast yet.'

I said: 'Helen will find you something.' I looked at the others. 'You can all clear out. I've got some work to do.'

I managed to get rid of them and sat for a while at my desk, riffling through the pages of Rupert's manuscript. The room was quiet about me, and beyond its walls there was the reassurance of muffled, ordinary sounds. A car passing in the street, a cistern flushing, a distant 'cello's hum. This sensual world was calm.

I endured it for a long time; perhaps ten minutes. Then I dropped the manuscript from my impatient, weary fingers, and went out to find Piers.

BOOK III

CHAPTER FOURTEEN

AUTUMN BROUGHT LITTLE or no relief from the general buffeting of wetness and wind that had characterized the summer. Day after day was sunk in the salt ocean of nature's unquenchable misery; the edges were damp and the heart of things was soaked in tears. The waters falling endlessly from the heavens made me think of the waters that rose to cover a sinful earth. That myth's symbolism was not inapposite now, when every hour saw another inch of our forefathers' laborious artefacts whittled away by the surging tide of human guilt and misery and despair. Occasionally the sun would catch the jewelled spire of some great relic so that its beauty echoed and re-echoed against the lowering horizon in brief and concentrated glory, before the lapping waves devoured it. Occasionally the flood appeared to recede, but the moment's illusion was lost almost at once as the hollow curved up to a new crest of destruction.

But in this deluge most of us had, if not arks, at least rafts. We bobbed high enough, and even gained some exhilaration from the view of toppling spires and domes. We were dry; we were – for the moment – safe. It occurred to me once that this, too, might have its relevance in fable. Had others before found boards and lashed them together? Were there even some who survived, perhaps, for thirty-nine days before the grey waste of water at last overpowered them? It was an idle thought. We knew now that, whether the Flood were real or not, the Ark, undeniably, was an illusion. And thirty-nine days gone by would leave no hope on the fortieth morning. These waters would not drain away.

My own raft, at any rate, had gained several inches' buoyancy. I ran fifty thousand of *Smoking Guns* and was able to wire Dublin within a fortnight for another hundred thousand. Its successors did not quite succeed in repeating that success – I had to find another author and although competent he lacked Rupert's assurance – but they did more than satisfactorily. I found myself able to indulge again in small luxuries. A decent suit, a *Britannica*, a case of Scotch obtained at under three pounds a bottle through Piers's discreet agencies. I even toyed with the idea of getting a new car.

I thought very seriously of getting a new flat. Since giving up my rooms in the Albany my wanderings around the environs of South Kensington had been capricious and frequently resumed. My stay of over eighteen months in Regency Gardens was more than twice as long as any in the preceding four years. I had thought this accidental – caprice decreeing exceptions even to its own sway – but now, considering, I realized that unwittingly I had put down roots. Man's attitude to the groups in which he finds himself varies with his nature; between the extremes of locking (or trying to lock) the door, and banging desperately on it for admission. But there is always the moment of realization that one is in place again, a familiar and expected figure with conventional rights and conventional liabilities. Britton still occupied half my room. I could have repudiated the mask of easy-going tolerance that had been put on me by Helen. I could have thrown Britton out or stamped out myself in virtuous wrath. Neither course seemed worth the emotional trouble. I didn't really object to Britton being there. I had as much space as I knew what to do with. There were moments, of course, when I felt, as a desperate urgency, the need to get away from every familiar face and gesture around me, but I did not forget, either, how much I still needed them. Now I might want privacy. Next week privacy might again wear its different, terrifying aspect of loneliness.

Olivia still kept the small room down the stairs. She spent a lot of time in it. The nervous excitement provoked by her crisis with Piers had settled, it seemed, into a lethargic moroseness.

She went out to work in some office or other, and occasionally she went round with the rest to the Regent or the Little Lion. Once or twice, I realized from the good-nights exchanged on the stairs, Britton managed to persuade her to go out with him, on some undefined jaunt. But more and more frequently I passed the door of the little room and glanced in to see her lying along her narrow divan, hair untidy, shoes scuffed off, her face turned away from the stairs and the outside world. She still came to the Wednesday séances.

The rest of the inhabitants of Number 36 went on much as they had done before. Blodwen's arrival had been a surprise impact but her calculating vulgarity was rapidly absorbed into the general atmosphere of the place as all our other unique and surprising personalities had been before her. If she wrought any change in it our observations, involved as they were in the scene they watched, failed to notice them.

The only one on whom she had any clear and positive effect was Leslie. As his fresco slowly assumed obscure and painful shape on the basement walls he spent more and more time with us, sleeping with Lulu or on another of Helen's inexhaustible supply of camp-beds beside his work. He had an attic somewhere in Oakley Street but he used it as little more than an accommodation address. His attitude to Blodwen was surprising. She treated him, as she treated most men and the few women she disliked, with amused contempt; in contrast he displayed a surprising deference, accentuated by an obvious physical yearning for her that contrived to be at once open and furtive.

Both sets of séances continued. They began to develop individual and recognizable characters. Mondays were chiefly concerned with direct communications, warnings and prophecies. Wednesdays, with Howard and Olivia, were the evenings of paranormal tomfoolery; a tomfoolery tinged occasionally with a seriousness belying the title, but, broadly speaking, tomfoolery enough. On an evening cold with the drawn-in chill of a damp October day, Howard arrived to join us in Piers's room carrying a long cardboard trumpet under his arm. I was comfortably wedged in an arm-chair with a glass of brandy. Olivia sat on the edge of the divan, her features relaxed into sulky apathy. Piers was fiddling with a connection to the jointed, angular table lamp on his desk. Blodwen, on the other side of the divan from Olivia, was mending a ladder in one of her stockings in meticulous and unusual silence.

Howard said: 'Well, here it is!'

His voice had a pleased, self-satisfied note. I stretched my hand out and took the trumpet from him. I weighed it in my hand; it was very light. Howard had painted bands in luminous paint at either end; in the subdued glare of electric light they had a stale, sticky look.

I passed the trumpet on to Olivia. She examined it with dull, careful curiosity.

'Where are you going to fix it?' she asked.

Howard pushed one of Piers's chairs into the place where the table normally stood. Standing on it he was able to reach up almost to the ceiling. He glanced down.

'A screw in here. I'll need something higher, though. The table.'

Piers said: 'We might as well get the table out now anyway.'

We rolled the carpet back and put the table in place. Howard climbed on it, balancing precariously for a moment. He began to screw a brass hook into the ceiling, bringing down at first a fine cascade of plaster dust. While he was doing this Piers was tying strong thread around each end of the trumpet, leaving a good loop length by which to suspend it. He passed the result up to Howard, who hung it cautiously, patting the trumpet into a hovering equilibrium with light, adjusting movements. It rested directly above the centre of the table, a megaphone for the Invisible. Blodwen looked up as we stood back, admiring it.

'What's that for?' she asked.

Howard said, lightly insolent: 'What does it remind you of?'

She glanced at him contemptuously. 'As far as you're concerned – nothing.'

Piers walked across and put his arms round her from behind, cupping her heavy breasts and half-lifting, half-forcing her to her feet. Upright she was by several inches the taller. He kept one arm about her, as though reluctant to let her go.

He said: 'Time you took your things next door … unless you want to sit in?'

She shook her head, her dark, extravagant curls brushing against Piers's face. Her face twisted wrily.

'Not likely.' She turned round so that she faced him.

'I think I'll trot round to the Regent. See you there when you've finished?'

As she was talking she reached for his inside pocket to get his wallet. We had all witnessed the procedure before. She normally took it out, peeled off as much as she wanted, and replaced it with a tolerant, acknowledging kiss. The difference this time was not very great, but somehow I found a large significance in it. Piers gently restrained the reaching wrist. He took his wallet out himself, gave her a pound, and put it back. He patted her affectionately and pushed her away. I saw a faintly puzzled look on her face as she found her handbag and dropped the note in it.

She went, as usual leaving the door open behind her. Howard slammed it, and came back to pull a chair up to the table and sit on it. He gazed with interest at the trumpet, rotating very gently in an eddy of air. It was two or three feet above our heads; one would have to rise from one's chair to reach it. I finished my brandy and went across to stand beside him, the palms of my hands resting on the table top.

I said: 'Do you really think we'll get Direct Voice?'

Olivia said: 'I don't.'

She had got out of the habit of setting her hair; it was no longer a silken yellow floss curving, clinging, about the softer curve of her cheek. It was thin straw now and the line of her face no longer compellingly taut, but just a little flabby.

Howard said: 'It's worth the try. No harm in having a few extra props about the place. Gives us a professional air, anyway. What do you say, Piers?'

Piers said: 'Direct Voice? Whose? And if a disembodied larynx can make any kind of sound at all, why should it need a material amplifier?'

Olivia said: 'It's all incredible.'

She spoke more emphatically. She had taken to repeating Piers's remarks of late; in this respect alone did she show any forcefulness. Normally she was careful also to avoid passing opinions before he had spoken. I imagined that in the past Piers must have made some scathing comment on Direct Voice which she remembered.

Piers smiled towards her, mockingly polite.

'Of course, so many things are, aren't they?' He switched to a more general gaze. 'I've got something I think might interest you. I'll put it on.'

He took a twelve-inch gramophone record from the cabinet beside the radiogram. I noticed that it had a plain white label carrying hand-written information.

'What is it?' Howard asked.

Piers put the record on the turn-table. He lifted the tone-arm back, clicking it into spinning motion. Holding the tone-arm between thumb and finger, he said:

'It's an S.P.R. thing. The record of a Direct Voice sitting someone ran up at Tavistock Square once. I forget which medium and they've left it off the label as well.'

I said: 'You mean the S.P.R. vouch for it?'

Piers smiled. 'No. Not quite. It was a full blackness sitting and they hadn't rigged up their infra-red cameras and things then. For interest only. Listen.'

He set down the tone-arm. There was the hiss of the revolving needle, punctuated by the usual heavy scratches of amateur recordings. Piers turned the volume up and they became even louder. I listened, inattentively. The first whispering speech was barely distinguishable from the scratchings. But the effect of it, issuing from the radiogram's heavy, ornate speaker, brought me forward in an involuntary movement of apprehension. Howard got up from his chair and Olivia came across from the divan. We twitched on strings towards that crabbed, shivering voice as it rose and fell above and below the level surge of surface noise. It was joined by another, unnaturally loud – presumably one of the sitters interrogating. I listened, beginning to pick up the thread of the conversation.

The loud voice: '... to hear you again. Mrs. Purley is with us this afternoon. She does so want to know if you have seen anything of Lionel, lately. I suppose he won't be able to come through to-day?'

'No. Not to-day ... There won't ... but he wants to send his love to all.'

The whisper had dropped below audibility but it rose to a clear firmness on the latter half of the sentence. The bland confident voice of the sitter resumed:

'I've been thinking over what you said last time. About the true path, the Way, being found through the Heart. That's very inspiring.'

The whisper was almost querulously weak.

'Yes. That ... the answer. I found that. Everyone finds ... on this side. The Heart is the key. That's the message ... to give.'

I heard the record through with sick, impatient disgust. I could imagine the setting so well – the large, dusty room blacked out to hide the heavy furniture, the dusty volumes of the *Proceedings,* the too legible faces of the sitters. Three-quarters of them intent, persuaded, listening to the new Gospel being preached. But it was the thought of the others, the mocking quarter, that for some reason nauseated me. That forgotten, individual afternoon was here in the room with us, its trust and scepticism re-created along with its rustling, muted platitudes.

Piers said: 'It's double-sided. Want to hear the rest?'

Olivia looked at him uncertainly, probing to find his wishes. She began to say something equivocal; I cut across her words.

'No. We've heard enough, Piers.'

Howard said: 'A bit on the invertebrate side, wasn't it?' He moved back restlessly to his chair, and looked up at the hanging trumpet.

'I shall be surprised if we get anything like it, though.'

Piers was arranging records for our own sitting. With his face turned away from us his voice had the same flat, cruel intonation that it had in the dark.

'We never know,' he said, 'do we? Until we try.'

As he turned round I was surprised to see that his face was serious and unsmiling.

Beneath the tawdry sway of 'Scheherazade' we sat together in the known but never familiar dark. These days we rarely had long to wait for the manifestations. A grating of wood, the tiny flail of frost in the air, and the table began its bucketing motion. It maintained its activity for about five minutes. We had some orthodox rapping; Ming identified himself and there were some attempts at messages that were no more than fragmentarily meaningful. Then the lull fell, a lull broken occasionally by creakings and shiftings of the table, but for the most part solid, and boring.

Howard said: 'Perhaps they're straining at the trumpet.'

Piers said restlessly: 'Something should happen. These Wednesday do's are degenerating. We want something for our money.'

I said softly: 'Because our money is time …'

Olivia cried out. Her voice was nervous, but not convincing. She said: 'What touched me? Someone touched me.'

Piers's tittering laugh answered her. 'We didn't. I didn't.'

She said, hopelessly: 'Perhaps it was nothing.'

Something or nothing? Touched or not touched? I reflected, aware of my own large flesh exposed and alive to ambiguous stimuli, crawling with minute and imprecise sensations. We sat, all four of us, our imaginations drawn taut by darkness and evocative music, waiting for mystery to tap our expectant nerve-ends. But there were stimuli at nerve's beginning as well. A vast complexity of motive and counter-motive. 'These Wednesday do's are degenerating. We want something for our money.' And quick despair, reacting response, leaving their snail trails of confusion and uncertainty. It wasn't only Olivia who was open to that charge.

The table began jumping again with a startling spontaneity that might have been ironical comment on my self-doubts and hesitations. In this there was no unsureness. The table thudded heavily on the bare boards. I was aware of my own innocence at least. There were external stimuli here all right, and not of my causing.

Howard spelled the message out:

TRU ... BREATHING TRUMPET.

He said: 'What does that mean? I don't hear it breathing.'

Piers said: 'I think ... Wait a minute.'

As generally happened our hands had relinquished their contact once the phenomena started; it was an abandonment that created, of course, several more loop-holes for doubt to peer out through, but the increased doubt was a lesser strain than continual hand-holding would have been. I now only heard Piers's chair creaking, enabling me to guess that he had risen from his seat. His voice, when he spoke again, came obliquely down.

He said: 'I've got my cheek against this end of the trumpet. There's something blowing through all right.'

Howard said: 'Hang on. I'll listen at the other end.'

We heard him scramble to his feet also. He went on:

'I can't feel anything ... Yes, I can! Something's blowing through.'

'Now?' Piers asked.

Howard said: 'Yes! Your end, too? But how can it?'

I was looking up. The two bands of sickly phosphorescence wavered uncertainly, the larger pointing towards Piers's chair on my left. Their light was not sufficiently strong for me to detect anything of the two faces attentive at either end. Piers's voice came down again:

'Now?'

'Now!'

Olivia said uncertainly: 'What's happening?'

I said: 'It's quite simple, Livia. There's a very little man in the middle of the trumpet blowing air two ways at once. He must be double-headed.'

The last record of 'Scheherazade' clicked to its end and my voice sounded louder in the silence than I had meant it to be.

Piers said: 'Want to try it, Tenn?'

I said: 'Why not? Swing it round. Livia and I will listen in on the Unknown.'

I had to hold the large end of the trumpet to prevent it from swinging away from us. I held it against my cheek conscientiously. Nothing happened. Olivia said:

'Anything at your end?'

I pursed my lips and puffed a breath of air towards her. She gave a little cry.

'That was me,' I said. 'I was just seeing if the little man was in the way.'

Piers said: 'Try it alone, Tenn. Sit down, Livia.'

I heard her sit down and stood, for some reason obedient to Piers's command, holding the trumpet's edge. Almost at once I felt the pulse of warm air against my face. It came in gusts as though from lungs racked by the unaccustomed effort of breathing. In a lull Piers said:

'Well? Nothing?'

'Something,' I said. 'Certainly something.'

I felt the gust again and heard it expand into the sharper edge of speech: barely audible, barely intelligible, a whisper challenging. A call: 'Tenn!'

I lunged as sharply as I could, feeling with my hands for the other end of the trumpet. They closed on vacancy. There was nothing there; nothing anywhere.

Nothing but the memory of a whisper in a voice I thought was dead.

CHAPTER FIFTEEN

It was many years since I had known that easy familiarity with sleep which is the prerogative of youthful or contented minds. On this particular night I expected it to come hardly, if at all. It was surprising that I fell asleep so quickly.

We had broken up around nine and had an hour in the Regent before it closed. We found Blodwen there, along with Helen and Cynthia, Leslie, two or three indeterminates (chiefly as to origin but also, for that matter, as to sex), and, teetotally chain-smoking in front of a glass of lemonade, Britton. He looked up to greet us with more enthusiasm than the others felt or thought proper to show.

'How'd it go?' he asked. 'How'd it all go?'

He motioned Piers eagerly to a place beside him. I stood at the bar ordering drinks. I heard Howard replying:

'Wonderful prophecies. Foreseeing all – the typist home at tea-time.'

Britton's voice said: 'Seriously?'

Cynthia said: 'Typist? What typist?'

'The one who was with us in the ships at Mylae,' Howard replied. 'Not – never – my elegant sister. No young man carbuncular for her.'

Cynthia said: 'I don't think these séance do's are good for the boy, do you, darling? They over-excite him.' The remark was addressed to Helen. Busy with collecting the drinks I didn't hear her reply. Howard was excited. I hoped he wasn't going to start one of his unequal engagements with Cynthia; it moved me both to pity and resentment watching them. I took two Worthingtons over to where Piers was sitting beside Britton and inserted them gently into the conversation that had sprung up between them. Piers was saying quietly:

'... no voices – but it certainly felt like something breathing. Oh, thanks, Tenn.'

'Another lemonade?' I asked Britton.

He shook his head, his hand curled quite tightly about the glass.

'We've had puffs of air before,' he said, 'without any kind of trumpet.'

'This was warm air,' Piers told him. 'Wasn't it, Tenn?'

I nodded, drinking my beer. For some reason I had begun sweating and, as always, my physical discomfort and distaste upset me. I touched my face surreptitiously with the back of one hand but it was dry enough. But despite this small reassurance I felt my perspiring largeness naked and obvious to the world of cool, dry pygmies.

Britton said: 'You two ... You're in both sets of séances. That's where the twisting goes on. Anyone could see that.'

His tone was joking, but it was the weak, forced humour of someone making the best of a bad job. He must, I realized, feel excluded. But to feel exclusion as an emotion implies a corresponding desire for inclusion. Did Britton have that? I observed him smiling at Piers. There was unease beneath it. It might just have been the unease of the uncertain humorist.

Piers looked at him steadily.

'Why two? Why not one? Do you think there's anything that's happened in the séances that one person couldn't have engineered on his own?'

Once again he had surprised and provoked me. Sitting, still sweating lightly, in the Regent and later strolling back to Number 36 with the rest, it was on this that my mind interminably revolved. That faculty of his for taking the razor-edge of suspicion, lifting it into light and then as sharply blunting it with his casual, hammering steel. It was characteristic but it never failed to astonish me. My thoughts raced in a repetitious and interwoven network about their central point; resolving no problem, coming to no conclusion, but simply obeying the laws of their own strange, mazy motion. It was because of this relentless rat-race of consciousness that I was even less than usually hopeful of sleep. When I woke, some time in the night, it was with another shock that I realized how swiftly sleep had come, and remembered the dream that had followed on its heels.

I was at Thirl again. I knew that as one knows things in dreams, with an awareness transcending all the irrelevancies and blatant falsehoods of individual objects. The objects, as usual, were in nonsensical juxtaposition. A room furnished, more or less, with the furniture of my double room at Number 36. But the room itself was the big conservatory, and one end of it was stacked with the high tiers of potted plants that we cleared out the summer my mother died; the summer of 1919. Sunshine pressed its way through the glossy tangles of evergreen, to fall at last in haphazard patterns of weariness on the red and white tiled floor. There was the old, unforgettable sense of preternatural coolness, more deeply shaped by the thought of the heat outside, and the old smell of dust lightly powdered on aspidistra and geranium. That smell was once for me the symbol of all enduring things.

I was looking for someone.

Not, at first, with any idea of urgency. It was more an anticipation of a presence than a feeling of its absence. Someone was coming in to see me. Not my mother. Despite the apparent evidence of the sun-obscuring ranks of plants, I knew that she was dead. I awaited someone – admitting it with dream morality's easy frankness – more real and more important. Secure in expectation I busied myself, contentedly alone, with different tasks and trivialities. They melted lightly one into another, aspects of dream forming and dissolving. What did not dissolve was the sureness that someone else should be there with me.

It did not dissolve, but gradually it changed. Anticipation faded, and the knowledge of absence sharpened and grew strong, bringing with it anxiety and a need for action. The tasks and trivialities dropped away. I began to hunt and in so beginning was committed relentlessly.

In dream I searched the house. I hunted in a shifting rainbow of time, three or four Tennysons at least – from the stumbling, grave-minded boy among the potted plants to the later, obese flat-dweller – inextricably woven together on the thread of their common desire. Space, too, was flexible, though in narrower degree. Climbing the backstairs from the kitchens, hoping somehow to surprise the unformulated quarry, the worn, wooden steps leaped into a long, exaggerated, heart-pumping agony. And then, as suddenly, were lost as I – we? – found myself translated to the warm, rose shadows of the second floor landing, where it was late afternoon and the slanting sunshine through the bedroom windows gently underlined the emptiness there. The whole house was empty. That Tennyson who had once – on one occasion – known it so, was briefly the controlling aspect. But the crucial emptiness was not of one time or one aspect of memory. It was of one person.

In the garden, perhaps? In the orchard? Gazing from the nursery window now, but finding no better success. Only the slow drift of leaves against the darkening summer sky, and pollen in a yellow haze suspended above the shadows on the fishpond.

The stables, then. Winter here, the long trail of icicles from the frosted eaves and the bulbous, tapering stalactite above the large water-butt. Life, too. The patternless harmony of horses, shifting, stamping in their stalls; their rich smell and their long, unhumanly individual and personal faces stretching out incuriously to watch the intruder. I ran – lightly, quickly! – up the wooden steps to the loft, where it was summer again and the hay newly stacked and rich with the very essence of clovered afternoons. A rat, momentarily poised on the corner of a high bale, leaping off with all the sharp grace of concentrated action to whisk away into the shadowed corner. But nothing, no one, else, and need still more acute for each new empty scene.

I returned to the house across the lawn. The house itself was swathed in thin folds of mist, giving it a strange appearance of tallness, even of gauntness. Under my feet moisture sprayed from the uncut grass. I crossed the flagged path and pushed open the door of the conservatory. The old bronze doorknob was cold and rather moist. Inside the conservatory I stood silently for some time, watching the array of puritan plants marshalled in their pots, and aware of the mist pressing against the glass, huddling close on three sides and pallidly breathing on the roof. It was a very dark afternoon and the gas-jets were flaring unevenly in the chandelier near the door. The gas-jets, I remembered, went a few years before the plants did.

I was content to wait now. I waited, relaxed on small haunches, in the west corner, the one from which the mechanical airship used to set out on its jerky, wire-suspended flight towards the patient Rodney. Water dripped from the cracked pipe overhead, meticulously falling to meet the stained patch of tiling beside my right foot. I could set the very hour to that impression. The framed Craxton leering from the incongruous wall was from a different hour, but was not strange on that account. All hours were here.

I waited until the door opened and I woke with a shock, sweating, in my ordinary bedroom in Regency Gardens. Even in the vivid aftermath of dream I could not remember who it was that I had known would come through the conservatory door. But I knew who had come. I lay back in bed, breathing heavily, remembering the door opening and Piers's small figure advancing across the threshold to meet me. From the dream that remained; that and the sight of the graceful rat leaping in its own unfathomable flurry of motives from the rich, high platform of hay.

For some time I lay awake, sweating and trying to think. In the sharp chill of the night the evening's beer had gone to my bladder and I got out of bed and stumbled up the half flight of stairs to the bathroom. As I came out I saw the narrow shaft of light on the stairs above me. There was a light in Piers's big room and the door was just ajar. I listened and heard the resonance of speech, low-pitched, unvarying, unhurrying – Piers's voice. There was no sound of interruption or rejoinder from Blodwen. I stood there for a moment with the sweat drying on my flesh in the night air, before I turned and went down again to my own room.

In the morning I had a back ache. I lay in bed for some time after a subdued clattering from the other side of the partition told me that Britton was up. In the segment of sky visible above the cold roof line opposite, a Parthenaic procession of cloud wisps galloped towards some frozen festival. Their individual uniqueness as well as their tattered anonymity engaged me. Curl and spiral, twist and sliver. Air and dust and moisture flinging itself forward in determined, irrelevant self-pursuit along the immobile precipice of wet slate. I watched in a kind of stupor, a lassitude compounded of the slow ache twisting my spine and the immediate, comforting warmth of the blankets. I felt that there was little chance of breaking out of it by my own volition. When Britton brought a cup of coffee in I greeted him with some warmth.

He brought the cup over and I took it from him. He sat down on the bottom of my bed.

'You're generally up first,' he reminded me. 'Feeling all right?'

I drank the coffee. Helen's coffee was always a revelation. The ache seemed to subside.

'Just a pain in the back,' I said. 'Thanks.'

'It's cold.'

He looked cold. He was rubbing his hands slowly together. But there was some nervousness about his movements, too.

'Last night …' he said.

I drank some more coffee. I was feeling better and my mind was opening to its usual small guilt at being in bed when others were active; even as modestly active as Britton.

'Yes?'

'That was rather a silly joke of mine – that you and Piers might be faking the séances.'

I said: 'You'd be a fool if the idea hadn't occurred to you. It didn't matter. You weren't hurting our feelings.'

I wondered what he was after. It certainly wasn't that.

He said quickly: 'But by the very nature of these things we've got to trust each other in them. That's obvious, really.'

I said with some interest: 'Have you explained that to Piers?'

He said: 'It doesn't need explaining.' He paused. 'There is something I want to talk to him about.'

I waited for him to go on. I didn't have long to wait. He leaned forward, burying his hands into the folds of my eiderdown.

'I'd like to come in on the Wednesday séances. Howard would probably be willing to change. There wouldn't be any objection to that, would there?'

I said: 'So it's getting serious?'

He asked: 'What is?' He looked so genuinely, innocently uncomprehending that I almost thought I might have somehow jumped to a wrong conclusion. Unravelling more warily, I said:

'You want to join the circle of Piers, myself and – Olivia. That's right?'

He flushed a little. He said frankly:

'We've been seeing quite a bit of each other – you probably know. It just seems silly to be sitting in on different evenings. It isn't as though it matters to anyone else.'

'No,' I said. 'Windowless monads, entirely surrounded by water.'

He laughed, with his familiar, past-youthful boyishness.

'I'm with Donne, not Leibniz. But you don't need to apply the general to the particular all the time. I'm sure the others wouldn't mind.'

'Then you only need to ask Howard to swop with you.'

He said with less ease: 'I will. But I'll mention it to Piers first.'

'Yes,' I said. 'Now you know you have my blessing.'

He said quickly: 'Of course you have as much say as anyone. I'm glad you think it's a good idea.'

He looked as though he were ready to move. I shifted slightly in bed myself and felt a renewed pain stab across my kidneys. I wanted to get up but this irrelevant physical malice tilted a fragile balance towards a further delay. I handed Britton my coffee cup to put down on the chest-of-drawers.

'I think it's a good idea,' I said, 'but how do you think Olivia will take to Presley?'

He got up from the end of the bed and walked with his slouching step across the room. I thought he might be going out but he turned at the edge of the carpet and came back towards me. He stopped beside the bed again, looking down at me from the puzzled, uncertain height of his personal isolation.

He said: 'Is that a necessary question?'

'No,' I said. 'Never mind.'

He continued to look down at me, searching for something. 'It's too ordinary for you, Tennyson. You don't deal in that kind of innuendo.' He paused, waiting perhaps for me to put in some explanation or disclaimer. 'I think I know what you are getting at.'

I said: 'That coffee was a tonic. I ought to be getting up soon.'

He smiled suddenly with an anxious, placatory warmth.

'It's me, isn't it? Not Olivia? You think I've given up the idea – of going to Presley.'

I said: 'Have you?'

'I don't know.' He half turned to look out of the window towards the flickering, grey sky. In profile I could see more clearly how his face was beginning to jowl. 'Quite honestly, I've been getting out of the habit of thinking about it. I wonder why that is? Now … Yes, I still intend to go. I intend to go, all right.'

'Regency Gardens is still only a transit camp?'

He said: 'The world's a transit camp.' I smiled and he laughed. 'I say some pretty trite things, don't I?'

'You're getting more self-critical,' I told him. 'Two months ago you would have said that and meant it.'

'I still mean it.' He hesitated. 'I think I'm beginning to tread carefully again. Do you know what I mean? It scares me a little.'

I said: 'Again?'

'It happened at the University,' he explained. 'I'd never left Presley before except for day trips to Blackpool or New Brighton. Not even for a week's holiday – we could never afford it. I'd been confident enough there. But in London ... even at the far from elegant college my Exhibition ran to ... I really don't think you can imagine what the provincial lout has to go through when the edges start being knocked off as late as eighteen.'

He was very calm and objective, and I distrusted that. One's adolescence is the most personally unique of all one's ages; it is never possible to laugh at it very light-heartedly.

I said: 'But you must still have had a lot of confidence. Writing poetry, solving the problems of philosophy ...'

He said: 'Of course. But that made it *worse*. Don't you see? Everything was being shaken up, overturned. Old certainties went down like ninepins. It didn't make me any more secure to know I was taking a hand in the bowling myself.'

'But at any rate you got them all down – and set up the right ones.'

He glanced at me and smiled.

'That puzzles me too. I was in on all the mid-'thirties intellectual fashions. In America I thought things out more carefully. I know the answers to any questions Lulu or Rupert can put me. I don't know why I'm beginning to tread carefully again. I can't even get hold of anything that's wrong.'

I said: 'You've been in the wilderness, haven't you? Rupert was saying something like that shortly before you arrived. He expected you to return in the full blossom of mature genius.'

'Yes, he wanted something. Something out of his own apocalypse. And Lulu – she still seems to think there's a chance of rehabilitating me for the cause. But they're part of the old fashion-plate, aren't they? They don't worry me.'

'You were too long in America,' I said. 'And too remote.'

He coloured. 'Remote? The war?'

'The war was neutral. It didn't have any effect in itself; apart from the effect produced by a slow broiling in boredom and futility and petty discomforts. It's not that. It's just – the second generation after Einstein.'

He said patiently: 'I don't get it.'

Feet clattered on the stairs outside. I recognized Howard's whistle, lifted in a phrase from the last movement of the Oboe Quartet. I said to Britton:

'There'll be time – before you go to Presley. Throw me my dressing-gown? I'm getting up.'

The pain hit me again as I lifted my legs out of bed, but I had made up my mind now.

CHAPTER SIXTEEN

On Saturday there was chaos. One of the Irish printers had somehow managed to mix up my private and registered addresses, and despatched an entire consignment of *Range Round-Up* to Number 36. They were dumped on us shortly after breakfast, parcel after parcel filling the hall and overflowing into Helen's room and even up the stairs towards Olivia's cubby-hole. Piers came up from breakfast to find me blundering helplessly amongst them. He sat down on a convenient pile, smiling.

'Delaney's a bloody fool,' I said. 'I told him particularly over the 'phone that he could send telegrams and letters here for urgency, but the magazines must go to Shaftesbury Avenue. Look at this!'

He said: 'It doesn't matter. Saves a few hours, anyway. I'll 'phone Griggs and have him bring the van round.'

I was still angry, and a little frightened. 'When a sub-post office gets a pile like this for a private address, it's noticed. We don't want to advertise the scheme.'

He said: 'I shouldn't worry. You're not doing anything illegal, yet. Are you?'

Rupert came silently up the stairs from the basement. He surveyed things warily, found a parcel breaking open at one end, and eased a copy of *Range Round-Up* out of it. He carried it upstairs with him, reading the first page as he went.

Piers said: 'All the same, you really ought to have other strings to your bow – just in case.'

The pain in the kidneys which had caught me on waking two days previously had since then been intermittently troublesome.

It stabbed me now and I sat down on another pile between Piers and the door.

I said shortly: 'In case what?'

'I've been reading Helen's newspaper,' he said. 'The situation is critical. There's too much sterling leaking out. Someone is bound to think of plugging the holes eventually.'

He had picked out a copy of the book himself and was flipping over the pages.

I said with over-done cynicism: 'More prophecies?'

He turned the book over again to look at the cover.

'Not so bad. Not so very bad. The red's a little out of register, but not too much for our kind of customer. I think you can 'phone Delaney to start another run. Another twenty-five thousand to be going on with. I'll let you have a cheque for these.'

As usual he had his cheque-book with him. Although he was resting it on his knee, his small, precise lettering ran evenly along.

'Prompt enough?' he asked.

I took the cheque. His inquiry had been unassuming, but it was still like accepting an instalment of salary. Other strings? But the same bow. He was looking at the cover again, holding it away from him at arm's length.

'Make it fifty thousand,' he said. 'I like it.'

Blodwen came up from breakfast, with Britton close behind her. She was bulging badly out of her scarlet dressing-gown.

She said: 'My God! What's this?'

Piers said: 'Business. Go and get dressed.'

He stared after her as she moved away upstairs, her body shifting through its usual pattern of curves beneath the red silk. He said thoughtfully:

'I think I might buy a camera some day.'

I kicked one of the parcels lying beside my feet.

'Well, these are yours now. That's all I'm concerned with. You can get rid of them as soon as you like.'

165

He pulled another copy out of the bundle that had already been rifled and tossed it over to me. I caught it awkwardly. 'With the middleman's compliments,' he said. 'It'll go very nicely on your bookshelf – beside *Trend*.'

It was a very small gesture, but like all Piers's small gestures it carried a significance with it. I wondered just what the significance was.

'Why not?' I asked. 'They're both honest jobs.'

Piers laughed. 'I always like the expressions you use, Tennyson. By the way, I'd like you to meet me with the car to-day. There's something I'm picking up.'

I was finding his obliqueness more irritating than usual. I nodded towards the stairs.

'Does Blodwen know about it yet?'

'No, not yet.' He looked at his own hands with secret, smiling thoughtfulness. 'I like preparing little surprises for people. I was thinking I might arrange for Howard to join the Monday séances.'

'So that Britton can come in on Wednesdays? He's asked you about it then?'

'No,' Piers said. 'No, he's not. But he will do, won't he? And we want everyone to be happy. I've not seen much of him just lately. Do you think he's contented enough here, Tenn?' He paused. 'There's no reason why he shouldn't be. There's no reason why we all shouldn't be.'

It was a long time since I had been tempted to impute real sincerity to any remark of Piers. Yet I did now, for a moment.

I said: 'There's a chance, isn't there, that Howard might resent the switch, unless it were very tactfully explained to him.'

And the old, familiar Piers smiled in thin-lipped anticipation. He stood up.

'Just one more gesture, one more act of service towards a selfish world. I might as well get on with it. And 'phone Griggs.' On the small landing by Olivia's room he called back.

'Lunch at Maxard's. One o'clock. All right?'

I said: 'I can spare the time. But just what is it?'

If he made any answer I didn't hear it. Helen and Cynthia came up from the basement together. It looked as though Cynthia might even have been helping with the washing-up. She went into her room with a small exclamation that was more one of weariness than astonishment at the state of the hall. One of the doors to Helen's room had a pile wedged against it. Helen had to come past me to reach the other door.

She said: 'Tenn, this is dreadful.'

I admitted it.

She said: 'It worries me, Tenn. You know, the lease stipulates against using the house for business purposes.' She stared helplessly at the parcels, each with its neat, mimeographed label: Tennyson Glebe Publications Ltd., 36, Regency Gardens, S.W.7. 'There's such a lot of them.'

The front door was standing open. The milkman came up the path and deposited his usual clutch of strangely assorted bottles beside the brass scraping-blade.

'Mornin', Mrs. Drage. Early Christmas this year?'

I watched him carrying the cradle of empties away. His horse had got its front legs up on to the pavement and was sniffing interestedly at the evergreen hedge. The milkman clipped it back into the road.

I said: 'Why worry? No one is going to hold you responsible. You can't watch your lodgers all the time.'

She said helplessly: 'I'm not supposed to sub-let either.' She stood on the threshold of her room, holding the doorknob. I watched bewilderment being replaced by opportunism.

'Tenn – you might let me have another month's rent.'

I kicked one of the parcels. 'They're not mine you know. They're Piers's.'

Embarrassed, she said: 'Oh, dear.'

The helplessness might never have been absent. Her face crinkled into small lines of worry. I had a feeling of helplessness myself watching her. But I was not going to be chivvied by Helen's dependency. I said ruthlessly:

'Why not get it from Piers? I've had to get used to his being mixed up in my affairs.'

She said gently: 'Yes, I know, Tenn. I can manage, anyway. Cynthia's going to see about a job with someone next week. I'll manage all right.'

She smiled and went into her room with plump, pathetic dignity. I followed her a few seconds later to give her five pounds.

Griggs brought the van round about half-past ten; looking down from my balcony I saw him and the boy loading the parcels into the back while Piers instructed them. He got in the front with Griggs when they had finished. Just before the van drove off he looked up to me, confident that I would be there, looking out, and waved and smiled. I went back into my room, closing the window against the early winter chill, and got down to some work.

The main item was 'phoning Delaney. Surprisingly, the lines were clear and I was through to him within ten minutes. His comfortable, smothered Dublin voice:

'Is that you, Mr. Glebe? This is Michael Delaney – Delaney's Printing Works. That is you, Mr. Glebe, is it not?'

I told him again: 'Yes, Glebe speaking. Look, Mr. Delaney, the *Range Round-Ups* have arrived.'

He broke in on me. 'This is Delaney's Printing Works. Is it Mr. Glebe?'

'Yes,' I said. 'You're Delaney and I'm Glebe. We know all that.'

He said, contritely and more distorted than ever: 'I'm apologetic, Mr. Glebe. It's the drink. I'm just a bit dthrunk.'

The gambit was familiar, down to the exaggerated initial slur on 'dthrunk'. He was apparently never sober. I could understand that well enough in a small Irish jobbing printer, but his unvarying and endless apologies rather surprised me.

'The *Range Round-Ups*,' I said patiently. 'They've just arrived.

But you sent them to the wrong address. They should have gone to Shaftesbury Avenue. You sent them here, to Regency Gardens.'

His voice shook up into a squeak of surprise.

'But I know they were addressed to Regency Gardens. I helped the lad with the labels meself, Mr. Glebe. Thirty-six Regency Gardens – was it the wrong number, maybe?'

'Look. Have you got some paper and a pencil?'

I heard him breathing heavily while he fumbled. He said 'Yes' at last.

'Write it down, then. All books for Tennyson Glebe Ltd. must go to Shaftesbury Avenue and not – *not* – to Regency Gardens. Got that?'

'Shaftesbury Avenue,' he repeated obediently, 'and not – *not* – Regency Gardens.'

'And you can run another fifty thousand straight away. Clear enough?'

'Fifty ... thousand ... *Range ... Round-Up*. Did yer like the cover, Mr. Glebe?'

When I had got rid of Delaney there was the mail to deal with. I had picked it up the previous afternoon after three days in which I hadn't called at the office, and there was quite a large batch. The bills were easy. It was still a novel pleasure to be able to write covering cheques straight away. And a guilty one; I knew Piers's views as to the lunacy of settling accounts within six months of receiving them.

Some of the fan letters were interesting. There was one written from Dalston, in angular, violent handwriting with words run together and individual letters broken apart.

'I have Read westerns for more than Twenty years but Must feel tell you How Much I appreciate your Present Series which are amongst the Very Best I have remember Reading especially "*Itching Triggers*" a Very fine yarn inded. I Have read also "*Smoking Guns*" and "*The Bar-P Possee*" wich were Very fine Yarns if there Are any others similar please send for wich I enclose p.O for 1.8 pence, or Return same. Thanking you in Advance.'

I re-read it in fascination. It was like eavesdropping on some alien universe, more wild and foreign than Delaney's fantastic Irish drunkenness could ever be. Other minds might weep at a sunset, at the proud, pathetic tilt of an architectural line, at a Beethoven quartet; or genuflect before altars, homely or exotic. A man might find the meaning of his life in the Arctic wastes of thought or on passion's spreading equator. But above this shambling diversity of taste and tendency it was the gaudeamus from Dalston that captivated and delighted me now. 'I have Read westerns for more than Twenty years.' A score of years in which the grey smoke from Dalston had merged into the vaster greyness of the London sky, but all that time a bright flame flickering. 'Thanking you in Advance.' My own gratitude was as genuine. I found the other four Westerns we had produced and bundled them into a large envelope, along with the tattered postal order and a note of cordial greetings to Dalston's literary Stylite. I was writing the address when Howard came in.

There was something unusual about his appearance. I looked at him carefully. His blue corduroy trousers were gaping a little more widely from the tear at the knee, and the strap on one of his sandals was tied up with yellow plastic wire, but there was something else as well. I found it fairly easily. He had had his hair cut; his neck looked thinner and more defenceless than ever.

He came to the point immediately.

'Tenn, have you been giving Helen money again?'

I said patiently: 'If I had, Howard, I shouldn't be under any obligation to tell you.'

He went over to the piano and seized on the head of Goethe.

'I know damn well you have. There was nothing in Cynthia's handbag last night and three quid this morning.'

I said: 'Did you …'

'The bitch came in before I had a chance,' he said gloomily. 'I'm broke, Tenn. Come on, you might as well support the entire family.'

I found two pounds for him. I said:

'I think I'll keep an account and send it in to your father. His practice is more lucrative than my publishing.'

Howard rolled the base of Goethe over the keys with his right hand and picked out a melody with his left. It was quite competent boogie-woogie.

'Father?' he said. 'I've got no father. Not to speak of. Not like you legitimate bastards. Tenn?'

I made some noise of affirmation. I was glancing through the latest manuscript from my stock writer. It was labelled *The Hop Scotch Brand – And a Small Bicarb of Soda For Me, Please*. Sellars took his Westerns very seriously; the titles were the one little joke he permitted himself. I riffled through the pages for the necessary identification and wrote in a more fitting title – *The Brand Of The Circle T*.

Howard said: 'I hear I'm to move over to Mondays from Wednesdays.'

I looked up. 'Has Piers spoken to you about it already?'

He crashed some stormy chords. 'Christ! Another swindle? I thought he was a bit too pally about it all. Don't you two love playing the pocket Neros?'

I said: 'It's not for us. Britton is keen on the change. It doesn't make any difference as far as you're concerned, does it?'

He said sulkily: 'Couldn't something be arranged in the open, just once? I think it's bloody silly, anyway. We were just beginning to get things happening with our circle; now we are to bust it up so that Holy Joe can tickle his fancy in the dark. It may take months to get things going properly again.'

'Or this small re-arrangement,' I said, 'might be the key to open wide the gates of Hell. Who knows?'

Howard held the bust in one hand, gazing at it with rapt attention while his free hand strummed what might have been fragmentary Beethoven. He murmured:

'The bells of Hell ring ting-aling-aling, for you, but not for me. Tenn, seriously, man-to-man, don't you think the way Helen treats me is a bloody scandal?'

His darting mind! But always from island to familiar island; from grievance to grievance. Without, for the moment, seeking anything for myself – neither gratitude nor approbation nor even immunity from torment – I wanted to help him. But there was no clear way. Condemnation would only raise another island in that surly sea of self-pity where sympathy must lead him to wallow. I trod delicately, and in that wary progress the original impulse died, swiftly and imperceptibly.

'Does it matter very much? You manage all right. After all …'

And already in its place there was the familiar mild embarrassment, the anxiety to avoid any kind of awkwardness. The other might never have existed; was beyond even imagination's recollection.

'After all, I'm twenty, I'm old enough to look after myself.' He moved his hands along the piano keys furtively, striking occasional soft notes in the treble. 'I dream of large, warm, comforting women at nights. That's a bad thing, isn't it, Tenn?'

I began falsely: 'As a large, warm, uncomforting man …'

Howard said: 'You say some queer things at times.'

He was looking at me with a friendly, curious expression. I remembered a meet at Lowen Hill, when I could not have been more than thirteen, and Bluebell, a small-boned, quizzical, red-and-white bitch. When I pulled her ears in the yard behind the Anchor she looked worried and ingratiating. During the morning she picked up three scents that left the rest of the pack casting aimlessly, and ran them to three deaths. I could remember a high bank of blinding gorse, blotted with blood.

He said at last, ending a silence:

'Anyway, there's always practice. I can hug my 'cello.' His smile twisted, becoming carefree, sunny. 'I'm just a big kid, aren't I?'

There was still a lot I should have done when Howard had gone, but I didn't feel like it. I read a novel for about half an hour, and then went over to the Regent. There was no one there except Tony behind the bar, and he was too busy polishing his nails and brooding over his own unimaginable wrongs to talk much. I drank whisky until half-past twelve, when I got the car out and drove with exaggerated slowness in to Maxard's. Piers was waiting for me. We had some more drinks with lunch and I gave him the wheel when we came out.

He drove northwards, telling me about his latest deal; in nylons. I listened only half-attentively, dulled beyond curiosity by drink and a heavy lunch. I had some mild interest in our present destination. He drove out to the remoter reaches of St. John's Wood, and pulled in at one of the streets of suburban-type, semi-detached villas that proliferate there. He left me for about ten minutes. He came back down the gravelled drive, between the wired-up standard rosebushes, carrying a wicker basket. He put it down on the seat between us, and opened the top very gently.

'Have a look,' he invited.

In the basket there was a half-grown Blue Persian cat. It looked up at us, unsure and frightened, but silent. Piers closed the lid again carefully. As he began to drive off again, he said:

'It's The Cat.'

CHAPTER SEVENTEEN

The Cat settled down fairly quickly at Number 36. Within forty-eight hours she was sufficiently at home in her new surroundings to be displaying manifestations of character of apparent reliability. Leaving on one side the blindness and wilful prejudice of those who would deny individual personality to cats (and especially those who, in contradistinction, profess to find subtlety in the mass servility of dogs), there is an informed body of opinion that tends to generalize as to types. I had myself held to this habit. Persian and semi-Persian toms have a shaggy, mysterious, brooding majesty; their queens are soft, vain selfish minxes, graceful and cruel flatterers. It was to the latter category that The Cat was so obvious an exception.

She was graceful and charming enough. She had the felicity of a kitten along with the elegance of the cat. Her topaz eyes gleamed with a soft brilliance, set off by the soft blue smoke of her fur. It was her character that surprised. There was a kind of diffidence in it, an innocence. She accepted the attentions that surrounded her without that complacent arrogance that I had learned to associate with her type; instead with an air of friendly astonishment. Howard commented on this, lying prone on the carpet in Piers's room, his right hand engaging The Cat in mock battle.

'If only women were a tenth as graceful,' he said, 'and a hundredth part as unselfconscious.'

Blodwen, passing from the double divan to the dressing-table, paused to rock one slippered foot across the arch of his back. He looked up incuriously at the Amazonic curves towering above him.

She said: 'You look the kind of pansy who would play with cats.'

I glanced at Piers. He was sitting hunched up in his favourite arm-chair, the one Olivia had liked, watching The Cat in its desultory skirmishing with Howard's fingers. He gave no sign of having heard anything. Blodwen went on to elaborate her point with a remarkably obscene jest; but he paid no attention.

Howard said wearily: 'Oh, go away, go away.'

She went a few minutes later, noisily off to the Regent. She must have passed Helen and Cynthia on the stairs, and possibly even Olivia who arrived about half a minute after them. The circle about The Cat widened. Lulu came down to verify that she was to attend the evening's séance (having apparently heard a garbled account of the changes), and joined the rest on the carpet. The Cat accepted them all, amicably and without pride.

Piers caught my eyes, and came across to where I was sitting in the other arm-chair. He perched beside me on the arm, so that we were in a physical proximity that normally we both avoided.

He said: 'She's pretty, isn't she?'

I nodded. Lulu was saying:

'... the *sweetest* little angel, aren't you?' She had had her hair re-permed and its grotesque curls hid her face as she crouched down towards The Cat.

Piers added: 'I like to see homage paid to beauty.'

I felt the thinness of his arm, almost the bone of it, against my shoulder. I said:

'Especially when you have the lease on it?'

Of course I was remembering Jane and Hilda and Olivia. I expected the tolerant smile with which Piers usually greeted any reference to his transient lecheries. But unwittingly I had stirred something. I saw the small face lengthen into unresponsive blankness; the physical pressure between us was relaxed from his side. It was a fleeting revelation. In a second he swayed back towards me; the sharp, familiar smile returned.

He said: 'This is my first lease – on beauty.'

We both saw Olivia's face jerk up from the circle around The Cat, anxious, unsure, uncertainly half-smiling. She had been straining to listen; the degradation was quite startling. I thought of Britton. Piers smiled, his gaze directly on her.

'A tenth as graceful, and a hundredth part as unselfconscious.'

She looked uneasily hopeful for a moment, trying to fathom the reference, but gave it up and turned back to the others. Piers kept his eyes on her, examining the falling lines of her figure almost as though professionally. He said, a little later:

'I've got a proposition for you, Tenn.'

I said: 'Well? I don't mind listening to anything.'

He slipped quite quickly from the arm of the chair and stood in front of me. Olivia looked round again to see what was happening. Piers said:

'Come in next door. We can talk there.'

I hadn't been into the back room since the days of Olivia's tenancy. Blodwen, clearly and surprisingly, was more tidy in her ways. The room had the musky, scented smell of feminine occupation but lacked the even more usual disorder. There were no stockings nor underwear over the backs of chairs, no scattered powder nor hairpins loose on the small dressing-table; not even a garment drying on the rail beneath the hand-basin. Except for a copy of *Gone with the Wind*, open and face down on the divan, the room was impersonal.

I sat on the divan myself. Piers leaned against one corner of the dressing-table. He took a rolled-up magazine from the inside pocket of his jacket and gave it to me.

'Have a look at it,' he invited. 'It's interesting.'

I unrolled the magazine and smoothed it out on my knee. The title was cursive, red on black: *Paris Nights!* Beneath it, against a yellow background, a travesty of a woman flung limbs and breasts, in defiance of anatomy and gravity, to all points of the erotic compass. In the bottom right-hand corner a miniature, monocled, top-hatted man leaned on a swagger cane and peered up towards the few areas of flesh partly concealed. Inside there were similar sketches in black and white, dotted between short fictions with such titles as 'He Stole Her Panties' and 'The Mole on Her Hip'. In the top right-hand corner, '75 cents' was white inside a splashed red star.

'And this,' Piers said.

This was *Studio Snapshots*, on octavo art, price Three and Sixpence. Photographs. On the cover a full-bellied nude woman was leaning forward and away from the camera. Inside there were other posed nudes, with a distinct emphasis on buttocks.

Not accepting the obvious, I said politely: 'Well?'

Piers took the two magazines from me and slapped them together.

'This is where our money is,' he said. 'Three and sixpence. What would it cost to produce, Tenn?'

I took *Studio Snapshots* from him again and looked at it critically.

'What kind of run?'

'As a starter – ten thousand.'

I said: 'I don't know what the photographs cost; probably about ninepence a copy.'

'Retailing at two shillings,' he said appreciatively. 'That would do nicely. Over six hundred. Very comfortable.'

I said: 'You're going into publishing?'

He smiled, cynically, patiently. 'Don't fence, Tenn.'

I said: 'I'm not fencing. I think I'll stick to Westerns, though. I'm doing well enough with them and there's no risk.'

Piers said: 'Risk! I could sell fifty thousand – and will within a few months. I just believe in feeling my way.'

I said: 'That's not the risk I was thinking of. I'm just not interested, Piers. I do mean that.'

He didn't say anything for a moment. He flicked the copy of *Paris Nights!* between his disproportionately large fingers. I felt that it was important not to be too emphatic; simply casual. I got up from the divan and offered him the magazine I still had.

'Thanks for the offer,' I said.

Piers said: 'I warn you, Tenn. Your Westerns. With every good will I couldn't sell them at one and sixpence – not even at one and three.'

I said: 'I'm not raising the price. What gave you that idea?'

He smiled. 'Your future printing bills. Even in Scotland you won't get a printer to compete with Delaney. You couldn't put them out under one and six.'

I sat down again. 'You might as well tell me what it is,' I said.

He had a newspaper in his inside pocket as well. He marked the heading – DOLLAR LEAKAGE TO STOP – with his fingernail, and gave it to me. I read it quickly. Gaps in the import regulations ... unrestricted, unlicensed despatch of printed matter, especially from Eire ... in future only single, separately-wrapped copies of any publication to be accepted for postal transmission.

Piers said: 'You could have Delaney post them one by one, but I doubt if it would be economical.'

I said: 'You knew this was coming off?'

It was an unnecessary question. Anything fitting in so well with Piers's intentions was to be regarded almost as his private design. He made no reply. I went on:

'I'll find some way. Anyway, I don't fancy ... these things.' I gestured.

Piers smiled. 'Moral grounds?'

I said: 'I don't think prison life would suit me. I'm not built for it.'

Piers said: 'Don't worry; these are inside the law. Nude photographs are educational as long as you don't show genitals or pubic hair. The other line' – he fingered *Paris Nights!* thoughtfully – 'can promise anything as long as it doesn't perform. You compromise virtue and leer at its *décolletage* but you leave it triumphant in the end.'

I looked at him curiously. 'Brave advice – from a middleman. But it's the publisher who's answerable.'

He nodded approvingly, small head wagging wisely on small body.

'That's a sound comment. Now – how about that partnership?'

There had been hints, of course, but the reality amazed me, I hedged:

'Glebe and Marchant Pornography Ltd.?'

When he took that seriously I knew quite certainly that he was serious about the whole proposition. He said:

'Private names would be a disadvantage in quite a number of ways. It would have to be something else. What about the Ming Press?'

It is logic that gives madness verisimilitude. Piers was being very logical. I found it impossible to think of anything to say. The only genuine emotion I was able to recognize was pleasure – yes, and gratitude – that Piers should want me as a partner in anything. I had never really believed there was anything in his hints but his usual casual mockery. Now I found the reality so overwhelming as to obscure the projected basis for association.

Piers slid off the edge of the dressing-table and came over. He put a hand on my shoulder.

'Think it over,' he said. 'We'll talk about it later.'

He left the room without looking back. I stayed for a few seconds before going myself. I paused on the landing. The door to his other room was closed, but I could hear the chatter of voices from beyond it. I went downstairs to my own room. There was no one there. Britton had left a volume of Annie Besant open on my bookshelf. When I went over to remove it, my attention was caught by the five slim volumes of *Trend* on the top shelf. I picked one out and examined it curiously. Tennyson Glebe Publications Ltd. An article on the significance of existentialism; one of the first in the little reviews on this side of the Channel. And a good one, too. Glancing through it I was surprised at the clarity of the writing. By Anthony Stewer. I remembered seeing Anthony in the Little Lion a few weeks previously. He was talking rather loudly about a new job; getting the point of view of the Meat Packers' Federation into the Press with the help of a big advertising agency.

I put *Trend* down. It was a long time ago, but some things were even remoter.

1940, for instance. Late spring 1940, at Thirl.

I'd known some bee was buzzing as soon as he arrived on leave. That was a great year for conversions, for leaps from weakness into all kinds of strength. And there was some kind of strength in Tim, sprawling in an arm-chair in the library, accepting the Scotch and soda I poured him; a strength that was not the conventional strength of his youth and uniform. He talked about the squadron as he generally did, cheerfully, unselfconsciously admitting me to his bright world from my drab one; but there was something underneath, a drifting cloud below the surface. Something was troubling him. It didn't come out until late in the evening, after dinner.

He pushed the port back to me. He said:

'We had a rather queer do last week-end. A kids' party. Orphans – and all crippled, one way and another.'

I said: 'Bit out of your usual line?'

Tim nodded. 'Yes. The C.O. found out about it. The people at the Hall had always run an annual do for the kids in this home. But the Hall's empty now, closed. They would have been disappointed. So we had one at the station for them instead.'

When he paused, I waited. He went on:

'It was damn queer, Tenn. I hated the idea of it. I've never been able to stand cripples. Remember when George took on that lad with the withered arm to help in the gardens? I went any distance out of my way to miss seeing him. The thought of it made me sick. And I felt a bit like that about this party. I very nearly wangled a duty to keep me out of it.' He looked at me, grinning uncertainly. 'I didn't though. I remembered I was twenty-three. I went.'

He lifted his glass, held it importantly against the light,

sloshed the port in small waves against the side.

'I wouldn't have missed it,' he said. 'It was great fun. Great fun. There were only about forty of them and as many of us – we just about had one each. I landed a little girl. About eight, fine yellow hair, and a back like a corkscrew. We got on fine together. Her name was Susan. We had a great time. The lemonade flowed like water.'

I let him go on. With Tim that kind of small joke was often a lead for something more serious; a nervous verbal gesture. He said, talking more slowly:

'About this war, Tenn ... I've been scared a lot. Not so much of getting wounded or going for a proper Burton, but the idea of being smashed up, perhaps burned, and then patched into any kind of shape by one of these plastic blokes. That's worried me a lot, off and on. Perhaps it's just the brooding but I've had a sort of premonition that something like that would happen. It was a lot easier to imagine being pushed around in a wheelchair with a hood than being done properly, or the war being over. And I always felt that whatever happened I wouldn't have the nerve to commit suicide. That was really what got me.'

He took the port and poured more into his glass. He looked up, his face unlined and confident.

'Now I don't give a monkey's cuss about any of it. I just don't care. You can't imagine how good that feels. We did close formation landing on Wednesday and I sang like a bird the whole time. It isn't only the fear of what might happen now that's gone. Something has come in its place' – he glanced at me defiantly – 'something solid.'

One of the advantages of being with Tim lay in the shortcuts we knew and exploited between our individual selves. I knew what he was talking about.

I said: 'So, after the war ...'

'It's as good a thing as any. And if I were a cripple myself ... very suitable.'

'You used to have bigger ideas,' I said.

Tim shifted his chair back restlessly.

'I feel that I've been cut down to size somehow. It was long overdue. Tenn – you can help in one way.'

I nodded slightly.

'They're pretty short of cash. They've had to retrench already; unless they get some real help they will have to fold up. I could manage a bit, but what with mess bills and things ...' He paused and amended it. 'And women and things – you know how it is.'

'About how much?'

He looked at me seriously. 'Five hundred will see them through till the war's over, if the war's over next year.'

In my remembering, that pulled me up. In April 1940 a level-headed young man had said that, and a level-headed brother, of early middle age, had thought it reasonable. How long ago!

I didn't want to stay any longer in my room. It was almost time, anyway, for dinner; the early dinner of the séance evenings. I went out on to the stairs. Cynthia was coming up. She said huskily:

'We thought it might be fun to introduce them.'

She had put Brock's lead on, and he was obediently following her up the stairs. I let them pass, and went after them, bored and vaguely curious. All the others were still in Piers's room when we arrived; all but Piers himself. In the centre of the carpet The Cat was licking a dainty flank.

Helen said: 'Brockie dear, this is The Cat.'

Cynthia released Brock from his lead. He stood still for a moment, raising his front paws off the ground in a gesture of mild, benign astonishment, his snub nose sniffing towards this new acquaintance. The Cat paused in her toilet and watched him. Brock began to move towards her, warily and delicately, pausing at each step in his characteristic pose of attention, a front paw hanging in space. As they reached touching distance Lulu cried:

'Oh, no! They'll fight.'

But Brock put out his slim, probing tongue and, with a tender gesture, touched The Cat's fur. And The Cat, still friendly and innocent but no longer diffident, leaned forward to rub against the badger's coarser coat. It was one of those rare occasions of completeness and melodrama that life ironically flings in to tilt the scales against our patiently, wearily acquired realization that completion and melodrama are non-spontaneous and artificial. It was Helöise and Abélard.

The door opened and Blodwen came in. She had managed to have a fair number of quick drinks; her face was flushed. She began: 'What about dinner?' and then saw what we were looking at. 'What have we got up here? A bloody menagerie?'

The others, their attention divided between the animals and Blodwen, did not see that Piers had come in quietly behind her. He was looking at the animals too. And he was hating them.

CHAPTER EIGHTEEN

THE SWITCH OF Howard and Britton between the two séance groups did not have the bad effect Howard had postulated; rather the reverse. The new groups settled down as smoothly as their predecessors and Ming was almost continually present with each of them; on the point being put to him he expressed his disembodied approval of the change. Olivia and Britton were obviously happy about it. They were going about together quite a lot; Olivia lost some of her nervous strain and took a renewed interest in her appearance. When she dropped into my room early one Wednesday evening she looked more like a delicate, fluffy rabbit than she had for months past. She was wearing an electric-blue woollen frock tightly dirndled along a deep waist band and loose about the shoulders and in the skirt. It was one I hadn't seen before and it suited her.

She said: 'Oh! I thought Joe might be in.'

I had finished the work I was doing and was killing the hour remaining before dinner. I waved her in, pleased to have company.

'Have a drink? He's only gone for a haircut; should be back in ten minutes.'

I made gin-and-lemons for both of us. She sat on the arm of my chair drinking it, friendly, almost flirtatious. She was of the type of woman that responds to sexual admiration with vague and impartial largesse. They appear to store it and then, like some sensitized plant, discharge this sensual warmth on the nearest convenient reactor. At the moment I was convenient; any male would have done.

She demanded: 'Tell me what happened on Monday.'

I shrugged. 'Some more messages. From the Other Side.'

We had been getting a few conventional spiritualist messages, passed rather contemptuously by Ming. They were very much alike; some kind of identification, a formal greeting to a relict, occasionally details of the manner of death. Olivia said:

'Addresses?'

'And names. Very circumstantial.'

'London area?'

I nodded. She said warily:

'I suppose Howard looked them up?'

We had been quite excited when one of the early ones had checked in the Telephone Directory and Howard, ringing up, had got in touch with a widow of three months, fitting neatly into the séance formation. But further research had revealed that all the London departed had had their names and particulars in the obituary columns of various newspapers, easily accessible at the local library. Any one of us could have looked them up beforehand. And the occasional extra-London spirits who declared themselves invariably managed to give particulars that had verisimilitude but no value. We had written to two or three and the letters had been returned 'Address unknown'. We still checked the details where we could, but we knew they didn't prove anything.

I said: 'You look well in that dress, Livia.'

She leaned over and stroked the thin hair on the crown of my head.

'I feel well, Tenn.'

'Liking your job better? Resigned to a life of toil?'

She laughed. 'Oh, that. Not really. But' – she glanced down at me – 'Joe's a great help. I feel …'

I said: 'Yes?'

'… Somehow as though he were leading me into freedom. He can be very sweet.'

I said: 'I'm glad then.'

She leaned further over, her body brushing against mine.

'But you don't really like him, do you? Why don't you, Tenn?'

I said: 'You aren't interested in my opinion.'

She said gravely: 'I am. I value it. And I'm puzzled. I can't see why you're so cool towards Joe and so pally with a filthy little swine like Piers.'

I looked at her. She was very earnest. Her hair was falling felicitously over the side of her face; a pleasant effect, and I was glad that she marred it by sucking her short upper lip into her mouth as she brooded on the mystery of my ways. The combination of charm and ugliness, equally unconscious, fascinated me. She gazed more directly at me, and I said helplessly:

'But why do you want to understand my reactions? It isn't likely that you could; any more than I could understand yours. We're different people.'

'But Piers! You only have to be with him five minutes to realize what a tick he is.'

I said: 'I thought it took longer than that.'

She looked blank for a moment, and I wondered if she might not have been able, in some incredible way, to sponge her memory clear like a slate, forgetting not only my awareness of her association with Piers but the very factual existence of the association itself. Then she smiled, a knowing and rather furtive smile.

'You aren't blinded by instincts though, Tenn, are you?'

I asked curiously: 'Was there no more to it than that?'

She declared emphatically: 'No more. It's not handsomeness or virility. Nothing so simple. It's the helplessness, the little-boy-lost business. You probably don't notice it but it's there for women. We want to take him in our laps and give him suck.'

Her voice rose until she was speaking quite loudly. I said:

'Well, I'm glad you can see it clearly now.'

She nodded her head in simple agreement. She said:

'But that still doesn't explain why you put up with him.'

I got up out of my chair.

'It's time for dinner. I think we might as well go down. Joe probably won't bother to come up now – he may be with Helen already.'

On the way down I thought about Olivia. She descended the stairs in front of me quite jauntily. I wondered if she was finding her way into some kind of freedom, with or without the guiding hand of Britton. Even at the séances now she had his defence, such as it might be. Piers had not pricked her lately with his venom, but it was difficult to believe that that had anything to do with Britton's presence. Briefly I caught myself wondering that Piers should apparently be complacent about losing his grip on her; and then wondered that a thought so implicitly melodramatic should ever have entered my head.

Britton was in Helen's room and Olivia joined him while I carried on down to the basement. Helen was laying the table. She smiled at me and nodded vaguely towards the kitchen.

'Aren't they perfectly sweet, Tenn?'

Badger and cat were lying on the small rug in front of the stove. Brock's delicate tongue was caressing The Cat, licking gently along her fur. I was watching them when Piers appeared in the other doorway. He must have been able to hear the noise of Helen's activity in the communicating room, but just as clearly he did not see me where I stood partly hidden by the great linen cupboard. He spoke softly to the two animals.

'So that's where you are. That's something we'll have to put a stop to, isn't it?'

He moved into the room. I realized that he would be bound to see me, and was embarrassed by the idea. At least it seemed like embarrassment, which is so often twinned with fear. I moved forward myself, as though I were merely coming through from the dining-room and nodded to him casually.

Piers said: 'Tennyson. The man I've been looking for. I picked your mail up.'

He gave me a small handful of letters. I was surprised. It was an errand he had performed once or twice before for me, but not recently. He watched me while I opened them. The last one, officially franked, was from Customs and Excise, Holyhead.

'We have to inform you that we are holding eighteen parcels

consigned to you as addressee from Dublin, and containing printed books. If you will forward to us particulars of the Import Licence in respect of these goods, we will arrange their further despatch. Import Licences in books are issued by the Board of Trade, Department C ZX11, on the basis of a quota fixed in proportional ratio to pre-war imports from the same country. Where no Import Licence has been obtained, the consignment must be regarded as an infringement of the import regulations, and the goods concerned are subject to confiscation.'

They were, Sir, my obedient Servants. I showed Piers the letter. He nodded.

'Eighteen. That's less than five thousand; some of the rest might get through. Didn't a batch arrive yesterday?'

I told him: 'Eight thousand.'

'They aren't organized properly yet. You might break even.' He laughed. 'A clear profit if you don't pay Delaney's bills. You're not likely to need him again now, are you?'

I said: 'It looks as though I'm going to need a steady job with a salary.'

He touched my arm. 'It's not that bad.'

Helen called us through to dinner. Olivia and Britton came down; and Cynthia and Rupert. The others were apparently out for the evening. Wednesday, I remembered, was one of Lulu's party nights; she would be coming in about eleven-thirty, drunk with the dialectic and gin and French vermouth, to inquire about the séance. She would probably have picked up Leslie on the way. I looked at his fresco. He was working on the wall with the window now. He had already stripped it, and on the right-hand side grotesque guesses at roses, halfway between Matisse and Matthew Smith, rambled high and aimlessly into a winter, or at least an off-white, sky. I turned from it to the first wall he had tackled. The distorted, pseudo-Biblical, pseudo-Freudian creation was not endearing itself to me with the passing of time. I thought I could still detect traces beneath the crab-woman of the tail Blodwen had provided, but it might have been imagination. I didn't go close enough to make sure.

Dinner was rather a quiet affair altogether. Olivia and Britton were in a lull of their mutual talkativeness and discovery. Helen and Cynthia were as placidly silent as they usually were when lacking the stimulus of Howard's malicious envy. Rupert never bothered to talk while eating, a minor extension of his normal reticence. Piers crumbled his bread gently between his fingers, his eyes reflecting far back under his sharp brows. I myself had quite a lot to think about.

Olivia, Britton, Piers and I went upstairs together after dinner, Olivia carrying a tray with coffee and Piers carrying The Cat; he had pried her loose from Brock's protecting paws. We were surprised to find Blodwen in Piers's room, lying on the divan in a red silk blouse and russet tweed skirt rucked halfway up her massive thighs. She looked up as we came in.

Britton said: 'Not wanting any dinner?'

She shook her head. 'I had a gutsy tea at Gunter's.'

It was her usual robust voice, but she did not usually seem to think that questions from Britton deserved any answer; she despised him only less openly than Howard. Piers put his head on one side, regarding her.

He said: 'Well?'

She said: 'Hello. I thought I might join you in the spook-hunt for a change.'

She was speaking just a shade fast. Piers looked at her, coolly deliberate.

'We work in groups of four. Count us. I'll let you know in advance when we're going to have another mass sitting.' She still lay there, but it seemed like a conscious effort. She said:

'That's all right. I won't interfere. If you like I'll just lie here and listen in.'

The door was open. Piers stood by it; he found his wallet and took a note out, waving it at her, beckoning and threatening. He smiled.

'Here's a pound. Go and have a drink for yourself at the

Regent.' And, bringing the childish pun out with contempt: 'That's your kind of spirit.' He paused slightly. 'I mean that. Blodwen.'

Blodwen looked from him round the small circle of our faces. She got up slowly and took the money from Piers, and went out.

In this new group Britton and I sat on either side of Piers; Olivia faced him. The cardboard trumpet eddied gently above our heads, the bands of luminous paint at either end a drab and sticky green while Piers's batteries of light bulbs were switched on. He put them out one by one, until there was only the focused brilliance of the desk-lamp at his shoulder, and shadows crawling gigantically across the high walls and ceiling. He said:

'Well, what music this evening? Any preferences?'

Britton said: 'Some Mozart maybe?'

There was still a trace of American nasal flatness in his intonation, though he had lost the more obvious aspects of accent.

Piers turned partly round, his shadow hunching hugely and grotesquely on the wall behind him. He said thoughtfully:

'I don't stock anything before Wagner. But I think a change might be a good idea. We'll try an assortment.'

He put half a dozen records on the auto rack and set the turntable running. A solo trumpet lashed out on a sustained note as he switched the desk-lamp off, and the floating splotches of marking paint leaped into crawling luminescence above us. It was a Louis Armstrong record that I had heard before. The trumpet clowned and danced its way through it, doubled ringmaster and buffoon in its own small circus.

Piers said: 'Yes. I think that's a nice change.'

The second record was jazz, too. It might have been Ellington, but I knew too little about it to do more than guess. Halfway through the table jumped under our hands, a satisfactorily violent explosion into activity, and Piers switched the volume down. A clarinet rose reedily, muted and far away.

There were a couple of addresses again. The first communicator, Ming told us, was William Persill who had broken his neck falling off a ladder two months before. He wanted us to write to his wife in Leyton. The other was a Japanese who had died by drowning. He gave an address too. It sounded convincing; Britton wrote it down laboriously in the dark.

Piers said restlessly: 'Any prophecies, Ming?'

The telegraphese from the paranormal spelled out:

RID OF BADGER.

I heard Britton's puzzled voice: 'That's a funny thing to say.'

Olivia laughed. I imagined it was intended to be scornful, but there was a nervous sound to it that destroyed the effect. I broke in:

'Anything for me, Ming? Which Labour Exchange do you recommend?'

The tapping, racing against Britton's alphabetizing voice:

SUCCESS MING PRESS.

Piers said: 'Yes, but when?'

SOON SOON SUCCESS SOON.

'Everything's going to be fine,' Olivia said. 'Aren't you lucky, Tenn?'

The table reared, and we spent about half a minute restraining its levitational urges. When it finally subsided it did so completely, relaxing into a wooden and unresponsive inertia. There was a slackness pervading the atmosphere. We sat for some time hardly talking, finding it an effort to speak, aware of the physical strain of drawing breath. The sequence of jazz records lapsed into silence, and with the removal of this last external measuring-rod time became entirely subjective and unreal, apprehended only in the moment's pulse of blood. We lay in that special kind of lethargy which occasionally comes with drink; the universe is moving about you, slowly, almost imperceptibly in its nearer objects, but with increasing speed out to the dizzily whirling stars on the outer rim – you are the hub and for you there is no such thing as motion. There is no action you can take or want to take; not even the moral action of judgment. If rapine and torture and murder were enacted before your very eyes it would all be part of the moving, meaningless, external world.

Piers at last brought time back to us. He said in his chilled, hidden voice:

'Aren't you about due for your little cylinders?'

His words released a longing for the taste and smell of tobacco that hadn't existed before; the desire flinging me out into the real and spinning world. I looked at Olivia as Piers switched the desk-light on. She, too, looked as though she had been dragged out of a remote and enchanted sleep. She looked back, compressing her lips. She made a small gesture of annoyance when Britton said innocently:

'I want a cigarette now; but only this minute. Like that light switching on.'

He passed Benson and Hedges round to us. Piers was looking at Olivia, smiling faintly. When Britton had held a match for her she leaned forward suddenly and blew a puff of smoke across the table at Piers. He made no move of avoidance or disgust. The cigarette smoke rose about his face, curling in sluggish grey twists in the strong beam of light. The other three of us, smoking, watched it dissipate among the ordinary flecks of air-borne dust; Britton looked embarrassed and uneasy but too unsure of what was happening to say anything.

When we stubbed our cigarettes out, Piers said quietly:

'O.K. Ready for another try?'

Britton said: 'Yes.' He hadn't seen anything. I was afraid myself, afraid for Olivia. She sat looking at Piers for a few seconds.

'All right,' she said, 'switch off.'

The extinguished light was still throwing its green and pink blobs of afterglow in front of me when the table began its savage, impatient dance. But there was no violence, no twisting and lunging at the known victim. Britton alphabetized softly.

TRUMPET, it said. TENN TRUMPET.

For a moment I was too happy in my relief to take it in. Piers said:

'Something for you, Tenn. You might as well listen.'

I got up awkwardly and reached for the swinging trumpet. It had been tied a little too high and it was difficult to hold it against the side of my face. When I got it there I felt the smooth chill of cardboard, but nothing else. There was no warm air, no warning breath, but the voice seemed to speak at my ear, remote and tiny and as real as the surge of thunder. I listened, holding the trumpet, unaware until it was all over and the light switched on again that I had crumpled the strong card convulsively between my hands. I must have been looking very dazed. Britton said sympathetically:

'Who's Tim?'

I repeated it uncertainly: 'Tim?'

'You called the name,' Britton said.

I said nothing, thinking how often I had called it, silently, in six and a half years. When the séance broke up at last I sat in Piers's room after the other two had gone downstairs. I took out a cigarette and he watched me light it. He said very gently:

'Well?'

'From to-morrow,' I said.

He got a bottle of Scotch out and poured a large measure for each of us.

'Here's to it, Tenn,' he said. 'Our very good health, and the prosperous fortunes of the Ming Press.' He drank his own glass quickly and put it down on the edge of his desk. He looked at me casually, warmly. 'And we'll get rid of the badger.'

CHAPTER NINETEEN

THE DAY AFTER the Ming Press was signed and sealed into existence the rest of the consignment of *Range Round-Up* arrived. The only loss had been the eighteen parcels that Customs and Excise had notified to me; the final operation of Tennyson Glebe Ltd. showed a profit of between three and four pounds. For the new venture I had managed to put up a stake of seven hundred and fifty, and Piers had matched it. We took over the Shaftesbury Avenue registered address, purely, as Piers explained, as a temporary measure.

He said: 'I don't like this business of having to collect mail, and telephone calls being re-directed and all the rest of it. That's all right for mushroom publishing, but we're in this for something bigger.'

I said: 'We could run our own building up. About fifteen floors. That's if we could get a licence.'

Piers grinned. 'We will do eventually. But for a year or two we can make do with something smaller.' He looked round his room. 'A house like this would be all right. There are advantages in Kensington – business is moving out this way for one thing.'

I said curiously: 'A rosy future for pornography. Can you build the kind of thing you want on the basis of the sensual itch? A financial empire with a public convenience clientele?'

He said: 'Don't underestimate them, Tenn. I know what I can sell and where I can sell it. There's enough scope; it's just that nobody's tackled it thoroughly yet. We're in the bread and circus days now and our kind of circus has always brought the crowds. The other operators in the field have only stuck their toes in the water; they've always been afraid of legislation, for one thing. But things aren't tightening up – they're breaking down. At present our goods may only sell in rubber-shops and at street corners. But in ten years we'll have them on the station bookstalls.'

I asked him: 'What do you want me for, Piers?'

'I'm not a fool. I don't think the details are unimportant; I know they are the things that count in the long run. You're the publisher. I'll stick to the selling. We'll fit in nicely together.'

Altogether Piers seemed happier than I had ever known him to be, though happiness, perhaps, is a misleading term for the controlled nervous exultance that drew his thin lips so often into smiles. Brock was the only thing that seemed to disturb him now; and it was some time before I realized that this disturbance was real and no elaborate joke. Increasingly The Cat disappeared and was found playing with or being nursed by the badger in the kitchen, and no séance passed without some command or persuasion from Ming that Brock must go, but I couldn't take it seriously. The only action that seemed open to Piers, anyway, would have been to put down poison, and since The Cat's arrival that was out of the question. I didn't think of anything else until Helen said at dinner one night:

'We're getting rid of Brockie. Joe was right. It isn't fair to keep a wild animal in a town house.'

Howard looked up at her incredulously. 'What was that you said?'

'He should be leading a more natural life,' Helen said defensively.

Howard looked at Cynthia. 'Is this one of your ideas?' he asked roughly.

She glanced at him contemptuously before turning to Helen.

'When did you decide on this, darling? You didn't say anything to me about it.'

So the 'we' must have been herself and Piers; I was fairly certain Britton could have had no part in it, despite Helen's reference to him. The outburst when he first came had been a part of the pattern of his dogma which, if he still maintained, he kept strictly to himself. I had even seen him stroking Brock, with tentative affection. He said now:

'Oh, I'm not so sure. It might be less kind to send him back. He's never learned how to cope with a wild environment, with his natural enemies ...'

Piers said: 'The badger has no enemy but man. Do you really think it couldn't fend for itself in the country?'

Britton began weakly: 'Well ...'

Howard said: 'Just what the hell is going on? Whose animal is it that you are keeping or getting rid of as your fancy whims decide?' He turned with a conscious effort towards Cynthia. For the first time he was making an approach that was not an attack, appealing for her support. 'It's a family matter after all.'

Cynthia watched him critically for a moment. Her face ugly and more real under its cosmetic disguise; and seeing her thoughts made manifest in tensed muscles and wrinkling flesh I knew that Brock would go.

She drawled: 'The family? How touching!' She returned to her food indifferently. 'Do just as you like, Helen. I think you're probably right.'

Helen said uncertainly: 'Of course, we would miss him ...'

She looked at Howard where he sat pressing himself back in his chair with the tenseness of his humiliation, his thin face white above a shabby old red shirt. He caught her eye and looked at her in agony and anger.

'Let him go,' he said. 'We must keep the family unanimous.'

Piers said softly: 'The question is where. Hyde Park wouldn't quite do.'

It was strange that Helen could shield herself so completely from Howard's bewildered, angry eyes. Her voice was almost complacent again:

'We could take him back to where we found him ... but it was pretty well built up even then.'

I hadn't meant to say anything but in some way the idea of sitting silent any longer was insupportable. And, given the compulsion to speech, the rest was natural. I said:

'I have to go down into the country on Saturday – just the other side of Beaconsfield. It's good land. There's a badger earth that's been there for sixty or seventy years to my knowledge.' I looked at Helen, avoiding Howard. 'If you really have made up your mind, I wouldn't mind taking him down with me.'

Helen said: 'Oh, Tenn, that would be nice.'

Piers put his knife and fork down on his plate. His expression was thoughtful.

'Why shouldn't we all go down with you? It would make a nice trip. That is, if we wouldn't be in the way?'

I had let myself in for this. I thought of trying to put them off and knew with certainty that it would be an attempt without hope of success. It was far better to acquiesce. Something might turn up; if it didn't there was a chance at least of passing things off casually. I said:

'If you want to. The Austin will only hold five and that's a squeeze. Apart from that you're all welcome.'

Provisionally it was to be Helen, Cynthia, Howard, Piers and myself, but Lulu, when she heard about it, insisted on hiring a car to take another party along too. Britton wanted to go, which also meant Olivia, and Lulu herself talked Leslie into it fairly easily. She was getting a Daimler, so I shunted Howard into her party to relieve the congestion in my own car. It would also keep him away from Cynthia.

In Regency Gardens I had known quite a few planned jaunts evaporate as anticipation dwindled and boredom supervened and the thought of being a whole day away from the Regent and the Little Lion became intolerable; some within twenty-four hours. Nothing like that happened this time. When I brought the car round just after ten o'clock on Saturday morning the Daimler was already waiting, and even Cynthia was only a quarter of an hour from being ready. I waited, smoking a cigarette. The weather was as benign as I could remember it being all the year, the air soft and flushed with the memory of rain, the sky blue and white in an altogether summery pattern of bellying curves and spaces. It was warm, too, extremely warm for November. Cynthia came out in just a jumper and skirt, the three-quarter fur over one arm and the other hand holding Brock's lead. He padded cheerfully along in front of her, soberly eager for the outing.

She said: 'We'll sit in the back with him. You go in front, Piers.'

Leslie was driving the Daimler; theoretically he was to stay behind us but we had arranged to meet at the White Swan in Beaconsfield if we got separated, and at Notting Hill the long black car slipped ahead and out of sight. They were at the White Swan when we arrived, sitting in the big room, drinking various mixtures of gin and talking politics. Lulu, with her fatal facility for the wrong thing, had attempted to establish solidarity with the only obvious labourer present, a small, unhappy-looking man with large eyes and a large, expressive nose. He was saying defensively as we came in:

'Leave me alone, lady, just leave me alone. I voted Conservative at the Election an' I'll do as much again. You don't need to pester me.'

Brock sat down between Lulu and Cynthia, and looked up with his usual mild curiosity at the speaker. The man's gaze darted towards and away from him in flickering incredulity. Lulu began excitedly:

'But you don't understand ...'

The Daimler had to follow us the rest of the way. I turned off the main road, watching landmarks of fifty years spring up in postures so convincing that they might never have ceased to exist. And yet the road retreated, and they went again, back into the untidy drawers of the past, the drawers that can never be properly turned out. At Mickham's farm a figure led a donkey across the slope of Four Acre; a hunched and shambling figure that might have been Mickham himself if he had not died of pneumonia in 1923. There had never been much change in these parts, but this was the first time the absence of it had had the power to frighten me. The gap in the hedge just beyond Scar Lane. Surely the savagely proliferate years might have filled that void? I drew in at the edge of Lessill Wood, under the great beeches with black boughs stretched against the sun.

'The earth's just in here,' I told them. 'No more than twenty yards.'

They followed me in, keeping unnaturally quiet, their footfalls deadened by the fallen beech-leaves. Only Britton moved abreast of me. He said:

'Beech-nuts ... Did you ever eat them – as a kid?'

I nodded.

'Which is the stranger,' he asked, '– that they were worth all that trouble and patience then, or that they aren't worth it now?'

The earth seemed rather larger but it was substantially the same, and clearly still in use. Cynthia unfastened Brock's lead, and carefully took off his collar. He looked up at her mildly. She said to Helen:

'Got the bag, darling? I hope it's going to be all right.'

She put the paper bag down and Brock snuffed at it eagerly. She said:

'Come on, now. Walk away. I don't think he'll notice.' He did look up once, his snout sticky with cream-bun, but he returned immediately to his feeding, convinced, perhaps, that luxury and desertion could not possibly be conjunctive; it is not an uncommon conviction. We walked away quietly through the wood, and got into the cars. The sound of their engines starting up made a rook rise in squawking, irregular contours through the air from a nearby post.

It was less than two miles to Thirl. You turn a sharp corner to the main gate, and cars must slow down for that, although the gates themselves were removed in 1941. There was a board projecting from the lodge. I had not seen it before, and did not remember authorizing it. Piers read the inscription aloud:

THIRL MANOR

THE TIMOTHY GLEBE HOME

FOR CRIPPLED CHILDREN

He said: 'So you still have the power to surprise me, Tenn.'

I had warned Miss Wistreich that we should be coming; and she appeared at the top of the steps as the cars drew up at the front door. She usually kept one of the children with her on such occasions to abate her nervousness; to-day she had two. Her head jerked involuntarily on her frail neck as I introduced them all. She hid her face, as soon as she decently could, in turning to the children.

'And these are Janet and Cynthia,' she said brightly. 'Say hello to Mr. Glebe and his friends.'

Janet was a spindly, fair-haired child with a leg-iron. The metal flashed like silver in the sunshine as she bent her good knee in a curtsey. The other girl was smaller, with dumpy features and nondescript hair and only one hand. Our Cynthia bent down to her, her well-groomed head almost touching the untidy freshness of the child's.

'Hello,' she said. 'My name's Cynthia, too.'

In the Library Miss Wistreich poured out sherry for us; she had let the children go and her head was shaking more noticeably. Holding a glass uncertainly herself she said with determined light-heartedness:

'You mustn't forget the clock, Mr. Glebe!'

Lulu said: 'The clock? What clock?'

Miss Wistreich smiled twitchily. 'Mr. Glebe winds it up – it's a thirteen-month clock. It's in the hall, as you come in.'

I said: 'We'll see to it now. No, stay and finish your drinks, the rest of you.'

Miss Wistreich watched me as I wound the clock. Climbing down I said to her:

'Tell them to find their own way about. I'd like to go out for half an hour. Luncheon at one?'

There were children all over the place; half a dozen of them, playing some obscure game on the tiled floor of the conservatory, paused to watch me as I passed. Their voices, released again, followed me in shrill diminuendo as I crossed the lawn. I avoided the stables and went through the kitchen garden to the orchard. The little entrance gate had been repaired and newly painted. The orchard, as always at this time of the year, was ankle-deep in yellow, fallen leaves; they drifted out beyond its limits into the Little Meadow. I climbed the stile, marvelling that once the easiest way had been scrambling between the bars, and once – for a long number of years – I had vaulted it. I walked up the slope of the field, feeling the exertion of even this brief exercise. Near the brow the sun came out again, uncomfortably hot, and I felt the sweat tingle along my legs. I stood for a moment looking out over the rolling sweep of the land. Down to the right the river was high, swollen by the autumn rains following the wet summer. On the left, Lake Field was green and deserted between its clumps of thorn and stately sycamore. I turned that way, noticing that the mistletoe was thicker than ever in the sycamores, its tendrilled clusters bunched among the bare, winter branches like feathery nests of insubstantial birds.

The ground dropped sharply to the lake and the small wooden pavilion on a knoll at its edge. Miss Wistreich's improvements had extended even here. It was flanked now by a double row of young cypresses. I went to lean against the wooden rail, and read the inscriptions again.

> … *Placed here in Memory of Rodney Lucas Glebe, 2nd Lt. in the 21st Lancers, Killed in Action, September 13th, 1918. Mors Brevis, Vita Æterna.*

And below it my own addition:

> *And of Flying Officer Timothy Rennis Glebe, his Brother, Killed in Action, July 3rd, 1940.*

I stayed there for some time, looking at the gold lettering and the polished wood. I turned round when I heard the sound of someone approaching. There were two – Britton and Olivia. Olivia apparently realized what the pavilion was and stopped in confusion, pulling at Britton's arm. He came on, oblivious.

'What's this, Tennyson? A dovecot?' He read the inscription and said awkwardly: 'I'm sorry. Your brothers?'

I nodded. He said: 'I think we'll walk on round the lake. See you at lunch.'

Piers found me only a few minutes later. He came and stood beside me. He said briskly: 'So I've run you down, Tenn.'

I turned towards him. 'Yes, you've run me down.'

He said: 'It's still yours, isn't it? It's not in trust or anything? Nothing irrevocable?'

I said wearily: 'Nothing irrevocable. It's on a yearly renewal. August to August.'

Piers said: 'You provided the house and land – and the capital for upkeep?'

I said: 'They manage on the interest.'

He looked at me intently: 'On the interest? In these days?'

I began to walk away from the pavilion and he followed me.

He said: 'So there's absolutely nothing to stop you pulling out next August?'

'If I want to – nothing.'

He said with friendly patience: 'Don't think I'm unsympathetic, Tenn. I can see how this sort of thing can happen ... the emotive effect of strain. But let's look at it rationally now. You're not a St. Francis, are you? You've got no leper-kissing perversion. You're not looking for that kind of comfort.'

'No,' I said. 'What kind am I looking for, Piers?'

'With that kind of capital we could really do something. It makes all the difference.' We were out into the Little Meadow now and the house lay just below us, beyond the yellow and scrawled black print of the orchard. 'All the difference in the world.'

I said: 'You haven't answered my question.'

He took my arm. 'You didn't really mean to ask it, did you? You know which questions can have valid answers and which can't – that's one of your strongest points.'

We had arranged to leave at three. I saw Miss Wistreich in the Library just before that. She had got used to us over lunch and her head was fairly stable. She said:

'I hope you found everything all right, Mr. Glebe.'

I said: 'There's something I have to tell you, Miss Wistreich. I'm afraid it's going to be a disappointment.'

Her eyes focused distantly as her mind searched for possible set-backs; she was a woman who hoped for little, and it wasn't easy to find them. I said quickly:

'I'm afraid it's going to be necessary for me to withdraw my support after this year.'

She said after the briefest interval: 'Entirely?'

'I'm afraid so.'

She smiled at me, and then her eyes dropped and her head twitched again in a new spasm of nervousness.

'I would just like to say … how grateful I am – we all are – for what you have done, Mr. Glebe. We are so grateful.' It had always embarrassed her to thank me.

I said: 'Perhaps this National Health Scheme will …'

'I'm sure of it, Mr. Glebe,' she said quickly. 'There's nothing to worry about.'

I found the others grouped round the Austin. They were all excited and cheerful, except Piers. He stood by the radiator, his expression one of cold and disapproving reserve. I felt a pang of guilt and actually thought: 'What have I done now? How have I failed him?' I heard Helen's voice raised as I approached:

'The darling! We couldn't let him go now. We couldn't possibly.'

I looked with the rest. Brock was sitting on the driving-seat.

BOOK IV

CHAPTER TWENTY

DURING THE WEEKS THAT FOLLOWED, Piers seemed to have accepted his defeat over the question of getting rid of the badger. It was a trivial matter after all, but in the past it was the trivial that had always engaged his strongest efforts. Anyway, he made no further overt attempts to get his way about it; he showed a surprisingly persistent patience in recovering The Cat from its continued jaunts down to the lower regions. Neither of us had much time to brood. There was a good deal of work to be done on the Ming Press. One of the chief difficulties lay in finding a writer who could turn out the stuff we wanted. The line between the necessary salaciousness and indictable pornography was the narrowest of hair's breadths; contributors either modelled their shock tactics on *Tess of the D'Urbervilles* or rolled over into a gay and rollicking lechery that would have had us all in gaol within a week. I asked Rupert, and he promised to try his hand. But he gave me a blank refusal a couple of days later.

'It's so *pointless*, Tennyson – all these references to feminine underwear and glimpses of chunks of female thigh. Boys, now, would be different.'

I said: 'Thanks. I'll bear that in mind.'

We found the right kind of thing at last, and an illustrator, and a printer willing to be persuaded that we had some idea of the law and were not trying to ruin ourselves and him. Advance copies of the first issue – *Cutie Stories* – arrived about the middle of January. I had modelled it faithfully enough on the magazine called *Paris Nights!* which Piers had originally shown me, even to the legend '75 cents'. As Piers had explained, we not only had to take over from those journals whose import by parcel post had been banned along with my Irish Westerns, but also to satisfy a taste that had been pre-conditioned to think of America as the sensual paradise. We had to accept their conventions. Nyloned co-eds flitting, with adequate pauses to display camiknicks and brassieres, between campus and drugstore. Everything was already established. '75 cents' whetted the appetite, and was additionally useful in enabling retailers to fix their own price and profit over and above the one and sixpence we got. 'Printed in London' appeared in six point at the foot of the inside back cover.

I was looking at it, brooding over a tilted frame, when Britton came in.

He sat down in a chair opposite, and leaned forward in a purposeful way.

'I've had rather a surprise meeting, Tenn. Someone you know. Miss Wistreich.'

I said: 'Here? In town?'

He nodded. 'In Brompton Road. We had a coffee together in a Lyons'. She's looking round for help for the Home – from next August.'

'She told you then that I shan't be able to support it in future?'

He said hastily: 'Not as a criticism …'

I interrupted him. 'I know Miss Wistreich.'

He marvelled, his solid, solemn, pouching face almost achieving expressiveness.

'And you told her last November – when we took Brock down. But why? For God's sake, why, Tenn? What's behind it?'

'The simplest reason,' I said. 'I shall need the money.'

'But it's not the kind of gift you can take back! Don't you see that?'

'Loan,' I explained, 'not gift. Can't I?' I looked at him. 'You came here in August and I offered to put you up in the other half of my room – for a week. It's now January. I haven't put you out and I'm not putting you out now. But you really mustn't try to monitor my actions.'

'Normally I wouldn't. But this is different. You endowed the Home as a memorial to your brother; you gave up practically everything you had and came to live a shabby, scratching life in this sort of place. And now, nearly seven years after that gesture, that action, you try to revoke it. It just isn't possible.'

'Actions if you like,' I said. 'You can talk of actions. But not gestures. I don't live in your world. I'm not a tiny imperishable fragment of the perennial deity. There are two actions that contradict each other. But it is the earlier one that needs an explanation, if either does. I'm no more immune from emotional brain-storms than anyone else. But observe that even then I didn't slam the door. I made over an interest that was annually renewable. It specifically wasn't irrevocable.'

He said softly, in a kind of holy hush: 'We all hedge, always. We try to keep one foot in the door. But the thing itself is real – the gesture is real.'

I said: 'Let's leave it at that. We aren't talking the same language. We're out of different fashions. You still belong to the 'thirties. There's been a war here.'

He flushed. I still had the copy of *Cutie Stories* in my hands. He leaned across and ripped it away from me – the cover tore across a tight red satin rump.

'And this is what you want money for? To invest in the production of this kind of copron? What's the scale? How many of these balance with a week's food and shelter for a child with a club foot?'

I went over to take the magazine back from him, and he permitted me to do so. I threw it over on to my desk.

'Have a drink,' I said. 'Or have you been drinking already?' He watched me while I poured Scotch out, and perfunctorily refused the glass I offered him. 'Now. If you insist on all these emotional tags, and if you're determined to identify my actions with your own social ethic – how many of the children at Thirl do you imagine will starve as a result of my withdrawal of the money they've been using?'

He sat watching me in silence, his stubby hand tightly clenched.

'It can't have dawned on you,' I went on, 'that there's been a change since your Presley days. The foundations are being laid of the Welfare State. There is a distinction between fifty crippled children being a charge on my property and a charge on the members of the State in which they live, but I should have thought that as a social ethic the latter was more defensible. Which do you want – the patronage of charity or a penny on every hundred thousandth pint of beer?'

'Charity ...' Britton repeated, almost to himself. 'There abideth ...' He shook himself, more than ever like a large, bewildered dog. 'I'm beginning to see things.'

I looked at him inquiringly.

'Piers is behind it all – I can see that now.'

I said wearily: 'Behind what?'

'Behind all this corruption.' He stood up and went over to the balcony window. 'I wonder why it hasn't been obvious all along?' He turned round again and stared at me. 'Have I been afraid of him?'

Warning him, I said: 'Don't get melodramatic. You have a strong tendency that way. You used to write melodramatic poetry.'

'Melodrama's a relative quality, isn't it?' He laughed. 'A leaf out of the Marchant Relativist Handbook! Is evil relative too? Is filth relative?'

I finished my drink and levered myself out of the arm-chair.

'Think it over,' I said. 'And then – put your questions to him yourself.'

I went out, leaving him standing by my window. It was after eleven o'clock so I found myself heading towards the Little Lion which had recently regained its popularity. Some of the others would probably be there. I considered this and turned right to the Regent. I wanted another drink but I wanted it in peace; if possible in privacy. I pushed open the door of the Saloon Bar.

There were only three people in it, sitting at the table under the palm. Piers, Cynthia and Lyle McAdams.

McAdams greeted me with a roar.

'Tennyson, Tennyson, Victoria's linnet! Have a drink. Do you want to buy a good coat? A very good coat?' He examined me critically and began taking off the expensive, partly-worn tweed overcoat that hung loosely about his own narrow shoulders. 'I think it'll be a fit. I'm sure it'll be a fit.'

Piers had beckoned Tony over for another round; they were drinking rum and I joined them. I said to McAdams:

'Don't bother. I don't want one.'

He protested indignantly: 'But it's very good – from the R.A.C. No shoddy stuff.' He had a look at the maker's label in the lining, and tried to show it to me. 'There you are – made in New York. You can't get this kind of stuff in England.'

'Where have you been the last six months?' I asked him.

He dipped his tongue into the rum and drank it down. 'Brixton again.'

Cynthia laughed admiringly. 'Lyle – you are a devil.'

'And now,' I asked him, '– back in the caravan?'

He laughed, his infectious Irish laughter. 'Would you bloody well believe it – they've put up prefabs all round it. Comes in handy when I'm short of milk. And not a thing touched; not even a window broken. There's honesty still in Earls Court.'

'Looking for a job?' Piers asked him.

'I think I might resume my histrionic career,' McAdams said. He giggled. 'Did I ever tell you of the time I had a part in *The Monkey's Paw?*'

He had, twice or three times. Surprisingly, Piers said: 'Go on.'

'It was a travelling company – one of those that works the provinces with double-headers for value, a one-act curtain-raiser before the big show. I got the part of the soldier who sells the old man the paw – you know the play? Now the old man was played by a Greek, a very hasty-tempered individual with a very strong sense of dramatic propriety.' 'Propriety', in McAdams's brogue, was a beautiful word. 'He was strong against the drink, too, and he never took very kindly to me. Well, this night I'd been out with the boys and when I got back it was nearly time for my cue and I got changed and greased up in the devil of a rush. I went on stage with as much noise as a regiment instead of one Sergeant. And it wasn't until I was well and truly on that I realized I'd forgotten to bring the paw.'

He paused to laugh in anticipation at his own anecdote. Piers was smiling gently and watching Cynthia, who was contorting her face in genuine sympathetic delight. McAdams, I thought, looked rather seedier than he had in the summer, but he still had charm enough.

'Well, there I was, properly flummoxed. What's *The Monkey's Paw* without the paw? I waited till the old woman was speaking, and I whispered to the Greek: "I've forgotten the paw." He and the old woman were sitting at either side of the stage fire – one of those old-fashioned country grates, it was, with a pan of sausages supposed to be frying on top – and he looked up at me cock-eyed from his chair. "What's that you said?" "I've forgotten the bloody paw," I told him again. "You can't have!" he said. "Well, I bloody well have," I said. He had to take a cue himself at that point, and there the two of us were batting dialogue at each other, and him giving me looks like cannon-balls, and every minute a minute nearer to the time when I would have to produce the monkey's paw and hand it over to him. And just at the crucial moment I had one of my brain-waves. I bent down between the pair of them, pretending to spit in the fire, and grabbed one of the sausages out of the pan. You might say I'd saved the situation. Turning to the Greek, I said my line: "Well, here it is – but don't say I didn't warn you." And I slipped the cold sausage into his hand.'

He threw his head back, showing his teeth. They were his only really good feature; large and beautifully white and regular.

'You should have seen the look on the Greek's face! It was as much as I could do to totter off the stage.'

We had been duly appreciative – Cynthia overwhelmingly so – for McAdams told his tales well. But he enjoyed them enough himself to be quite oblivious of outside reactions. He was still gurgling to himself over it when I got Tony to bring another round of drinks.

Piers said to Cynthia: 'Have you ever visited Lyle in his caravan?'

She shook her head, watching McAdams and still smiling with him.

'Come round!' McAdams said. 'Come round, the lot of you.' He glanced at Cynthia, and let his eyes dwell on her. What cosmetics didn't do for Cynthia's face, smiles did. She was looking quite pretty. 'Come round now,' McAdams insisted.

Piers said: 'We might as well.'

I think the thing I most envied Piers for was his ability to step right outside his normal character and yet remain convincing … For most people it is a laborious, never-ending struggle to establish their reality in the chaotic universe of human relations; they develop tones of speech, mannerisms, catchphrases, all designed to reinforce that precious, longed-for assurance of identity. They type themselves willingly with that end in view, and to side-step for a moment is to jeopardize everything. There are weak characters, of course, who never manage to reach that stage, but Piers wasn't weak. And he stayed real all the time. Being friendly with Cynthia, whom in the past he had quite casually disregarded, encouraging her to join him on a visit to McAdams' caravan, in which he could have no conceivable interest; in all this he was still Piers, still a whole. But a mystifying one. Was Cynthia, perhaps, to succeed Blodwen?

McAdams said: 'Let's kick along then.'

The other two got up. I said:

'I'm going back in a moment; I've got something to do.' I looked at Cynthia. 'If Helen comes shall I send her after you?'

Cynthia wrinkled her face. 'She won't. Don't bother anyway.'

I realized that I had been seeing mother and daughter together less frequently in the past weeks; and when they were, there was less evidence of the physical intertwinings and mutual, caressing endearments that had distinguished their relationship. I could even put a date to the estrangement, if estrangement were not too strong a word. On Cynthia's side, at any rate, signs of affection had been less noticeable since the planning of the trip to Thirl.

When they had gone there was the opportunity to have a drink in peace. I took another rum and drank it slowly. But now with my object achieved, I felt lonely. There seemed no point in staying in the Regent. Moreover the drinks had sharpened my self-assertion. I became aware of an obscure sense of grievance; was I allowing myself to be driven by Britton out of my own room? I walked back righteously to Number 36.

Helen heard me on the stairs and put her head out of her room.

'Tenn! You haven't by any chance seen Cynthia.'

I said: 'By chance, by divinest providence, I have. She and Piers have gone back with Lyle McAdams to his caravan.'

Helen said: 'Oh. Thanks, Tenn.'

Britton was still in my room; he had been joined by Olivia. She had a happy, complacent look about her that I mistrusted. She sprawled in one of the arm-chairs with her legs swinging over the arm.

'Not at work to-day?' I asked her.

Olivia smiled. 'A theoretical headache. I have to take a day off now and then to maintain my sanity.'

I said heavily: 'You should join Joe in the idle rich. Would it be terribly rude to ask you, Joe, precisely what you do live on?'

'No, I don't mind.' He looked at Olivia. 'I brought quite a few dollars over with me. I've been spending them. I'm afraid I got a bit careless about money. There didn't seem to be any reason to hold on to it, then.'

'Careful,' I said. '*Mit Weile treten*. The Love of Gold is the Murder of God. That's the one that Billy Blake left out.'

Olivia seemed bemused, but she was still secretly triumphant about something, and spoiling for a fight. She began:

'I'm not religious, Tenn, but …'

'I know,' I told her, '– some of your best friends are bishops.'

She looked beyond me to Britton. 'He's only a bit squiffy, Joe. It's that little tick, Piers …'

'My name? I'm sure I heard my name?'

Piers stood on the threshold. As usual he had come in silently. Olivia broke off, but went on swinging her legs with deliberate carelessness. I said:

'What happened? You're back quickly?'

Piers smiled vaguely. 'I left Cynthia there. But this is more interesting. What was it I prevented you from finishing, Olivia?'

She threw a second's look at Britton; reassurance, confidence, and pulling the stool out of the ring-corner. He leaned against the wall under my Craxton. He said slowly:

'You knew Tennyson was withdrawing his support from the Crippled Children's Home?' Piers nodded. 'It was your idea, wasn't it?'

Piers's glance flicked thoughtfully at me. 'I think I made the first suggestion.'

Britton said: 'We all sin, almost all the time. But we sin mostly through weakness; the sins of omission. I don't think that's true of you, Piers. I think there's something so nasty about you that I would call it positively evil. I can see your hand now in a lot of things that are wrong about this house. You are not only corrupt yourself, but you can find delight only in the corruption of others.'

Piers smiled, looking not at Britton but openly, knowingly, at Olivia.

'Am I? Do I? Did I corrupt you, Livia? You gave every sign of enjoying it at the time.'

He let his gaze travel back to Britton. Britton faced it, calm except that his mouth was trembling a little. He said:

'No. You lose in this. You can't provoke me to violence, not even by that. Olivia and I are out of your reach. All your filth and twisted cunning haven't the power to touch us now.'

Piers was still smiling. He said:

'I'm wondering about something. You've been here a long time, Joe. Nearly six months. We've seen a lot of each other. Now revelations don't happen; we know that. You've known what you thought of me. Why haven't you said something about it?'

'Revelations do happen,' Britton said. 'But in this ... you're right. I've felt – I've guessed before.' He put his hand across his mouth, and slowly drew it away. 'Why haven't I said anything?' He looked at Piers squarely. 'I think because I've been afraid of you.'

'Fear,' Piers said. 'It crawls inside you, doesn't it, Joe? It agonizes and torments you – it always has. It drives you to what you think is God. It has always been with you and it always will be. It stopped you writing poetry' – he paused slightly – 'and all through the war it kept you in New York, away from the bombs, away from the warring armies.'

Britton's mouth was working again, more violently. He said nothing. Olivia jumped up from her chair to face Piers.

'He fought in Spain,' she said. 'He fought there. Even if he lost his nerve afterwards that's genuine; he can't be blamed.'

Piers said gently, looking at Britton: 'I know about Spain, Joe. I know a lot of things and I know about Spain. Shall I tell Livia what happened at Escurial?'

Britton said in a choked voice: 'No.'

Olivia said: 'Yes! Whatever it is, it can't make any difference. Tell me. Then see.'

Piers said: 'Shall I tell her, Joe? Shall I tell her about Pedro?'

Britton didn't look at Olivia. He was shaking.

He said: 'No. Please don't. Please don't.'

Piers smiled at Olivia. 'When it's put like that – I don't think I can reveal a secret. Do you?'

He gestured towards Britton with one hand, a showman exhibiting. Britton turned towards Olivia at last; the child disgraced, betrayed, hopeless, and still hoping for shelter. She looked at him, and shivered with the force of her repulsion.

She said to Britton: 'He's right. Oh, God, he's right! I can't …'

She turned and ran from the room and down the stairs. Piers went after her unhurriedly. He called down the well of the staircase:

'I'll see you later, Livia, in my room.'

He came back. Britton was still standing against the wall. His face was composed now apart from his eyes. He was blinking continuously. Piers said:

'I don't think Olivia needs to go out to work. We can use her as a model; she has a good figure.'

I found myself looking out of the window. Something was happening there. It had been very cold all morning; now it was beginning to snow.

CHAPTER TWENTY-ONE

During that day there were two or three abortive snow showers, transient and leaving no traces behind them. The first true fall took place during the night; in the morning the snow was white and even on the narrow strips of front gardens, grey and churned into frozen ruts and channels in the wide road between. The cold was savage. When it was not driving in blind spurts under the lash of the east wind it lay, a damp, embracing chill, over the frozen snow. The snow turned to glassy ice, and more snow fell, and the cold did not break. Day drifted into sleety night, night into frozen day, and the cold remained. January died, but except on the calendar February came to no birth. Warmth and generation had taken leave of the world.

Out of doors, muffled and hooded, people trod carefully, stumbling on the fretted iron snow that lay in roads and gutters and extended in glassy crystal waves on to the pavements, slipping where it had been levelled and polished into a few feet of smooth and even treachery. Along Old Brompton Road the buses plunged and skidded like slow, lugubrious mastodons, feeling their way pessimistically towards Knightsbridge, or in the opposite direction towards the even more discouraging chill wastes of Putney.

I went abroad infrequently myself. Piers went in every few days to pick up what mail there was for the Ming Press or the defunct Tennyson Glebe Publications; apart from occasional trips with the rest to the Little Lion I stayed at Number 36, contesting the pervasive, inexorable cold in my room with an inadequate two-bar electric fire. Piers came in one morning and stood by my chair looking out of the window. It was snowing, tiny flickering flakes interspersed with bursts of sleet. He said:

'It's cold down here.'

I nodded. I was reading the *New Statesman* and an inside chill matched the freezing bitterness outside. It was so eminently sensible; a sober, appraising chronicle of progress into chaos and bestiality. The objectiveness was there; only at the very edge of the abyss did the writers close their eyes and preach the invisible bridge, the bridge fashioned from man's own bootstraps to carry him over to Paradise. I was too old now, and too cold, to make that leap of faith.

Piers invited: 'Come up to my place. It's a little warmer. I want you to give me a hand, too.' He smiled. 'I've got a camera.'

Following him upstairs I said: 'A camera? What for?'

It was very warm in his room; he had had an extra power point rigged up for his various electrical devices and he was running three large fires from it. Blodwen was sitting in front of one of them, her back against the divan, darning Piers's socks. She nodded at me as I came in, but her eyes followed Piers.

Piers said: 'Do you know anything about cameras?'

I looked at the one he was showing me. It was an old studio model in polished light wood, with a hood and various accessories, mounted on a heavy iron tripod. I shook my head.

'No. But I don't imagine you bought this on the chance that I would.'

Piers laughed. 'I have done a bit of photography. This is a very nice job. Beautiful lens. It will serve our purpose.'

I realized what he was talking about, and was surprised at my own obtuseness in not having appreciated it earlier. Piers went over to the big cupboard where he kept the séance equipment – the trumpet, the variable red light and the rest – and fished something out. He brought it over to show it to me.

'What do you think of this. I rigged it up last night.'

It was quite an impressive arrangement; a wooden box about two feet square and eight or nine inches deep, lined inside with silver foil and studded with 150-watt light bulbs connected to a dangling length of flex. There was a handle for holding it. He said:

'Eventually we shall have to rig up a proper studio. Meanwhile I think this might give us enough light.' He went back to the cupboard and returned with a length of dark brown velvet, threaded on a steel expander. 'And this makes a background. You can clip it on these hooks.'

He stepped back to examine it. The velvet was stretched across the angle of two walls, about five feet wide and eight or nine feet high.

Piers said thoughtfully: 'That should do.' He looked round; Blodwen had dropped the socks and was watching us. 'All right,' he told her. 'You can strip now.'

She glanced at me. I was still holding the home-made nest of arc-lamps. I realized now what the assistance Piers had requested from me would entail. Piers seemed to detect the various hesitations about him. He said impatiently:

'How do you expect me to do it on my own? I can't hold the light and see to the camera at the same time. Not with this camera.' Blodwen got up and began to go towards the door. He said: 'For God's sake, you can take them off here, you're not a schoolgirl.'

She paused, and then went back to the divan and began pulling her frock over her head.

I said: 'Do you think all this is worth it? We can buy nudes cheaply enough from photographers who specialize in them. It isn't even economical.'

Piers said: 'It is going to be economical. Make no mistake about that. You're a partner in a business concern now, Tennyson.'

With his flat precise voice it was difficult to tell which word was accented – 'partner' or 'business', or whether both were. I turned away from Blodwen unrolling her stockings.

'A partner,' I agreed. 'The partner who holds the light.'

A swirl of snow brushed ineffectually and briefly against the window glass. The sky was dark and unfriendly. Inside, in front of the nearest electric fire, The Cat lay stretched, presenting her paws and silky flanks to the orange glow. There were two or three lights on in various parts of the room. It was all very cosy and domestic.

Blodwen came over and stood between us, nude. Her hips were better than one could have expected, massive but shapely and with no rolls of fat, but her waist was rather thick and her breasts drooped heavily. Piers examined her body with critical attention.

'We could try a straightforward profile first. Left side, I think. Put your left hand behind your head. No, don't grip your neck – just let it rest. Chin up. All right, Tenn, if you plug in to the wall point ... There's a switch on the handle.'

I connected my instrument and came back to where Blodwen was standing in front of the draped screen. Piers said: 'Switch it on.' She blinked in the glare of light that sharply illuminated every line of her body, every small blemish on her skin.

Piers said: 'Better have the light slanting downwards – can you get on a chair?'

I got one, and teetered on it precariously, holding the box of lights at arm's length. It was a foolish situation, I thought, for a man of my age and size. Poised as I was I could not avoid looking down directly into Blodwen's upraised face. Our eyes met, mutually blank. Piers put his head under the hood, and I was almost surprised that we should continue to exist.

He said: 'Now.' The camera shutter clicked. His muffled voice said: 'I think that's right but I'll try it again with a longer exposure.'

He appeared again after the second click. His fine, pliable brown hair had been pulled down by the hood into a fringe across his forehead.

'Give her the chair, Tenn,' he said. 'We'll take one sitting.'

We had arranged and re-arranged her body and taken about a dozen shots when Howard dropped in. He did not immediately see what we were doing. He said:

'Has anyone seen Cynthia since last night? Hello! Filthy pictures? Can I help?'

Piers had fitted Blodwen up with a transparent plastic mackintosh; she was sitting back-to-front on a chair with her left side to the camera. Howard came over and looked at her curiously.

I said: 'What do you want Cynthia for? I didn't know your fraternal instinct was so strong. I haven't seen her at all to-day.'

Howard said: 'She strips better than you'd think, doesn't she? Sure my co-operation isn't wanted?'

Blodwen said: 'Oh, for God's sake go away and play with yourself!'

It was her usual kind of rejoinder to Howard, but I detected something more than ordinary contempt in her voice; there was humiliation and a deeper bitterness. Piers appeared from under the hood and she looked to him as to a deliverer who might as easily torment. She looked away again from his comprehending smile.

Piers said: 'What's this about Cynthia?'

Howard shrugged. 'Helen's anxious. She thought she was just lying in late but now she's found her bed hasn't been slept in.' He glanced out of the window at the frigid sky. 'Helen thinks she might have frozen to death battling her way back from the Lion last night.'

Piers said: 'Or she might have found refuge in some other warm bed.'

His glance darted, watchfully amused, between Blodwen and Howard. He knew, I was sure, the peculiar humiliation a woman must feel when made naked in the presence of her enemy; the more the enemy has been hitherto despised the greater the shame. I could sympathize with Blodwen as I had never been able to do before. She could not hide her nakedness in any way without further abasing herself. In fact she leaned forward across the chair-back, flaunting her heavy breasts, and my sympathy deepened into a heart-wrenching identity. To refuse cover at the last, to stand in the open ready for all blows and all contempt – that, perhaps, was the best and saddest thing a human creature, male or female, could ever do.

Howard's attention had been distracted from her. He said to Piers:

'Do you think she might have found a man?'

His eyes had the look of someone renewing a lost desire which imagination has long since reduced to a tattered, hopeless platitude.

Piers said indifferently: 'She might.'

He looked at Blodwen fully. She had known the worst and, as far as it was possible, adjusted herself to it. She sat across the chair, her arms still lightly tanned from the previous summer and shading into the white of her shoulders and breasts. Piers turned to Howard again.

'She's not here, anyway.'

Howard came back to his surroundings. 'No.' He grinned.

'You could go and look for her,' Piers suggested.

Howard said: 'I could. But to hell with her.' His attention had been caught by Blodwen again. 'What about taking one of her lying on her back with her knees and arms up?'

Piers said: 'We're not looking for extra staff at the moment. You can run away. There's something you can do, though. Tell Olivia she can come up now.'

Howard looked at him, weighing the strength of his decision. I expected him to leap into one of his quick, resentful rages, but he didn't. He turned quite readily towards the door. 'I'll tell her …'

I said when he had gone: 'Olivia will be at her office.'

Piers said: 'Not to-day.' He went over and lifted Blodwen's arm, shifting and fixing her body as though she were a jointed doll. 'Can you get down on your knees, Tenn, so as to get the light flooding *up*? Yes, just like that.'

Britton knocked on the door and came in. He took in the situation and had begun to back out with some stammered apology, when Piers called him:

'Come in, Joe.'

Since the occasion of his abortive rebellion against Piers, Britton had tended to avoid both of us. He had come to the séances as usual but apart from that he had kept to himself. He came into the room, fumbling with his rimless spectacles. He said inadequately:

'I don't want to interrupt anything. It was just that Helen asked me ... I was looking for Cynthia.'

Piers was smiling sunnily. 'Everyone's looking for her this morning. We've just had Howard here. Come in, Joe, and sit down. You know how Helen is about Cynthia; she gets nervous if she doesn't see her every two minutes. Come in and get warm and help us with our chosen work.' He regarded Britton innocently. 'Lying on her belly, with her arms folded under her breasts, looking up to the camera – would that be a good angle, do you think?'

Britton put one hand on the knob of the door. His voice was weary:

'Let me go. I'm not fighting you any more. Just let me go.'

Piers said: 'Sit down. This is the only warm room in the house. And Livia will be coming up in a moment.'

Britton took his hand away from the door. He said:

'Olivia? For ... ?'

Piers said with calm firmness: 'Sit down. On the divan.'

Britton obeyed him slowly. Piers gave him a look of understanding and satisfaction, and turned back to Blodwen, She was staring blankly at Britton as he sat down, hiding in apparent shamelessness her private and unwanted sensitivity.

Piers said: 'Right. Get her a couple of cushions, Tenn, to lift her shoulders off the floor a bit. Now, look up. I don't know whether I can get sufficient dip on this camera; we may have to drag the small divan in from next door.'

Britton paid no attention to our rites. His rather square body, drooping on the edge of the double divan, had a subtle distortion somewhere in its lines; not hunch-backed exactly, but with a vague wrongness of contour and shape. His face looked as mournful, but less puzzled than it had. It was as though he knew what was happening to him, and the knowledge didn't help matters. He said: 'Piers.'

Piers turned towards him quickly.

Britton said: 'Did you mean it – that Olivia's coming up here?'

Piers nodded. 'I thought you might like to wait.'

Britton said: 'Look, I'm deadly serious.' There was a dull agony in his voice; he spread his hands out in the unconsciously melodramatic gesture of real pain. 'If it's me you're gunning for – you win. I'm not opposing you any longer.' He paused and swallowed. 'I'm sorry about the other day.'

Piers's eyes were cool but amused.

'I didn't know you had such pride in you, Joe. To credit my artillery with one objective, and that yourself.' He went on adjusting the legs of the tripod. 'And – looking at it academically, of course – even if that were so you haven't begun to understand the meaning of surrender. You make implicit claims, if not demands. Surrender makes no claims.'

Britton said: 'Nothing – I want nothing for myself.'

'What are you?' Piers asked. 'Something cold, that needs warmth? Something hungry, that needs food? Surely you realize that the only meaning there is to you is in the desire that looks for satisfaction? For subtle satisfaction.' He turned his head, his acute ears listening. 'That will be Livia.'

She saw all of us in the room, but it was Piers to whom she turned. She was wearing a blue satin house-coat, zipped up the middle. She glanced from him to Blodwen and back again. Her hair was combed into fluffy, clinging curls, and she had made up her face.

She said: 'Ready for me?' She hunched her shoulders. 'A good job it's warm in here.'

She put her hand up to the zipper on her house-coat. Britton cried out:

'Livia! Don't do that.'

She hesitated in her action. Britton got up and walked towards her. He put his hand out gently to take hers as it rested against the hollow of her throat, but at that she moved violently away from him.

He said pleadingly: 'You can take any revenge you want on me; any at all. But you mustn't do anything that will hurt yourself.'

She laughed. I had never thought her particularly soft, but I hadn't guessed she could be so hard. Piers looked at her with more admiration than he had shown for months.

She said: 'Revenge! What a damn fool you are, Joe.'

She took the metal clip between her fingers and unfastened the house-coat, bending forward to unclip it at the bottom. Straightening up again she slipped her arms out of the sleeves, and dropped it on the floor behind her. Her body was very shapely, swelling in symmetrical curves from a small waist. She stood with her hands on her hips and looked at Piers. It was a posture of frankness, but it did not remind me of Blodwen, who had now taken a cue from Piers and retreated to put on a dressing-gown. Blodwen had flaunted her nakedness because defencelessness was the only means of defence she had; there had been no pleasure for her in it. But Olivia was clearly and provocatively revelling in it. She put one foot on the chair and leaned over her thigh to examine it. Her toe nails were coloured a dull crimson.

She said: 'Blast! I've smudged them. I thought they'd dried.'

Piers said: 'The camera won't mind. Stay like that. Give her a horizontal light, Tenn. Unless Joe would like to take over from you?'

Britton had slumped back on to the divan. His dejection irritated me, as his naïve hopefulness had in the past. Blodwen went past him to get her slippers and I saw her hand touch his head with the merest flick of encouragement. The gesture surprised me; so did the realization that her emotional perceptions could be so acute. Britton did not look up, and Blodwen took up her work-basket and silently returned to her darning.

Howard burst in ebulliently.

He said: 'Has everybody come up here for warmth? The rest of the house is like Greenland's icy mountains. Hello – a new artiste?' He examined Olivia appraisingly and she looked back calmly at him. 'I didn't know you had such talents, Livia.'

She said with cool irony: 'Don't you wish you had a body you wouldn't be ashamed to be seen with?'

Howard laughed. He was bursting out with joy. At this moment nothing at all could touch him.

Piers said: 'Did you find Cynthia?'

He laughed again. 'I found out where she is.'

We gave him our attention; even Britton looked up, drawn out of his private misery.

'She's where she spent the night,' Howard said, 'in Lyle's caravan.' He went across and kissed Olivia with sexless bravado. 'She's gone. She's left us.'

CHAPTER TWENTY-TWO

D<small>AY BY DAY THE WEATHER</small> tightened its grip on the city, flattening its steel-grey hand on it, the razor-tipped fingers of the wind curling down from the iron sky to probe into street and alley and niche. The frozen snow, swept hours or days ago into drifts against houses and walls, grew shabby as London stone. In the roads the rutted, dirty ice formed miniature lunar landscapes, over which cars and buses travelled with increasing difficulty. The rune of ice endured.

I thought of similar spells which Nature had cast in this same place in earlier days. Not among the jovialities of history – the slowly roasting ox, the banquets on the Thames – but in the old, pre-Roman days when the marshes had stretched, stiff and dark, on either side of the vast frozen river. Glass-brittle reeds splintering under the plummeting body of the wild goose, stricken in mid-flight through the drab, unending sky. That was the kind of death, I thought, that stretched about us now. Individual organisms might still draw breath within it, but the thing at the heart was dead. Even when the children came snowballing and shouting down Regency Gardens, the snow took their voices and muffled and distorted them. They still had a kind of cheer, but it was the strange, high-pitched cheerfulness of the wake, with death its origin and death at its root.

I walked one day in the park with Rupert. There had been a fresh fall of snow, and the long avenues gleamed beneath the snow-branched trees. The park itself was transformed; old landmarks had been lost and new created. Somehow and inexplicably we found ourselves standing before Watts's glorification of physical energy. Behind us our trail stretched away, hieroglyphic, through the snow.

Rupert looked at the statue morosely. Horse and man were crowned with the feathery white.

'How I hate the Victorians, Tenn,' he said. 'All that florid confidence.'

'Don't be too hard on them,' I told him. 'It wasn't of themselves that they were confident; they were quite remarkably self-critical. It was the future – it was us they believed in. The millennium was perhaps fifty years away. 1947 would shock them far more than it does us. They really believed in it.'

Rupert said: 'Quite simply, it's unjust. They had the confidence; we have the disillusionment. It all stems from that. On the one hand the output of Browning, Tennyson, Swinburne. On the other, the Joseph Brittons, the W. H. Audens, the David Gascoynes, the Rupert Harbingers. We are only minor poets, too, but we under-produce as much as they over-produced.' He paused. 'In two hundred years' time, what chance will we stand against them?'

I said maliciously: 'I remember ... you thought there really might be a synthesis – a deliverer coming from the wastelands – a new Shakespeare ... only six months ago, in this park.'

Rupert smiled. 'It wasn't the same park, was it? That was the end of summer; this is winter. Joe Britton? I still think his was the finest talent of the 'thirties. He had not let himself be fooled into continuing writing during the war. He was coming back, renewed and fortified from the wilderness. He might have been anything, and I have a romantic turn of mind.'

'So Britton isn't the answer?'

'He's part of the question,' Rupert said. 'The timidity, the hesitation, the sterility of the rest of us – all that is easier to understand than Britton's talent flickering out like a candle and Britton himself retreating into stupidity.'

I bent down and childishly scooped snow into a ball, childishly moulded it and threw it at the horse's bronze magnificence. It stuck, a lop-sided star on the noble forehead. Rupert watched me, like a disapproving stork.

We turned to walk away through the long avenue, sullied only by our own earlier footprints. The sun came out and threw false, lovely gold between the regular trees. Away towards the Round Pond a spaniel frisked, apparently alone. Its blackness leaped against the pervading white; its shrill barking split the calmness of the air.

Rupert said: 'I've got a job, by the way. With the British Council.' There was someone with the dog; a withered, elderly man, muffled in a greatcoat and scarf, carrying a lead. He called, and the dog came to heel. 'What an artistic age we live in.'

When we got back to Number 36 I let him go upstairs and went in myself to Helen's room. She was sitting with her feet up on her divan under the window and Howard was sitting on the floor beside her, his head against her legs.

I said: 'That window-sash in my room still doesn't fit; there's a howling gale blowing through it.'

She said listlessly: 'I know, Tenn. Mrs. Bessborough said she would bring her brother round – he's a carpenter.'

I said firmly: 'You told me that a week ago. My rent's paid up three months in advance. You have some obligations, as well as privileges, as a landlady, you know.'

She said: 'Don't bully me, Tenn. What time is it?'

She began to look round in a helpless, searching way, for a clock. It was on the mantelpiece. Howard said quickly: 'It's just turned eleven.'

Helen said: 'We always used to have tea about this time in the morning.'

'I'll make some,' Howard said.

He got up eagerly and went out. We heard him running downstairs to the kitchen. Helen still sat, propped against cushions, staring out of the window.

I said: 'He's very attached to you.'

She looked round sharply. 'I don't appreciate him enough?'

I said: 'I don't think you do.'

She put down her embroidery. 'You don't know who his father is, do you?'

'I think I do,' I said. 'Sir Clifford? He let it out one day.'

'Sometimes people guess from the physical resemblance. It's very strong; it always has been. And in some ways their characters, too … Have you ever met Clifford?'

'No. I've heard of him, of course. From his reputation one wouldn't imagine there was much similarity.'

She laughed. 'Poor Howard! He would never get a name for being cool and ruthless, would he?' She hesitated. 'Tenn, have you ever wondered what kind of private life a man like Clifford might have?'

I said: 'I should think that a man whose strong point was ruthlessness would carry it over.'

'That's what I thought,' she said, '– when I met him. You can't have any idea, Tenn, how I worshipped that sternness, that incisiveness. In the mid-'twenties it was like finding a waterfall in the desert. He took things as he wanted them, and when he took me I was entirely happy. I never dreamed of marriage.' She smiled. 'You didn't know that both Howard and Cynthia were bastards?'

'I didn't know that.' I sat down on a convenient chair. 'And he left you? I gathered a different impression from Howard.'

'He didn't leave me,' she said. 'I left him. I stuck it for three years and I left him when Cynthia was born. I couldn't stand it any longer. You see, he fell in love with me, shortly after I went to live with him. It was a loathsome, clinging affection. Where he had acted before, now he tried to insist; and the insistence was vitiated by his dependence on me. I began to despise him, and eventually I hated him. He tried to persuade me to marry him when Howard was born – "to regularize the position" – but I wouldn't. I took his name for myself and the baby, but I wouldn't marry him. At that time he was just beginning to establish his reputation for ruthlessness at the Bar. And at home the masterly advocate was no more than an embodied whine. The worse I treated him the more he cringed. Sometimes I would drive him over the edge, into blind rages – that's how Cynthia was conceived – but after them he was even more abject.'

I marvelled at the secrets of placid, calm Helen, now placidly, calmly revealing them.

'I was willing to let him see the children,' she continued. 'But he wasn't really interested in them; he tried to utilize them to get me back. So I stopped the visits. He used to write a lot of letters, too. I told him that if he confined himself to one a year I would answer them. He still does write.'

She looked past me towards the door leading to the stairs.

'Howard's terribly like him. The physical resemblance would be enough by itself, but the fawning's there, too. I've been unlucky with my men.'

'Unluckier, perhaps, than you think,' I said. Helen looked at me. 'You didn't leave him until you had Cynthia. And for nearly twenty years, Cynthia has been enough for you.'

She was shaken out of her calm. Her large brown eyes flickered.

I said: 'Do you know yourself, Helen?'

She whispered: 'No. I don't want to. Don't tell me, Tenn.'

Howard brought tea for the three of us. He went to sit down again beside Helen. They were still sitting silently together when I left them and went upstairs.

It was Wednesday; in the evening, of course, there was a séance. I went up early to Piers's room – in part, at least, for the warmth – but Olivia was already there and Britton arrived soon afterwards, so we made an early start.

For some time there was no result; only the table creaking, an occasional sharp rap, a gust of cold air blowing round us. The room was cooling, anyway, as the fires had been switched off for darkness. Then, as quite often happened, things began with a kind of accumulated rush; the table tilted suddenly towards Olivia, leaped, and thudded and bounced as though trying to shake itself to pieces. Ming was with us.

There were ordinary questions and answers. The cold was not going to break – not yet. No – in answer to a frivolous query from Olivia – there was no such thing as temperature on Ming's side. Yes, he had been late because we had started early – but time was not the same there. It was too difficult to explain. Britton asked nothing, said nothing. Olivia had taken over the alphabetizing.

Piers asked: 'You still think the Ming Press will be a success?'

The decisive affirmative answered him.

'The new booklet we're preparing,' Piers said. '*Nudes on View*. Can we sell twenty thousand of it?'

NO. TWELVE THOUSAND.

We had asked the table for advice before, but never on so practical a point. I was a little disturbed by it. The paranormal making large prophecies or giving chatty weather forecasts was one thing; detailed publishing instructions were another. I felt some relief when subsequent questions received jumbled, meaningless answers, and at last the table's straining and rapping died into a chill silence. We sat quietly for perhaps five or ten minutes. It was very cold by now, and I had cramp in one of my legs.

I said: 'We might have a break, don't you think?'

Piers said sharply: 'No!' His voice softened. 'Not yet.'

Olivia began to mutter a few seconds after that. I thought she was speaking to us at first, and said: 'What's that, Livia?' But her voice continued in a low, guttural monotone, a flow of sound that did not appear to have any verbal meaning.

Piers said: 'It's trance. I'm sure it's trance.'

His voice which usually in the darkness lacked inflection had a strange ring. I heard Britton say:

'No ... you mustn't. Livia! Wake up, Livia.'

Piers said: 'Better be careful, Joe. Trance-talkers or trance-walkers – you should know better than to try waking her up suddenly. Better leave her.'

Olivia's voice rose to a shrillness, like an oscillation swinging across a radio frequency, and died back to the monotonous gabble. Her hand was still in mine. It felt very cold.

Piers said: 'Who is it? Who's there?'

The gabbling paused, and went on again with a questioning note in it.

'Who is it?' Piers repeated. 'Tell us your name.'

There was silence; and from it the voice spoke clearly and effectively, urbane, rather high-pitched, the voice of an old man:

'Ming Chi Li. You know me, I believe.'

Piers did not say anything immediately. It was as though even he were at a loss. At last he said slowly:

'This is a better means of communication than the rapping. Altogether more effective.'

The old voice seemed to shake. 'But, alas, more difficult. To-night, at least, I cannot stay very long.'

Piers said: 'I'd like to hear it spoken – we are going to be successful?'

The voice repeated: 'We are going to be successful.'

The pronoun puzzled me. Piers went on:

'And in the other little matter – the affair to-day – that, too?'

'That, too.' It was much weaker. It hesitated and began muttering, too feebly and too rapidly to be intelligible. Then it rose again, in an accession of strength.

'Switch on the light!'

Britton cried: 'No! Think …'

Piers clicked the switch at his side and the light from the desk-lamp, beamed across the table, illuminated Olivia's face. We all turned to look at it. It was distorted out of all appearance of familiarity, the skin drawn tightly across high cheekbones from slanting eyes, the nose so thin that the shape of the bone showed through, the mouth very small and meagre-lipped. Her flesh had a yellow, faded look. As we watched it was as though a mask dissolved, and her own features began to show through beneath it. She shook her head and her eyes, which had been open all the time, suddenly blinked.

She said: 'Well?' She smiled. 'What's been happening?'

Piers looked at her narrowly. He prompted: 'You …'

'Did I doze off? I don't think I did.' She was genuinely surprised. 'I suppose I must have.' She shivered. 'I'm cold.'

Piers walked about, flicking the various electric fires on, and half a dozen lights.

I said: 'A very nice transfiguration trance, Livia. You were Ming.'

'It was very impressive,' Piers said, coming to stand behind her chair. He rested his hands on her shoulders. 'Nothing stagey. A very Mandarin voice – and you pronounced your R's properly.'

She twisted her head to look up at him.

'Was I? Honestly?' She hesitated. 'I seem to remember something now.'

Piers said: 'To think we've been harbouring a trance medium without knowing it. And a transfiguration medium, too. What do you think of it, Joe?'

Britton looked at Olivia. He said: 'For the first time I've been convinced of the existence of a fifth personality here with us.'

She smiled, half contemptuous, half embarrassed.

'Thanks. How did you think we had managed the rapping – with trained woodpeckers?'

We, the We exclusive. Britton said patiently:

'No, I believed that, too. I'm quite gullible. But I've never felt the sense of a personality before. I did to-night.'

Piers said: 'Yes. We can really start getting to know Ming from now on.'

Britton stood up quickly but clumsily. He knocked his chair and had to catch hold to prevent it from falling. He stood behind it uneasily, his hands moving on the wood.

'Not me,' he said. 'Count me out for the rest.' He looked at Olivia again, his eyes, under sad, contracted brows, searching for hers. 'There's something frightening about the whole thing. I suppose I can't persuade you to leave, too.'

It was not a question but a statement, a defeated statement. Olivia smiled again. 'I'm not afraid,' she said, 'of ghosts.'

Britton hunched his shoulders. Piers still stood behind Olivia, watching him.

Piers said: 'There's no contract, of course. You don't have to give a month's notice. But perhaps you could give us some idea of what you don't like.'

Britton said stubbornly: 'I've told you. I believe in Ming now. I believe in him as something more than a noise on wood. I'm convinced.'

'Well,' Piers said. 'So Ming is a personality. What then?'

Britton's gaze was still on Olivia.

'If he has personality,' he said, 'he must have motive. Bringing it down to the concrete, his intentions are either good or bad.' His eyes flicked up, to Piers. 'Do you think they are good?'

Piers said: 'Irrational dichotomy, false quantities, disregard of definitions – what an orator you might have been, Joe. What is goodness? Let's define it.'

Britton said: 'It's your quantities that are false. We're not talking about any finite object. Goodness is God. Goodness is absolute.'

'Absolute,' Piers said thoughtfully. 'And immanent?'

'No.'

'Transcendent?'

'Yes.'

'The Absolute Transcendent Good,' Piers said. 'God Himself. Suspended in eternity, in creative nothingness, slowly clasping His divine and figurative hands across His divine and figurative belly. While here, in time, subject to the tyranny of matter, the slavery of flesh, finite creation is tortured and deceived and murdered, and tortures and deceives and murders in return.' He smiled. 'Is there anything wrong with my picture?'

'One thing,' Britton said. 'Man can reach union with God. Men have.'

'Beyond the Wheel of Existence,' Piers said slowly, 'the Nirvana, the union. Listen, I am the Wheel of Existence. I bring a child to birth in one room in a slum. I make its first conscious sight the spectacle of its parents copulating between bouts of cheap spirits. I swaddle it with rags, I anoint it with urine and grease from the fish-and-chip papers. I freeze it and cripple it and give it a recurrent, festering eczema. While still a child I turn it into the streets, into a jungle teeming with stalking tigers. I bring it to adolescence under the weight of a string of complexes with Greek names, and incipient schizophrenia. What shall I do with it then? Shall I condemn it to a life of grinding poverty or phenomenal riches, of subservience or mastery? Will it matter, do you think?'

'There is a way,' Britton said. 'It has been done.'

'The Wheel of Existence,' Piers said, 'works both ways, but mostly one way. It redeems one; it crushes a dozen million. Can you sleep in peace at that halt on the road to Nirvana while millions suffer through a defect in will? Is that Justice?' He paused delicately. 'You can read: you can read Huxley and Isherwood and Heard. You can read them because you have been to a Grammar School and a University. But the Wheel need not have given you that quick turn of memory and imagination that won you the scholarship at eleven. You might be on a cotton loom now.' He paused again, making his effect. 'How many living in Presley will reach Nirvana?'

I once saw a truck run into the back of a bullock-cart in Tuscany. The bullock was thrown sideways out of the splintered shafts. It lifted its head out of its own blood, and lowed. There was as much surprise as pain in the noise. Britton fingered the chair uneasily.

He said: 'Even – even leaving that ... This question of Ming. You don't lock yourself in a sealed room with a creature of whom you know only one thing – that it can see in the dark. Do you?'

It was an appeal. Piers said reflectively:

'No. You don't.' He looked at Britton intently. 'You don't, if you're afraid of it.'

Britton didn't say anything for a moment. He put his hands together, almost as though in prayer.

'I'm not afraid of it,' he said at last. 'I'm not afraid of it.'

Piers smiled. 'Of course not. You'll be up here next Wednesday, at the usual time. Won't you?'

I sat for a while with Piers after they had gone.

'Something Ming said,' I told him, 'has been bothering me. He said "the affair to-day" was going all right. That wasn't business?'

Piers said: 'Very much business. You know Helen's lease on this house falls due for renewal next month? I've got her to sign it over to me. Ming was confirming that it would go through all right.'

I had given up sifting fantasy from reality, motive from action. I went over and got myself a drink.

CHAPTER TWENTY-THREE

By the third day following Cynthia's casual elopement the change in Helen was very marked. She had always been apparently casual, but the casualness had masked that deeper shrewdness that had enabled her to keep herself and the two children, without any other income than that derived from letting rooms in Number 36. But now her casualness was real, a quality of listlessness that depressed everyone who came into contact with her, except Howard. It was true, I learned, that she had signed the lease of the house over to Piers; a desperate act in view of the fact that her tenancy of it, coupled with the flat shortage, enabled her to charge the exorbitant internal rents by which she lived.

Howard alone at first seemed quite unconscious of any change. He seemed to think that the one obstacle to a life of ecstatically entangled maternal and filial affection had been removed, and where in the past he had kept largely to himself, practising his 'cello in his attic room, he now danced a continual and seemingly blind attendance on Helen. He did not quite dare to move into the room Cynthia had had next to Helen's, but he was always to be found in Helen's room when he was not out shopping for her. Coming up from the basement one morning I saw him going out through the front door with a shopping basket over one arm. He was still no better dressed than he had been; his threadbare raincoat had torn all down one side and he had crudely stitched it together himself with black thread. Through the open door the draught of air from outside struck along the hall with a precise and savage chill. I shivered as I turned into the relative warmth of Helen's room.

She was lying on her divan but not looking out of the window. She had been making an attempt on the copy of *Gone with the Wind* I had seen previously in Blodwen's room.

She said: 'Hello, Tenn. Was that you coming in?'

I went over and stood with my back to the fire.

'No. It was Howard going out. Shopping, I think.'

She said vaguely: 'I did mention some things we needed. They weren't urgent though.'

I said: 'The dinner last night was pretty terrible.'

'I know. I'm sorry.'

She wasn't looking at me; she was gazing at the ceiling. But I was determined to get some reaction out of her. I pressed her firmly.

'But any effect the situation has on the rest of us is unimportant. It's the major characters – you and Cynthia and Howard – that are important. What about them?'

She brought her eyes down to look at me. She smiled gently.

'How nice of you to worry, Tenn. Cynthia – well, she acted, didn't she? I imagine she must have wanted to. I know she felt I let her down that time I let Piers persuade me about Brock, without talking it over with her. It was the first time I'd ever done anything without telling her about it. I don't know why I did. I think – something Piers said.' She shook her head. 'I don't know. It seemed quite trivial at the time, but of course it wasn't. I realized afterwards that it wasn't. I did try to explain to her but … there was a kind of coldness. I couldn't get round it.'

She broke off for a moment before going on.

'I'm getting a garrulous old woman, aren't I? Anyway, Cynthia's all right. She must be; she must have done what she wanted. I just can't understand – Lyle McAdams. How can she talk to him? What can they find to say to each other?'

I said: 'That covers two of the characters – Cynthia and yourself. I did mention a third.'

'Howard?' She looked surprised. 'But he's in clover, isn't he? It's all he's ever wanted – to be in my company, to get Cynthia out of the way. Everything's perfect for him now. I should have thought that was obvious.'

'Helen,' I said, 'you don't realize what you are saying about yourself.'

She said, mildly interested: 'You like Howard, don't you?'

'Yes,' I agreed. 'I like him.'

Her attention drifted. She looked out of the window, into the Arctic wastes of the small front garden and the road beyond. She picked up *Gone with the Wind* again, but put it down without looking at it.

'Lyle McAdams,' she said slowly. 'I just can't understand that.'

The front door bell rang; someone whistled a few bars of 'Good King Wenceslas' through his teeth.

Helen said: 'Would you mind awfully, Tenn?'

I went out into the cold hall and opened the door on the even colder world outside. It was a telegram. The boy was cleaning his boots on the scraper in a freak passion for smartness.

He said: 'Telegram for Miss Cartesian.'

I said: 'Thank you, I'll take it.'

I gave the boy sixpence and took the envelope in with me. It was a cable, not a telegram. I hadn't seen Lulu go out. I called to her up the stairs: 'Lulu, cable for you.'

She made some indistinct reply, and I went back into Helen's room, leaving the envelope propped on the hall table. I heard her clattering down the stairs and a moment later she came in. She was wearing a voluminous dressing-gown of some unpleasant brown material, and her hair was untidily bundled up in a coarse red turban. As far as dress was concerned it looked very much like a new solidarity-with-the-shoddy-proletariat phase.

She said: 'I've come in here to open it. It's freezing in the hall.' She tore the paper with her long, painted, dirty nails. 'It'll be from Mipsi. She said she'd cable me from Paris. Ah, Paris! Just thinking of it is like a warm breeze blowing along the Bois de Boulogne.'

Parisophily was one of the more irritating traits Lulu had acquired from the rag-bag of intellectual fashions.

I said: 'I've known warm breezes to blow along Old Brompton Road, too. You're in the wrong season.'

I was watching her as she read the slip of paper. Emotions were kaleidoscopic on her face; incredulity, joy, triumph and naked fear. She said, after a moment:

'It's not from Mipsi. It's my father. He's dead.'

Although more controlled now, she was still looking pleased enough to make any idea of condolences ludicrous.

Helen said: 'You hadn't seen him for some time, had you?'

Lulu didn't hear her; she was reading the cable again with a concentration that was more significant than any facial expression. She had received bad news once – a letter from Leslie's predecessor telling her he had finally decided it wasn't worth it. Naïvely she had blurted the story to us at the breakfast table, but the letter itself, barely skimmed through, she had thrown into the stove – timidly, not angrily. Now she read the cable through repeatedly and intently. She said:

'He always thought he would live to be ninety. Do you know, I believed him. And he didn't reach seventy! He would have been seventy next week.'

I said: 'We all must go at last, and leave our children weeping.'

Lulu missed the point. She caught hold of one word.

'I could have had children,' she said. 'I could have married a long time ago and had children. André ... He came from Cherbourg. Father had wanted me to marry a business friend of his – a technical arrangement between them. When I wouldn't – it infuriated him to be crossed. He went to see André, and told him that if I married him I would bring no dowry and no hope of inheritance. André liked me. He would have married me with only a little. But nothing at all was too much.'

She paused, thinking of the sad, unchangeable, irrecoverable past.

'He thought that had settled matters,' she went on. 'When I still wouldn't obey him he put me on allowance. £150 a quarter if I stayed single and didn't live with anyone.' She looked at us as though doubtful of our credulity. 'He told me he would have agents watching me every so often to make sure I was living by myself. He wouldn't disinherit me outright; he preferred that kind of thing.'

I was sorry for her, but I was sorry, too, for old Cartesian, growing old in the crumbling upper rooms of his financial pyramid, a grey old tom-cat mousing his only daughter. They had withered together, in different attics.

Lulu said: 'I haven't enjoyed it. Having to have men up in my room for an hour or so; sneaking a night every now and then. But I swore I'd outlast him.' She laughed, laughter that degenerated into a fit of coughing. 'I didn't think it could be so soon. I really thought he would live till ninety.'

Helen said: 'You could have borrowed on your expectations.'

Lulu shook her head. 'He thought of that. The agents were to look for that, too. I wouldn't risk it. I always knew I'd outlast him.'

Helen said: 'Have you any idea – how much?'

Lulu said indifferently: 'It's hard to say. Not much under a million, I should think.'

'The Communist Party will be pleased,' I said.

She looked at me sharply, in a kind of fear.

'I'm not going to lose my old friends, Tenn. Don't think that. This isn't going to change me. I'm not going to let it change me.'

'I know, Lulu,' I said. 'I know.'

She said dreamily: 'But think of all the things I will be able to do with it. Everything, anything I want. And every pound a pound he had hoarded.'

I left her with Helen and went upstairs to my room. The panels were drawn back between its two halves and I could see that Britton had simply climbed back into bed following breakfast; he lay hunched under the blankets, his head almost covered.

243

He had taken lately to lying in bed almost all day, and when he did get up it was only to stand or lounge in morose silence. I went over and slid the partition into place. He didn't move at all.

I was busy for what was left of the morning. Lulu called in shortly after I had settled down, to say that Helen wouldn't be preparing lunch; she was going into town for a meal with her instead. I was invited, too, but I refused to spare the time. Instead I lent the heiress three pounds – neither she nor Helen had anything on them – and made my lunch of some biscuits I had in my bureau, washing them down with gin and lemon. I was still working when Howard came in, about two o'clock. He looked very nervous and his eyes were swollen; he might have been crying.

He said: 'You haven't seen her, Tenn, have you? She didn't give you any message?'

'Helen? Lulu told me she was taking her out for lunch. I thought … I assumed you would be with them.'

He shook his head, with a pathetic bitterness.

'I was out shopping. She wasn't in when I got back, and no note, nothing. I went along to see if she was in the Lion.' He hesitated. 'I thought she might have gone along to McAdams's caravan. I've been waiting downstairs.'

Waiting, wondering whether Helen was not even then pleading with Cynthia to come back. So the confidence had been a mask, the cheerfulness forced. He had not been blind to Helen's reaction to her loss. I realized that Howard was more of a hero and more of a coward than I had imagined. I put down the dummy of *Passion in Paris* and poured a drink and gave it to him. He looked at it doubtfully.

'It's all I have in,' I said. 'It's what you need, anyway. A booze on gin would do you a world of good at the moment. It would bring all that raging sorrow out into the open and you could have a good cry.'

He drank it down and I poured him another. He took the glass and began to smile.

'Well, blast her anyway. What possessed them to go out for lunch in this kind of weather? It wasn't just to avoid me.'

I realized how foolish I had been in thinking Howard, of all people, could have been deceived by Helen's apparently complacent acceptance of his attentions. This was the first time since Cynthia had left that I had heard him curse Helen. But I felt that I could not permit him to slide back like that into his old deceptions; the falseness of the whole situation jarred too savagely.

I disposed of his questions. 'They went out to celebrate. Lulu's come into some money.' Before he could make any comment, I went on: 'What are you going to do about things, Howard?'

He looked at me with a faint trickle of gin down one side of his chin.

'Do? Do about what things?'

I spread my words out as carefully as I could.

'You're very fond of Helen; she has very little affection for you. All the love she has is concentrated on Cynthia. I'm saying these things because you know as well as I how true they are; and you are old enough to bear looking at them in the light of the exterior world – the world of real persons sharing real events. It's a situation you've been familiar with all your life. Only recently it cracked; some tiff – the first tiff – between Helen and Cynthia was allowed to widen until at last Cynthia just went. You have been hoping that with patience and the aid of your own affection you could eventually take Cynthia's place. But, honestly, you know that can't ever happen.'

Howard said quietly: 'Why can't it?'

I looked away from him. On the other side of the road a black cat trod delicately along a snow-silted parapet. It paused to lick at something, and then went on, out of sight.

'Because everything about you reminds her of your father.'

He nodded his head two or three times, as though considering some theoretical proposition and tentatively approving it. I thought the calm was about to break, but it didn't. He gazed at me quite humbly.

'What do you think I ought to do, Tenn?' he asked.

'I can't tell you,' I said. 'Even if I knew I couldn't tell you.'

'No. I suppose you couldn't.'

He emptied his glass and childishly sucked the last drops from it, holding the rim between his lips so that the edge of the glass came up to cover his nose. Putting it down, he said wearily:

'It's only that I don't like going on my own. I don't think I can face it.'

I watched him. 'Going where?'

'To Lyle's caravan, of course. To fetch her back.'

Coward and hero were together again, but of course they always were. And a victory had been won; Howard was going forward. The rest didn't matter.

I said: 'You think she'll come?'

He nodded. 'If I go for her. You pointed it out, Tenn – people don't change so quickly or easily.' He paused. 'Lyle. I can't understand it happening in the first place.'

I said: 'Neither could Helen. I think it was because he made her laugh. Cynthia gets bored very easily.'

'Yes.' He smiled. 'And she'll have heard all his stories by now. She'll come back all right. I think I'll go along and collect her now.' He looked at me. 'It would be a nice surprise for Helen when she got back.'

The sky promised more snow. I got up.

'I'll come with you.'

He came over and squeezed my arm. He said gratefully:

'Thanks, Tenn.'

We muffled ourselves up. I borrowed an overcoat for Howard from Piers's wardrobe. We made our way over a surface of splintering, glassy ice to Lyle's caravan. It was parked on the edge of the pre-fab site and seemed to mock with its peeling paint and fantastic extensions and accoutrements the prim, rabbit-hutch simplicities beside it. Lyle let us in to an atmosphere of stuffy heat, irrigated by eccentric draughts. There was no sign of Cynthia.

Lyle gave us no opportunity to explain our visit.

'Cynth's out,' he said. 'I don't suppose she'll be long. Look, Tennyson, what do you think of this horological masterpiece? Elgin half-hunter, solid gold case – and have a look inside. See? Micrometer adjustment. That's a lovely movement. I don't mind sacrificing it for ten quid.'

I said: 'E.D.T., whoever he is, has cut his initials almost through the case. Perhaps this will teach him that all our names are writ in water. Remind me sometime, Lyle, to put you in touch with my fence.' His breath was strong with rum. 'We wouldn't refuse a drink: if you offered one.'

He reached into a cupboard, drew out a bottle and shook it. It was empty. As it was a whisky bottle I thought of suggesting that he should keep a stock of labels to match his breath, but the fiction that Lyle treated people occasionally was one of those small, necessary fantasies that ride out the rough winds of truth. He said engagingly:

'You're five minutes too late. I've just finished it. We'd send out for a bottle but the Lion's closed.'

'Never mind,' I said. 'Never mind.'

'Did you know I'd got a job?' Lyle said. 'A walk-on in *Red Roses for Me*. My luck's turned, Tennyson. I'm going to make a great impression when I walk on to-night.'

I said: 'If you're not too drunk to make it.'

He said: 'The drink never incapacitates me. I've only ever lost one job through drink, and that was a stroke of bad luck. We were doing one of those English country-house plays in Bath, and I was the butler. I had to walk on early in the first act, deposit a tray of drinks, and walk off through the door opposite. Well, the first night I was very drunk. I don't think I've ever been drunker. But I was walking as steady as a bull elephant and I had all the confidence in the world. I'd done it a dozen times at rehearsals. So I just picked up my tray, walked on, put it down, and walked off. They told me it was the funniest thing in Bath since Lady Routish split her corsets in the Pump Room. For some reason they'd changed the exits round – put 'em both on the same side. I went straight for where the door had been during rehearsals and walked right through the bloody wall. The silly buggers wouldn't see it was their fault. They said I ought to have been able to use my eyes.'

He was still laughing when Cynthia pushed the door open and came in. She saw me and said: 'Hello, Tenn.' She looked round for Howard. 'Hello, Howard,' she said. She was smiling thinly.

He said: 'Hello, Cynth.' He didn't seem to know what else to say. He blurted out: 'I thought you might want to come back with us.'

She arched her brows in amazement.

'I never guessed you were so fond of me. Did you, Tenn?'

I said: 'Do what you want to do, Cynthia. You know how things are.'

'Yes, I know,' she said. She looked round, considering, reflecting on her power. It was difficult to realize that she was only a girl of eighteen. She smiled again at Howard. 'You depend on Helen and Helen depends on me. Poor old Howard. Yes, I don't mind coming back with you.'

Lyle found the whole thing another of life's prodigal, blossoming jokes. The caravan was too small for both us and his amusement, and Howard and I waited outside while Cynthia got ready. Howard kicked at the frozen snow with the toe of one shoe.

He said: 'I got a piece of salmon when I was shopping. Helen loves salmon. Perhaps Cynthia would cook it for her.'

I had often wondered in what power resided; I had never found the problem so puzzling as I did now.

CHAPTER TWENTY-FOUR

A PARTY, UNDER THE CIRCUMSTANCES, was inevitable. It was a long time – three or four months – since the last one had been held at Number 36, and the fittingness of celebrating Cynthia's return and old Cartesian's death was underlined by the assurance that Lulu would, eventually, pay the bill. Tony brought a barrel of beer over from the Regent in the afternoon, and came back in the early evening to deliver the spirits and tap the barrel, which he had set up in the dining-room. I had gone down myself to watch him. Leslie was there, too, having returned from some jaunt with the passion to complete his fresco quite renewed. He was tearing the plaster from the last remaining wall. Tony gave the bung another inconclusive tap with his wooden mallet and rested his willowy figure against the wall, staring at Leslie moodily. In the kitchen, Helen, Cynthia and Lulu were cutting sandwiches. I could hear Helen's voice, raised vivaciously, and Cynthia's answering husky drawl. Lulu was very excited and laughing a lot.

Tony examined the thin fringe of foam around the edges of the bung. He fished the stop-cock out of his pocket, drove the bung in with one sharp blow, and had the tap wedged in with the barest spillage of beer into the basin underneath. When we had tried to do the same thing ourselves on the previous occasion there had been a miniature fountain of beer which it had taken several minutes to bring under control. Tony turned the tap and poured about an inch into a glass. He tasted it, smacking his lips together two or three times.

'Be all right in an hour,' he said.

He went over to have a closer look at one of Leslie's walls, and disappeared, shaking his head slowly, into the kitchen. Leslie paused in his labours.

'I'll have a glass now. I've got a thirst on.'

I drew the beer for him and he drank it. From next door, Lulu's rejoicing mirth squealed at our ear-drums. Leslie glanced in that direction.

'I think I timed my return very well. She's going to be a very popular girl from now on. I shall have to consolidate.'

'Yes,' I agreed. 'There will be competition.'

He nodded with sober confidence and, as though his mind had been directed by this consideration to where his duties lay, went through to the kitchen. At the same time, like a figure on a Swiss barometer, Piers came in through the other door.

He said: 'Will you come up to my room, Tenn. There are some things I'd like to run over with you.'

I was away rather more than an hour; when I came down again the party had started. It had already spread from the basement to Helen's room on the ground floor and would necessarily spread further during the course of the evening. I found Howard in the kitchen with a glass and a sandwich. He was breaking pieces off the sandwich and feeding them to Brock, who was lying on his feet and accepting what came his way.

I said: 'I'll join you. What are you drinking?'

'Gin,' he said. 'Just gin. Have a sandwich.'

I got myself some gin and mixed vermouth in it; I brought it back. Howard had crumbled another piece of sandwich away and was holding it down to Brock. Brock flicked his tongue out idly, and took it.

'They're good sandwiches,' Howard urged. 'Fresh salmon sandwiches. Try one.'

For Howard, I thought, how rigidly time must divide the hopeful – even though falsely hopeful – morning of the past from the desolate present evening. Would he have been happier remaining in that deceptive emotional twilight? He might; but it was too unstable a situation to have lasted anyway, and at least he had acted. I told him as much.

'Acted?' he said. 'Yes. I suppose so. But action doesn't bring freedom.'

'It's the beginning of freedom,' I said. 'You can't be free without action.'

He looked at me, suddenly jeering.

'No metaphysics, Tenn. We can't have metaphysics. Piers wouldn't like it.'

Leslie came through with an expression of determination on his wedge-shaped face. He pulled his black horn spectacles off, and gazed myopically round the room.

'Where's my Lulu? My lovely Lulu, scented and spiced and laden with Orient riches. My quinquireme of Nineveh, from distant Ophir. Where is my ostrich-feathered girl?'

He went out through the other door, and we heard him climbing the stairs, singing in his vague, lilting accent:

> *'Lulu was a Zulu,*
> *Every inch a Zulu,*
> *Lulu, that Zulu girl of mine!'*

Howard began playing with the badger, but he was restless and projected his restlessness on to Brock. He caught the animal's long, narrow head between his hands and spoke to it. 'Who is it you want? The Cat? All right; let's go find it.'

He went out, Brock obediently following him.

There was already quite a gang of people about, variously grouped, and I wandered round aimlessly for some time, listening to divers conversations. I was fascinated, although I said nothing myself and was uninterested in the things I heard. The fascination lay in the fact that I had stumbled again into that condition of wonder and paradox that makes the very spectacle of human life and thought and action a renewed and bewildering joy. Here, in this group, mortal, fortuitous bodies gestured and communicated to each other their separately conditioned reflexes; a series of interlinking causal effects weaving a pattern of Shaw and Sartre and Stravinsky and judgment and passion and snobbery and coughs and smiles and sneezes. And here another pattern of the same order was formed by minds swaying between the tremendous oppositions of Thanatos and Eros, with the added, complicating burdens of all that was most stark and terrible in the imaginations of the dramatists of Attica. And here an endomorph, with minor ectomorphic variations, discussed the price of whisky with an ectomorph proper and a mesomorph with ectomorphic fingers. And here souls, tied to irrelevant, decaying bodies, made plans for a visit to the dog-track. And all were units in the vast dialectical synthesis; and all were unique and individual souls, beloved by God.

I found myself listening to Lulu.

'... it's tied up in half a dozen countries and currencies – that's the beauty of it! No worries about getting permission to take it out. The francs are waiting for me in the Banque de France. And dollars.'

Rupert was sitting on the floor in one corner of Helen's room, his large feet projecting terminally at the end of his spidery legs, reading Keats.

I said: 'How's the British Council?'

He said: 'You, Tenn? Listen to this:

"I cannot see what flowers are at my feet ..." '

I heard him out patiently. 'Yes,' I said when he had finished the verse, 'it's a good stanza.'

'It's bloody wonderful,' he said. His voice was almost fervent and his eyes very liquid. I noticed a tumbler beside him, half full of something. 'And all it says is that he was too drunk or it was too dark for him to see where he was going, and he had to smell his way. That's absolutely all it says.'

I said: 'I haven't seen you doing your meditation lately, Rupert.'

'Meditation?' He looked around with discouragement. 'Is it worth going on trying to chisel out what little there is in me?

Load every rift with ore … What do you do when the mine's worked out?'

'If we're lucky,' I said, 'we never know when that's happened.'

I saw moonlight shining on the snow outside, and went into the front garden for a few breaths of fresh air. Temporarily, at least, the wind had dropped, leaving behind it an ordinary frosty night. The moon's cool brilliance lit up great banks of cloud on either horizon, but between them there was the gulf of infinity, and poised in it the uncounted stars and the moon itself. I leaned against the wrought metal frame that topped the wall, and felt the savage chill of iron burn through to my arm. I put my fingers out and touched it, and found it glassy with ice. The wind had dropped, but the world was still immobile in its crystal prison of cold.

The light from the windows in Helen's room mingled with and was lost at once in the wider, brighter moonlight. Here, in the small, square garden, the two were unequally compounded, the weaker lost within the stronger. In this arena the struggle went always one way; to my attendant eyes there was no struggle but simply the folding of one power of light about another, an unchanging, static scene. And yet each particle of light was separate and discrete and from each second to the next the result was in perpetual doubt. Electrons jumped at the crack of unknowable whips.

I began to be very cold. The frost was pervasive, penetrating slowly but relentlessly; I went indoors again.

For a brief space Lulu was alone, and I found her so. She was in the kitchen, ostensibly getting more sandwiches to take upstairs. Her sallow complexion was flushed with excitement and the drink she had had; her eyes sparkled. I had never seen her looking so radiant.

I said unnecessarily: 'You're having a good time, Lulu.'

She laughed, and even her voice was young.

'Oh, Tenn, it's marvellous! I'm only just beginning to realize how marvellous!'

Piers came into the room and she called out to him: 'Piers!' He stood before her, smiling.

'They tell me I have to congratulate you, Lulu.'

She said: 'This is something you didn't foresee! Ming didn't prophesy this!'

Piers was still smiling. 'Didn't he? You've got a poor memory. Don't you remember – "Lulu R.I.P. 1947"?'

'But that meant me,' she protested, 'not my father.'

'Go,' Piers said, 'tell them that at Delphi.'

Lulu was considering it. 'It might … I suppose it might be that.'

'And now that it's happened,' Piers said, 'what are you going to do?'

Lulu let her eyes become dreamy and remote, and rolled her head voluptuously across her shoulders. She said, in a crooning drawl:

'I'm going to do just what I like. I feel completely free. There's no limit to what I can do. Absolutely no limit at all.'

Piers said: 'It's a pity it's too late.'

Lulu stared at him. Her voice sharpened. 'What do you mean? How can it be too late? Too late for what?'

Piers spoke with warm and friendly confidence. He gathered us both into a flattering intimacy that narrowed the walls of the room, excluding the laughter and noise beyond. It was the kind of effect that an intervening stranger would automatically make ludicrous; but I had never known chance to make a fool of Piers.

'We know each other,' he said, 'don't we? You won't mind if I'm frank, Lulu, and you won't mind Tenn being here. You see, Lulu, what you want most of all isn't the things that money can buy, the luxuries and privileges and service. In that swamp you would drown, rather horribly. What you want is ordinary domestic happiness – a husband, four walls, the noise of children.' He looked at her with sympathy. 'It's too late for that.'

Lulu said defiantly: 'I'm only thirty-five. I'm not too old – even for children.'

'But whose?' Piers said. 'Leslie's? You didn't mind paying him to come up to your room in the evenings, but do you want him as a husband, as the father of your children? You know yourself better than that.'

She said: 'There are more men in the world than Leslie.'

'Yes,' Piers said, 'that's true enough.'

She went on, gathering confidence. 'I don't have to stay and take my pick in Regency Gardens. I don't even have to stay in England. I'm not tied down. I can go wherever I want. I can pick …'

Her voice died away as she considered the enormity of what she was saying.

Piers prompted her. 'Yes, you can pick …'

She started to say something, but stopped. Her face which had been alive, first with pleasure and then with rebellion, turned to cold, despondent clay.

'There are a lot of things that you will be able to do,' Piers said. 'You can have your face tightened, your breasts lifted … if we see you in a year's time we probably won't be able to recognize you. But inside it all, inside the expensive silks and the renovated, perfumed flesh, it will still be the same Lulu. And because of that all the men you meet will be Leslies. You will always pay them for being with you, and you will always hate them, and hate and pity yourself. Even living here, in one room, on an allowance, you were never able to persuade yourself that you were loved for yourself alone. How can you hope to do it in a hotel suite or a country mansion?'

He looked at her dispassionately.

'He has won after all,' he said. 'By dying at seventy he has willed you twenty years of unhappy vice. At fifty-five the illusions would have been dead; now they are just sufficiently alive to lift you from one peak of disillusion to the next.'

Lulu said in a low voice: 'I don't need to accept the money.'

Piers said: 'Don't you? What will you do, then? Give it all away and leave yourself penniless? Keep your present allowance perhaps? Or raise it a little to account for the post-war cost of living? Do you think that without money you can win love, and if you don't, can you face the prospect of poverty and loneliness together?' He paused. 'At least the money will give you comfort. I'm quite sure you will take it.'

She said: 'I don't want that kind of comfort.'

'No,' he said. 'But you will take it.'

Piers left us. Lulu watched him go. Diffident as I usually was of touching others, I put my arm across her shoulders now. She shivered and for a moment clung to me, her dyed yellow hair falling against my chest.

She said: 'I think I'd like to go upstairs – to my room.'

I said: 'Yes. Go and lie down. You need a rest.'

She broke away and looked at me. 'Would you come up with me, Tenn? I'll be all right once I'm there but ... I just can't face going up by myself, somehow. It's awfully silly of me, isn't it?'

I said: 'No, of course it isn't. You're nervous. Come on, girl.'

We made our way in silence through the groups of chattering people. At the foot of the stairs she hesitated.

'I think I'm all right now. It was just that I had a queer feeling for a moment – that something terrible was waiting for me on the stairs. I'm all right now.'

I said: 'I'll take you up, all the same.'

She stopped on the first landing.

'Do you think ... is there any chance Joe might be in? I'd like to talk to him for a few minutes.'

'We'll see.'

Britton had managed to dress, but he was nevertheless lying on the divan with a blanket pulled over him. He looked up, blinking, as I switched the light on. With hair and beard uncombed and the sides of his face unshaven he had a rough and turbulent appearance, but his voice was as soft and slow as ever.

He said: 'Tennyson ... Lulu ...'

'Lulu would like to have a talk with you,' I told him.

He pulled his feet off the bed. 'Why, yes, of course. I'm afraid it's cold. I'll put a fire on.'

I said to Lulu: 'You'll be all right now?'

She smiled at me. 'Thanks, Tenn. I'll be all right now.'

I went downstairs and had some more drink and drifted around. Eventually I landed up on a chair beside Leslie, in front of his third wall. We looked at it together for a while, in silence. The browns and dull reds and yellows were Gauguin, but the imbecilic, attenuated figures were Modigliani. It was a pastoral scene, a ploughing match, and the perspectives and formal, symmetrically-leaved trees owed something to Grant Wood. It was the nearest to representational art I had seen yet from Leslie. Breaking the silence, I said: 'What does it mean?'

Leslie laughed. 'Yes, what does it mean? What a beautiful pattern of influences, though! Do you know, I think I'm rather proud of it.'

I said: 'In the way a child is proud of the pencilled scrawl on a sheet of notepaper that it knows perfectly well isn't writing.'

'Well,' Leslie said tolerantly. 'It comes back to that, doesn't it? With everything.'

I was a little drunk. 'Thought ranging back to origin and thought ranging forward to purpose – have I stumbled on the real, the unchanging dualism that divides men from men?'

'Purpose!' Leslie laughed. 'By the way, where's my luscious Lulu?'

'She said she was going to bed early. I think she wants to rest, after the excitement.'

'Should I disturb her?' Leslie asked. 'A spectacled Porphyro to her tattered Madeline? Not to-night, I think. There's time enough – world and time enough. Joy can wait.'

I said: 'The ache's in my bones. I think I'll go to bed, too.'

Leslie began to say something, but stopped as I got up.

I looked at him. He hesitated for a moment. Then he said:

'It's a funny thing, but I've got quite fond of her. Can you understand that? It isn't the money at all.'

I went upstairs. I collected a towel from my room and went up the half flight to the bathroom. Somehow I didn't notice the strip of light under the door, and I tried it to find it locked.

Lulu's voice called from inside:

'I'm having a bath. Can you go downstairs?'

'That's all right, Lulu,' I said. 'Good night.'

'Good night,' she said. 'Good night, Tenn.'

CHAPTER TWENTY-FIVE

During the night Lulu died a Roman death. The bathroom door had to be forced and Howard and I found her in the bath, frozen into crimson ice. We chipped her body free and carried it upstairs in a blanket and put it on her bed. She had been one of those people, I remembered, who are disturbed by any sight of blood. Had she already, when she called good night to me through the door, drawn the razor blade across her wrists, and was she even then watching the warm water redden with her blood? No, I didn't believe that; she could not have kept the horror from her voice. But soon after, and she must have stifled the horror inside her, hearing the noise from downstairs of people laughing and talking, watching the scarlet curl out and lose itself in embracing pink.

Britton was in bed when I told him. He sat up in a tangle of blankets. He looked more shaggy and disreputable than ever, but he was alive. I was very aware of life as an attribute that morning.

He said: 'Did she? Oh, my God!'

'Did she stay long with you last night?'

'No.' He shook his head, his face crumpling suddenly into pain. 'No. She didn't stay long.'

He got up and began dressing, and half an hour later I heard him go downstairs and saw him from the window walking through the snow towards Old Brompton Road. The wind had risen again, and it drove small, sharp flakes in gusts across the sky. I watched Britton until he turned the corner towards Knightsbridge.

I didn't see him again until the evening. He came into his half of the room about half-past seven and I heard him sit down on the divan; as usual it creaked under him. I knocked and went in. He still had his overcoat on. Bright beads of melted snow gleamed on it and on the trilby he had thrown on to one of the chairs.

I said: 'You missed all the interviews and paraphernalia. It was a very wise plan to get out of the way. All the same the Inspector will want to see you to-morrow. A very patient fellow, the Inspector – you'll like him.'

He said: 'I didn't mean to be out so long. I walked. I walked a long way. I went into Brompton Oratory to sit down. I don't know when that was.' He stood up and pulled his coat off and dropped it over a chair before sitting down again. 'I'm quite a bit hungry. I suppose you haven't got anything to eat?'

'I've got some biscuits next door,' I said. 'I'll get them.'

He called after me. 'Tenn.' I stopped. 'If you've got a drink of something, too – I'd be obliged.'

During the day I had salvaged a bottle of rum and a half-full bottle of whisky from the previous evening's store. I brought the whisky and poured a stiff tot into a glass for him. He drank some of it and munched biscuits.

I said: 'This kind of unhappy event is supposed to turn you away from a life of debauchery, not into one.'

He said again: 'I walked a long way. I was very tired. I heard the sound of the choir as I was going past the Oratory. I suppose – yes, it must have been vespers.' He had another drink of whisky. 'I hadn't been in a church since I was sixteen or seventeen.'

'You are a Catholic?'

'Yes,' he said. 'Yes, I am a Catholic.'

Olivia put her head round the door. She spoke to me.

'We're going up now.'

I nodded, and she withdrew, closing the door.

Britton said: 'The music ...' He seemed to collect himself. 'Olivia? What was it she was telling you?'

'She was saying they were going up for the séance – to Piers's room. I'm going up myself in a moment. I don't suppose you want to come.'

His brow wrinkled as though he were trying to remember something.

'A séance? But it's only Sunday.'

I said: 'It's a matter of striking while the iron's hot – for communication. It was Piers's idea.'

He looked at me for a moment, shocked and incredulous. Then, unexpectedly, he laughed.

'Of course. Of course Piers would think of that.' He finished the whisky and put the glass down. 'I'll come up too.'

Olivia, Howard, Blodwen and Piers himself were in his room. There was the vaguest sign of surprise on Piers's face when he saw Britton. He said:

'Hello, Joe. I was wondering what had become of you.'

'I've been walking,' Britton said. 'I've been walking a very long way.'

Piers turned to Blodwen. 'You can stay then. Since there are going to be five of us anyway, there may as well be six. You do want to sit in, Joe?'

'I suppose so,' Britton said. 'She's lying in the room above us, isn't she? Since we are responsible for that it seems almost appropriate that we should try to call her up.'

There was only a faint irony in his voice.

Piers said: 'Responsible? How responsible?'

'She came to see me last night,' Britton said. 'I suppose Tennyson has told you about it. She found me lying on my bed. I had had my own world cut away from under me, and she tried to tell me about hers. She was desperate for some kind of help, some kind of reassurance. She told me what you had said to her.'

'I told her the truth,' Piers said. 'Didn't I tell her the truth?'

'The truth,' Britton repeated. 'The truth without charity, the truth without hope, the truth without love. With those no truth is unbearable, and without them truth is a mockery and a lie. She came to me for them – we can't know why, now – and I sent her away empty. That's the responsibility I bear. Only you know what your own is.'

Piers said: 'I don't like to see you become so melodramatic, Joe. It's not helpful. We can look at things sensibly, can't we? It's a pity about Lulu, but to commit suicide she must have been hopelessly neurotic. If it hadn't happened now it would have happened next week or next month or next year. She just couldn't face things.'

'We're all hopelessly neurotic, aren't we?' Britton said. 'But we don't all commit suicide. Next week – she might have done it, she might not. She did do it last night. That's the certainty.'

'Don't forget the Wheel of Existence,' Piers said. 'You can always get back on the following round.'

Britton smiled. There was a difference in his face. I remembered his smiles as being uncertain, betraying a selfconsciousness that was always diffident for all his emotional obtuseness. Now his expression was spontaneous, immediate, confident.

He said: 'No, it only goes round once. You convinced me of that. You have convinced me of a lot of things. You drove me on to the rocks all right.'

Piers leaned back against his desk, his body slackening into a curve of indolence that often paralleled a furious and attacking activity of the mind. He closed his eyes for a moment and opened them again.

'It wasn't hard, was it?' he said gently. 'A hypocrite, a coward …'

'Yes,' Britton agreed. 'A hypocrite – and a coward. I saw the war out in New York. And at Escurial …' He moved his head slowly, his gaze ranging over the rest of us. 'It had quite a ludicrous beginning. At that time Escurial was in Government hands and the rebels held the hills to the north, with desultory, guerrilla fighting in between. Pedro was a Basque. He and I … did most things together. We got picked up together by a gang of Franco irregulars. Their captain was a queer, moody Portuguese who had spent a long time in this part of Spain. The point of the whole episode was that he had a girl in the town. He made us an offer – our liberty for the girl. He might have welched, of course, but it seemed worth taking. One of us had to stay as a hostage; the other was to go in to Escurial, find the girl at the address he mentioned, and either bring her or a message from her back to the captain. There was no doubt about who went and who stayed. The captain shared the common belief that the English were the most consummate string-pullers. Pedro had to stay behind.'

Britton coughed; it was an unsentimental, business-like cough.

'I remember,' he went on, 'we said good-bye just outside the cave the fascists were using. We shook hands and I gave him my copy of the Oxford Book of English Verse to pass the time till I got back. He was learning English. I went off to Escurial. It was an easy enough journey; things were rather quiet just then. I went to the address the captain had given me. That was where I had my first shock. The girl's family had moved, a month before. No one knew where they had gone. They might have evacuated; they might not. They might be only three or four streets away. I should have gone back straight away; we would probably only have been sent back under escort – he might even have let us go, it was a sporting chance. But I thought that if I searched I might find her. I wanted to find her. Quite apart from anything else I was curious. I searched for three days without success. And on the fourth morning I had my second shock. Her name – it was quite an unusual one – plastered all over the local *Correo*, as having been found guilty, along with three men, of intelligence with the enemy. All four had been executed at dawn.

'I could still have gone back to the captain. I might have reached him before the news did. He might have believed me when I told him I had nothing to do with her being denounced.

The fact of my return would have supported my claim. At the very least, Pedro would have been all right. But I couldn't face it. I knew what the guerrilla fighters were capable of, and I was willing to let Pedro run the risk rather than hazard myself to save us both. The fighting flared up again the following day, and then it was too late. One of our units picked Pedro up as the fascists fell back. He could still be described as alive; he could even talk a little. Enough to tell the story before he died, on the way back to Escurial. I should have been shot, of course, but I was an Englishman. They just threw me out.'

'Your responsibility,' Piers murmured. He looked at Britton critically. 'What have you done to-day – joined the Oxford Group?'

Britton smiled. 'I see no advantage in public confession. But I felt I owed you all this.' His glance touched Olivia. 'All.'

'But you have been somewhere,' Piers said, 'during your long walk.'

'I saw a priest.'

'A priest!' Piers's laughter was mocking and precise. 'I expected you to jump through some kind of hoop, but Catholicism ... Is the fat, purple ghost of the Holy Roman Empire supposed to be an improvement on the Wheel of Life? For God's sake have some sense, Joe. Believe in your impalpable, absolute goodness if you like, but don't insult your own intelligence with the kind of thing that traffics in virgin births and transubstantiations of third-rate wine into the red corpuscles of divinity.'

'What do you believe in, Piers?' Britton asked.

'I believe in nothing,' Piers said. 'I believe in disbelief.'

'Nothing's a great deal to believe in. I don't think you can do that.'

'There is one thing I believe in,' Piers said. 'I believe in myself. I know I exist.'

'And the rest of us? What do we do? Jump through hoops?'

'Yes,' Piers said softly. 'The rest of you jump through hoops.

I hold them up – you jump through them.' He paused. 'I crack the whip.'

Britton took off his American spectacles and began to polish them on his sleeve.

'You're mad,' he said. 'Even those who point the way towards the kind of thoughts you have would think you mad for carrying them to that logical conclusion. You're quite mad and you have a madman's cunning.' He looked up at Piers again. 'I can't think why you are exposing your hand now.'

'Perhaps because you surprised me a little,' Piers said. 'I didn't expect ... you weren't brought up a Catholic, were you?'

Britton nodded. 'I'm surprised your information service failed at that point.'

'Well, then,' Piers said softly, 'I have you placed again. And once I have you placed I know I can handle you.'

He hitched his body up and sat on the edge of his desk, his legs swinging idly like a child's. He looked round us, thoughtfully, affectionately.

'Consider,' he went on. 'Consider Tennyson, a director of the Ming Press. Consider Olivia, model in the nude for a guinea an hour. Consider docile Blodwen. Consider Howard and Cynthia and Helen, who once had the lease on this house.' He paused. 'Above all, consider Lulu.'

'It's an attitude of mind very easy to get into,' Britton said. 'Most people, most of the time, can be pushed or led by a stronger will. It's a commonplace of human behaviour. But you've gone further, haven't you? Further back. Like the child kicking in its cradle, you think you are omnipotent.'

'There's a difference,' Piers said. 'Mine works.'

'No,' Britton said flatly. 'It doesn't. An animal defied you. Don't you remember the trip to Thirl?'

'Yes,' Piers said. 'I remember the trip to Thirl. A major opportunity cropped up and I let the minor go. There's still time enough.' He smiled at us. 'I'll have the badger destroyed within a week.'

Britton said: 'You won't. It's nearly over now.'

Piers's legs stopped swinging. He looked directly at Britton.

He said slowly: 'I want you to realize that you can't defy me. And you can't take shelter behind priestly skirts. I'm not being melodramatic. I'm simply stating facts to you. *I* kept you here when you wanted to go on to Presley. *I* smashed up that little liaison between you and Olivia. *I* drove you out from your neo-Brahminist refuge into the open. You can cite a badger that refused to go wild, but I did these things to you.'

Britton said softly: 'Never has it been easier. The weeds flourish where the flowers have been uprooted. As they reject the traditional, wholesome beliefs, men rush to embrace all the false gods that men or the devil have created. Mammon, Pride, Lechery, Sloth … But they offer no protection.' He looked at Piers. 'No protection against even the minor servants of Evil.'

Piers laughed. 'How your mind runs to capital letters, Joe!'

He slipped down from the desk, and this small action seemed to throw a doubt on the whole of the preceding conversation, a doubt even as to whether it had taken place. I felt as though we had all been plunged into some parallel world of fantasy, and that Piers had gathered us up and tossed us back into reality.

Piers said: 'After all, we came up for a séance.' He glanced towards Britton. 'Are you sure you want to sit in, Joe?'

Britton nodded. We prepared the room for the séance. There wasn't much to do; as usual Piers had fixed the black-outs beforehand. But there were six chairs to go round the table this time. We fixed them, while Piers put out the lights leaving only the single glow of the desk-lamp by his side.

'Music?' he said. '"The Planets", I think. Our old stand-by.'

I found that I had Britton sitting on my right side, opposite Piers, and Olivia on my left. As usual the light clicked off and the music drifted out into the confined and limitless dark. Mercury the messenger, patron of orators, and thieves, craftsmen and merchants. The flicking, silvery notes. For the first time since the gruesome business of the morning I realized acutely that Lulu was dead; that we should not hear again her naïve, laboured political arguments or her little squeaks of astonishment when the table began kicking under our hands. It seemed that Howard was experiencing a similar reaction. He said suddenly, in an edged voice:

> *'She sleeps up in the attic there*
> *Alone, poor maid. 'Tis but a stair*
> *Betwixt us …'*

He stopped and began to laugh. Britton broke in.

He said quietly: 'Never mind.' And then, obviously to Piers: 'By the way, where does Ming fit into your solipsist world? Does he take your instructions, too?'

Piers said: 'You fool! I am Ming.'

Britton said: 'I thought you might say that.'

Piers said: 'The Chinese Mandarin! All the table tiltings and the rappings and Olivia's face twisting – who else do you think did it? Have you never heard of telekinesis?'

'So that's all it was,' Britton said. 'Just Piers being telekinetic!'

I hadn't thought his voice had the mobility to develop so mocking an inflection.

Piers said harshly: 'I warned you not to defy me, Joe. Especially not here and now. Especially not in the dark.'

'Who uses whom?' Britton asked. 'Which is the spirit and which is the mouth-piece? A man creating a ghost, or a ghost inhabiting a man? Are you Ming? Tell me, Ming – what have you done with Piers Marchant?'

There was the sharp, jarring lull of a record changing, and at that moment the table began a slow, undulant rocking.

Piers said: 'I warned you!'

'Ming,' Britton repeated, 'what have you done with Piers Marchant?'

The rocking increased to violence. The legs began to lift from the floor-boards and crash back again. I had a sense of tremendous, oppressive power.

'All right,' Piers said. 'You want it. Ming!'

The table began to plunge in a furious paroxysm of motion, bucketing and jumping, lifting towards the ceiling and shivering back against the floor. Noises – raps and thuds – began to sound from other parts of the room, drowning the music of Holst in their own symphonic medley of brutality. Something whistled through the air and I heard Blodwen cry out, either in fear or pain. Beside me Britton got to his feet.

'*In nomine ...*' he began.

Piers answered in a kind of laughing shout.

'That won't help you. You're on my territory now.' Britton spoke more loudly: '*In nomine Patris et Filii et Spiritus Sancti jubeo te hinc partire ...*'

I could hear no more for the climactic thunder in the air about me and Piers's almost shrieking laughter. The table lifted higher than ever and lurched down and to one side, and then silence was like a lost haven incredibly recovered. I went over and found a light switch and put it on. Howard, Blodwen and Olivia stood grouped beside Britton.

Piers was lying motionless on the floor, with the table collapsed about him.

BOOK V

CHAPTER TWENTY-SIX

O F ALL PARTS OF LONDON the most gloomy, I think, is that half mile from which the three great stations despatch their northward expresses. Of the three Euston is the least dispiriting, but its despondent echoing spaces are bad enough. Overhead the rain swept steadily across the high roof. The air which outside had been dark and muggy was intensified inside in both respects by the fog of engine smoke.

Britton leaned out of the compartment window.

'When you get to Presley,' I asked him, '– what then? Do you still want to work in a mill?'

He smiled. 'No. I don't think so.'

'In that case – why go back?'

'The instinct was right enough. I've got to get back somehow – back to the point at which I went off the rails. Presley will help.'

'You can never go back,' I said. 'There's no way back at all.'

'I don't know. I don't know what one can do.' He pinched his beard between finger and thumb. 'I only know that a time comes when you can't go forward; when there's no way forward. All you can try to do then is to find your way back. They're friendly in Lancashire. They always were; I don't suppose they've changed. And the places will be familiar – the streets and alleys, the country round about, the traffic flooding along the main road, past the butcher's shop.' He smiled again. 'There might even still be steam-trucks. It will all help.'

A little further down the train someone got in and slammed the door and from this false alarm of departure ripples of confusion spread away in either direction. People climbed into compartments; visitors stood back.

I said quickly: 'There's one thing I'd like to ask you about. Just what do you think did happen on Sunday night?'

'What is there about it that troubles you?'

I spoke more slowly. 'For a time, while it was happening, I think I believed in … in diabolical possession, and the power of exorcism.'

Britton shook his head. 'That's nonsense, isn't it?'

'Yes,' I agreed. 'That's nonsense.'

'But the phenomena – there's no trouble about the phenomena. Extra-sensory perception is quite respectable now. Price's poltergeists, Seal's telepathy and prophecy, Rhine's telekinesis. I was astonished when Piers showed me how respectable they were. The séances as a whole don't bother you?'

'No.'

'Just that last one?'

I nodded. He had to move to one side to let a woman get in. When he came back, he said:

'Auto-suggestion. Piers practised it quite effectively as a part of his megalomania. He had considerable hypnotic power along with his other paranormal faculties. But it's a two-edged weapon, and paradoxically while his growing assurance of omnipotence increased its power against others it made it the more surely fatal should it ever be turned against himself. And it made it the easier to turn. Even before the lights went off it had begun to slip round in his hands. And when, on his own ground … The few words of Latin finished things off.'

'Yes,' I said. 'Of course, that's it.'

Britton smiled. 'At any rate, that's the comfortable explanation. We don't want to believe in witches and devils and sorcery. Do we? Nor in powers of good and evil.'

He was watching me with sardonic friendliness. The change in him during the past few days had been startling. He had the composure, at least, of the man we had expected six months before, the literary and political lion of the 'thirties. I wondered why I could still feel no real warmth towards him. The fumbling, the uncertainty, the melancholy self-condemnation, were gone, but something still jarred. Knowing him right and vindicated and triumphant, and knowing Piers wrong and broken, there was still no doubt as to where my affections lay.

Away at the remote end of the station the engine screamed off pressure.

I said: 'Is there any message for Olivia?'

'Give her my love,' Britton said. 'Give them all my love.'

I nodded.

'And look after him, won't you? He needs looking after. But you will.' The smile was still friendly, but the depth of irony in it made me feel uncomfortable. The train began to move. 'I know you'll look after him very well.'

I drove the car down the sloping ramp from the station with a feeling of lightheartedness. It increased when I reached Regency Gardens and went in at the front door of Number 36, wide open again to welcome the thaw. Halfway up to my room I found some difficulty in manoeuvring past the assortment of boxes and cases spreading out from the little room. Olivia was kneeling by the camp-bed in her slip, folding clothes.

She said: 'Oh, Tenn? Howard's with him.'

'What time's your train?' I asked her.

'Three-thirty. King's Cross. Were you offering to run me along?'

I said: 'I might be. In fact, I will. Joe sent his love.'

She looked up. 'Oh. Thanks.' She returned again to her folding. 'I gave him my address.'

I walked through the front part of my room past the opened partition to the rear half. There was no evidence remaining of Britton's long stay there. On the small divan bed he had used, Piers was lying propped up against the pillows. Howard was sitting on a chair beside him, and the doctor was putting his stethoscope away by the wash-stand. I smiled at Piers, and his deep eyes looked back, unblinking, from the imprisoning body.

I said: 'I saw Joe off. And Olivia to Scotland this afternoon. I might as well run a car-hire service.'

Howard said: 'Blodwen's been on again about wanting to look after him herself, upstairs.'

I stood in front of the bed.

'Listen, Piers. If you want to go upstairs you can. Just as you like, old man. Wink once if you would prefer to stay here with me.'

I watched his right eye close painfully and open again. In all the months I had known him it struck me for the first time that in his features he was something like Tim had been. I wondered how I could have failed to see the resemblance before.

Before he went the doctor called me round the corner of the room, out of sight and earshot.

I said: 'Well?'

'We'd better have him X-rayed, just to be on the safe side, but I'm more convinced than ever that there's nothing organically wrong. It's just a traumatic hysteria.'

'And how long is it likely to last?'

He looked at his watch. 'It's hard to tell. He should improve gradually, but it may be months before he can do much for himself. It may be longer than that. If I were you I'd get him into a nursing home.'

I said: 'I'd rather look after him myself.' I paused. 'I might take him down into the country eventually.'

Howard and I sat beside the bed for another half hour; until it was time to get his broth. I went down for it myself. Helen was preparing it in the kitchen and I stood watching her.

I said: 'The house will seem very empty to-morrow, Helen. Joe and Livia gone.'

'Yes.' She cooled a spoonful of broth and sipped it delicately. 'I wanted to talk to you about that, Tenn. I thought I might move Howard down into Olivia's little room and let off the top floor. There are a couple of nice young men I met in the Lion who want to keep to themselves. I'm terribly short just now. I can't understand it.'

I thought of trying to explain that I was already paying the rent for Olivia's little room, but decided it wasn't worth it.

'That'll be fine,' I said. 'Two nice young men who want to keep to themselves. That was really all we needed.'

She said absently: 'Yes, it will be very handy. I think I'll slip up and take a glass of milk to Cynthia. She's got a nasty head. This broth isn't quite ready yet, anyway.'

In front of the stove Brock and The Cat were lovingly entwined, lazily licking each other's coats.

I wandered into the dining-room while Helen was going upstairs. The thaw had broken through the first wall of the fresco, and dark splotches of moisture spread across the rose background and the grey and yellow tree. There was a small spot under the crab-woman's chin, turning her into a bearded lady. The feeling of well-being that I had had since I left Britton deepened into a kind of exhilaration. Time and weather, that between them have crumbled Da Vinci's 'Last Supper' into mildew and dust, worked here as everywhere. At the other side of the room Leslie was busy. He had plastered his last wall and was painting it in furious and intent silence. I stood behind him and looked at it. A river of bright gold coursed through an enchanted valley towards either a rising or a setting sun. On the green lawns of its banks, and in the dells and copses that stretched up either hill-side, youths and maidens walked or lay in paired and happy dalliance. And all the maidens were Lulu and all the youths, even to the black-rimmed spectacles, were Leslie.

Brixton Hill *January 1949–February 1950*

ALSO PUBLISHED BY THE SYLE PRESS

by Sam Youd

THE WINTER SWAN

In 1949, Sam Youd – who would later go on, as John Christopher, to write *The Death of Grass* and *The Tripods* – published his first novel. As he later said:

I knew first novels tended to be autobiographical and was determined to avoid that. So my main character was a woman, from a social milieu I only knew from books, and … [with] a story that progressed from grave to girlhood.

When Rosemary Hallam dies, what she longs for is the peace of non-existence. Instead, her disembodied spirit must travel back and back, through two world wars and the Depression to her Edwardian childhood, reliving her life through the eyes of her husbands, her sons and others less immune than she to the power of emotion. And the joys and the tragedies which had never quite touched her at the time now pose a real threat to the emotional aloofness she has always been strangely desperate to preserve.

'You remind me greatly of a swan, dear Mrs Hallam,' her elderly final suitor had declared, '… effortlessly graceful, and riding serenely over the troubling waves of the world as though they never existed.'

ISBN: 978-1-911410-06-5

www.thesylepress.com/the-winter-swan

by Sam Youd as John Christopher
with an Introduction by Robert Macfarlane

THE DEATH OF GRASS

The Chung-Li virus has devastated Asia, wiping out the rice crop and leaving riots and mass starvation in its wake. The rest of the world looks on with concern, though safe in the expectation that a counter-virus will be developed any day. Then Chung-Li mutates and spreads. Wheat, barley, oats, rye: no grass crop is safe, and global famine threatens.

In Britain, where green fields are fast turning brown, the Government lies to its citizens, devising secret plans to preserve the lives of a few at the expense of the many.

Getting wind of what's in store, John Custance and his family decide they must abandon their London home to head for the sanctuary of his brother's farm in a remote northern valley.

And so they begin the long trek across a country fast descending into barbarism, where the law of the gun prevails, and the civilized values they once took for granted become the price they must pay if they are to survive.

This edition available in the US only

ISBN: 978-1-911410-00-3

www.deathofgrass.com

by Sam Youd as John Christopher

THE CAVES OF NIGHT

Five people enter the Frohnberg caves, three men and two women. In the glare of the Austrian sunshine, the cool underground depths seem an attractive proposition – until the collapse of a cave wall blocks their return to the outside world. Faced with an unexplored warren of tunnels and caves, rivers and lakes, twisting and ramifying under the mountain range, they can only hope that there is an exit to be found on the other side.

For Cynthia, the journey through the dark labyrinths mirrors her own sense of guilt and confusion about the secret affair she has recently embarked upon. And whilst it is in some ways a comfort to share this possibly lethal ordeal with her lover Albrecht, only her husband Henry has the knowledge and experience that may lead them all back to safety.

But can even Henry's sang froid and expertise be enough, with the moment fast approaching when their food supplies will run out, and the batteries of their torches fail, leaving them to stumble blindly through the dark?

ISBN: 978-0-9927686-8-3

www.thesylepress.com/the-caves-of-night

by Sam Youd as John Christopher

THE WHITE VOYAGE

Dublin to Dieppe to Amsterdam. A routine trip for the cargo ship *Kreya*, her Danish crew and handful of passengers. Brief enough for undercurrents to remain below the surface and secrets to stay buried.

The portents, though, are ominous. 'There are three signs,' the spiritualist warned. 'The first is when the beast walks free. The second is when water breaks iron … The third is when horses swim like fishes.'

Captain Olsen, a self-confessed connoisseur of human stupidity, has no patience with the irrational, and little interest in the messiness of relationships.

'I condemn no man or woman,' he declares, 'however savage and enormous their sins, as long as they do not touch the *Kreya*. But anything that touches the ship is different. In this small world, I am God. I judge, I punish, and I need not give my reasons.'

Olsen's philosophy is challenged in the extreme when, in mountainous seas, disaster strikes: the rudder smashed beyond repair, a mutiny, and the battered vessel adrift in the vast ocean, driven irrevocably northwards by wind and tide – until she comes to rest, at last, lodged in the great Arctic ice-pack.

ISBN: 978-0-9927686-4-5

www.thesylepress.com/the-white-voyage

by Sam Youd as John Christopher

Cloud on Silver

A disparate group of Londoners are brought together by Sweeney, a mysteriously charismatic man of wealth, for a luxury cruise in the South Pacific – they know not why. Sailing far from the normal shipping routes, the ship drops anchor just off an uninhabited tropical island. Whilst its passengers are ashore exploring, the ship catches fire and sinks beneath the waves.

With no means of communication with the outside world and no hope of rescue, passengers and crew must find a way to survive. In the scramble for power that ensues, the distinction between master and servant becomes meaningless as the more ruthless among them clamber to the top.

The inscrutable Sweeney, meanwhile, sits alone on a hillside. Coolly aloof, he watches the veneer of civilization disintegrate as his fellows fall prey to fear, desperation, barbarity …

As for Silver Island itself, with its lush vegetation and exotic fruits, it had seemed like paradise. But as the days pass, a subtle sense of unease gains momentum, and the realisation gradually dawns that all is far from well in this tropical Eden.

ISBN: 978-0-9927686-6-9

www.thesylepress.com/cloud-on-silver

by Sam Youd as John Christopher

The Possessors

When the storm rages and the avalanche cuts off power and phone lines, no one in the chalet is particularly bothered. There are kerosene lamps, a well-stocked bar and food supplies more than adequate to last them till the road to Nidenhaut can be opened up. They're on holiday after all, and once the weather clears they can carry on skiing.

They do not know, then, that deep within the Swiss Alps, something alien has stirred: an invasion so sly it can only be detected by principled reasoning.

The Possessors had a long memory … For aeons which were now uncountable their life had been bound up with the evanescent lives of the Possessed. Without them, they could not act or think, but through them they were the masters of this cold world.

ISBN: 978-1-911410-02-7

www.thesylepress.com/the-possessors

by Sam Youd as John Christopher

PENDULUM

The sixties ... a foreign country: they did things differently then. Or did they?

An Englishman's home, supposedly, is his castle, and property developer Rod Gawfrey was incensed when a gang of hooligans gatecrashed his son's party, infiltrating the luxury residence that was also home to his wife's parents and her sister Jane.

He had no inkling then of the mayhem that was on its way, as the nation's youth rose up in revolt, social order gave way to anarchy, and he and his family were reduced to penury.

Jane hadn't seen it coming either, despite her professional and more personal connection to Professor Walter Staunton, the opportunist and lascivious academic bent on fomenting the revolution.

A pendulum, though, once set in motion, must inevitably swing back. And who would have guessed that Martin, Jane's timid, God-fearing brother, would have a key role to play in the vicious wave of righteous retribution that would next sweep the land?

ISBN: 978-1-911410-04-1

www.thesylepress.com/pendulum

by Sam Youd as Hilary Ford

SARNIA

Life holds no prospect of luxury or excitement after Sarnia's beloved mother dies: potential suitors vanish once they realise that marriage to the orphan will never bring a dowry. Yet her post as a lady clerk in a London banking house keeps the wolf from the door, and the admiration of her colleague, the worthy Michael, assures her if not of passion, then at least of affection.

Then the Jelains erupt into her humdrum routine, relatives she did not know she had, and whisk her away to the isle of Guernsey. At first she is enchanted by the exotic beauty of the island, by a life of balls and lavish entertainments where the officers of visiting regiments vie for her attention.

But Sarnia cannot quite feel at ease within this moneyed social hierarchy – especially in the unsettling presence of her cousin Edmund. And before long it becomes apparent that, beneath the glittering surface, lurk dark and menacing forces …

Her mother had scorned those of her sex who tamely submitted to male domination but, as the mystery of her heritage unfolds, Sarnia becomes all too painfully aware that the freedom she took for granted is slipping from her grasp.

ISBN: 978-0-9927686-0-7

www.thesylepress.com/sarnia

by Sam Youd as Hilary Ford

A BRIDE FOR BEDIVERE

'I cried the day my father died; but from joy.'

Jane's father had been nothing but a bully. His accidental death at the dockyard where he worked might have left the family in penury but it had also freed them from his drunken rages. He was scarcely cold in his grave, though, when another tyrant entered Jane's life.

Sir Donald Bedivere's offer to ease her mother's financial burden had but one condition: that Jane should leave her beloved home in Portsmouth and move to Cornwall as his adopted daughter.

To Sir Donald, Cornwall was King Arthur's country, and his magnificent home, Carmaliot, the place where Camelot once had stood. To Jane, for all its luxury it was a purgatory where her only friend was the lumbering Beast, with whom she roamed the moors.

Sir Donald had three sons, and Jane was quick to sum them up: John was pleasant enough, but indifferent to her. The burly, grinning Edgar she found loathsome. And Michael, on whom Sir Donald had pinned all his hopes, she disdained.

Sir Donald had plans for the Bedivere line – Jane wanted no part in them.

ISBN: 978-0-9927686-2-1

www.thesylepress.com/a-bride-for-bedivere

Printed in Great Britain
by Amazon